True Gold

TRUE GOLD

MICHELLE PACE

TULE
PUBLISHING

CHAPTER ONE

CONNOR

BLOODY

"COME AND GET it, ya pain in my ass." I whistle, and after snapping at one last trout, my Alaskan malamute, Runt, bounds along the wood planks of the floating dock, crossing the overgrown lawn. He pauses at the base of the porch steps, waiting for a second invitation. I make kissing sounds, and he lumbers up, sniffing at the remains of my meal. He tears into my leftover steak enthusiastically, and I ruffle his thick coat. Unsurprisingly, he ignores me just like he ignores the broccoli I left on the plate.

I kick my feet up on the knotty porch railing, enjoying the muted sky. It's August, so it'll be hours before the sun sets behind the cedar-covered hills. You'd think I'd be desensitized to this view, having grown up here, but the wild and unmarred beauty of the Kenai Peninsula lured me home after years abroad. Though my memories of Alaska are mixed and complicated, this land had been in my family for generations, and my mother always referred to this house on the river as her happy place. She's gone now, and there's no place I'd rather live after my jarring discharge from the army.

I'd planned to serve until I retired, just like my old man. Frankly, serving my country is the only career I'd ever considered. Unfortunately, injury ignores destiny, and one careless landing ten years into my career was all it took. Funny how losing focus, even for a moment, can cost you everything. Neither surgery nor months of physical therapy changed the fact that I was eighty percent of my former self, which wasn't enough for Special Forces. I was faced with two options: a desk job or discharge. I refused to go from Green Beret to paper pusher, so home I went.

My premature return crushed me but after a few months of feeling sorry for myself, I found a way to use my unique skills in the private sector. Leading tourists on hunting and fishing expeditions pays the bills, and I volunteer for Search and Rescue every once in a while so I don't feel like a total sellout.

As if on cue, the knee pain comes, and more scotch vanishes from my glass. I've just wrapped up a ten-day hunting trip with some skinny-jean-wearing assholes from Portland, who drove me to drink more than my bum knee does. I tolerated their cloying cigar smoke, not to mention their juvenile questions about how Eskimo pussy stood up against the "garden variety." Their shoddy attempts at hunter safety were another matter, and after three days, I'd been ready to ditch them like the Donner party and let Mother Nature sort it out. Somehow, I mustered up the discipline not to smother them all in their sleep, and they left grinning behind their handlebar mustaches and already planning another trip back to the last frontier.

I shake my head with a soul-rattling sigh. Suppressing the urge to shoot people who were a danger to themselves and everyone around them is taxing, but better than a nine to five in some factory. I earn a hefty paycheck keeping idiots alive so they can brag to their fellow craft-beer-guzzling hipsters how they've "conquered" Alaska. Lucky for them, I'm compensated very, *very* well.

My phone rings, and the interruption pisses me off. I need time off like other people need sleep. I haven't broken a barstool over anyone's head lately and I'd kind of like to keep it that way. After every hunt, I religiously schedule myself seven days of blissful solitude. Just me, a fridge full of beer, and my nightly date with Pornhub. Resolute about preserving my downtime, I let the call go to voicemail.

My ringtone starts up again, and I roll my eyes. Glutton for punishment that I am, I look at the screen.

An unfamiliar area code. A number I don't recognize.

An inexplicable chill runs through me, and I try to shake it off, but my gut tells me to answer, and my gut is never wrong.

I swipe the screen hurriedly, ready to chew someone's ass.

"Who is this and how did you get this number?"

A pause follows, and I hear her inhale. The intake of air against her vocal cords gives her identity away, and I go numb as I realize who's on the other end of the line.

"Connor?" My name from Lilah's lips wakes my slumbering temper, along with my dormant libido. Ages have passed since I heard her smoky voice, but I'd recognize it anywhere. My heart lurches and my knuckles crack as my hand clenches into a painful fist.

Delilah Fucking Campbell.

Fucking isn't actually her middle name, but it should be.

"Hello?" She sounds nervous, which is as rare as the birth of a white buffalo. Lilah's the cockiest person I've ever met, and after my time in Special Ops, that's saying something. My pulse thunders in my ears when I remember the way she strutted into every room like she owned the place. I realize I'm on my feet and pacing, and I blush. A simple greeting from her has me at the ready. Just like the old malamute resting beside my chair, I'm a well-trained dog responding obediently to her dinner bell.

Delilah had been my first friend. My first kiss. My first time. Vivid flashbacks of that particular night cause cracks in my icy reserve. Lilah's the only girl I've ever loved, and our disastrous breakup whipped my ass ten times worse than my piece of shit father ever had.

I hear Lilah release a frustrated breath through the tiny speaker in my phone, and I swear I can taste her as if we've just kissed. My temples throb in time with my pounding heart. "Connor? Are you there?"

"I'm listening." I fight to sound cool and detached. She has a lot of nerve calling me, but then she's always had balls of steel.

"It's Lilah." Her unnecessary introduction makes me

twice as furious.

"No shit." I'm tempted to hang up on her then and there. So much for keeping my cool. I hear her sigh, and flashes of her inundate me. The candy she always snuck into the movies, and how it tasted on her tongue as we made out in the back row. The way the guys in school gathered to watch her stretch at cross-country practice like frat boys at a strip club. How they thought she was playing hard to get, when she was just balls to the wall, so good at the things she deemed worth doing that she didn't get how average people could live with their mediocrity.

All this comes rushing back with stinging clarity. Once upon a time, Delilah was my everything. We used to be inseparable, a package deal…Lie and me against the world. I knew her better than I knew myself back then. Or at least I thought I did.

"I need your help." This isn't a request, and her audacity makes me laugh. After all the blood shed between us, she thinks she can just appear out of the blue and I'll do her bidding. If she's going to rip open this scab, I'm going to make it hurt.

"With what? That pretty boy you married needs *another* trophy?"

Score one for me.

I lean back in my chair and wait for her to tell me to kiss her ass.

The silence on the other end makes me wonder if she hung up. I pull the phone from my ear to look at the screen when she speaks again.

"I'm not calling to talk about Josh."

"Why the fuck *are* you calling me?" I snarl into the phone, sitting forward so suddenly that Runt flinches in surprise.

"You haven't heard…" Lilah's desperation is palpable and it brings a smile to my lips.

"Spit it out, Delilah. It's late and I have shit to do." Her name tastes sweet and the thought makes me want to punch myself in the face.

"I would if you'd shut up for five seconds!" Her confrontational tone causes a familiar stirring below the belt. Ignoring my dick, I take a pull from my glass to stall as I decide on a reply.

She sniffles, and my stomach plummets. I've been so caught up in my rage that I'd missed the grief woven in her voice. She sounds shaken, un-Lilah-like. "It's Mom. She's…missing."

I choke on the liquid I'm swallowing and cough to clear it. Lilah's mom, LuAnn, is my godmother, though Lu doesn't put much stock in God. She and my mom had been lifelong friends. They used to put Lilah and me in the bathtub together as babies, that's how far back this incestuous shit of ours goes. LuAnn is a living reminder of my mom, who passed three years ago, and she's also the only Campbell who'll still have anything to do with me.

"Wait. What? What happened?" Sympathy leaks out before I can contain it. To say that I'm conflicted is putting it mildly. I don't want to be kind to Lilah. The idea is so distasteful it makes my stomach churn. I want her to suffer, like she's made me suffer. I want her to *ache*. Sometimes when I can't sleep, I can still feel my hand around her throat.

But LuAnn? She's family. Things were rocky for her after I wigged out at Mom's funeral, but unlike her daughter, Lu doesn't hold grudges and she and I declared a truce.

"She took the plane out to make deliveries four days ago. She never came home." Lilah's words are heavy with implication.

I swallow past the swelling lump in my throat. We'd had one hell of a storm roll in four days ago, and The Bearded Douchebag Brigade, my assistant, Reynolds, and I were forced to sit out of our hunt for nearly twenty-four hours. Luckily, tourists don't camp, they "glamp," so we'd been stranded in the woods in style. I'd used the break to get blackout drunk, since storms make it impossible to sleep, and I'm out of all of my prescriptions.

Reality sinks in hard and fast. With rare exceptions, very few pilots go missing in the bush and live to talk about it. Not even tough-as-nails pros like Lu. Alaska is one brutal bitch, notoriously the most dangerous place on earth to fly. As much as it pains me to admit it, Lu is very likely dead and they just haven't found what's left of her yet.

"I called the local troopers, but those backwater assholes won't tell me anything. The clock's ticking and they're just sitting around with their thumbs up their fat asses eating donuts. I even broke down and called Boone. That was a nightmare. It took thirty minutes of one-sided conversation before he finally texted me your number."

Lilah's urgency wrestles me back into focus.

I'm no shrink, but I've picked up the basics in court-mandated group therapy at the V.A., and Delilah's clearly fluctuating between the steps of denial and bargaining. I'd say anger too, but she's always angry, so honestly, who could tell? I could try to reason with her, maybe even try to comfort her...but I reserve that kind of effort for friends, and Lie and I are barely acquaintances these days.

"This is the first I'm hearing about any of this," I finally admit, powerless to keep up appearances.

"I just found out yesterday," she states, and I blink, taken aback. Lilah and her sister, Andi (who's local), aren't on good terms, but it's mind-boggling that Lu's disappearance hasn't trumped their squabble. As the root cause of their squabble, I'm probably biased. Then again, these are the Campbell sisters, and stubbornness runs rampant in their family line.

"Can you talk to Search and Rescue? Find out who's in charge and get them to call me? Boone's a fucking brick wall..." Lilah barrels on, not even pausing for responses. I'm unfazed that her use of the f-word is still as liberal as my father's use of the saltshaker. "Maybe you can get the details on the territory they've already covered for the ground search? My flight just landed, so I have to rent a car before I can get on the road and up to True."

My head reels, partly because of the scotch and partly because I'm balls deep in a conversation with *the one that got away*. As she blathers on with her demands disguised as requests, my hands shake and I place my glass on the rustic porch railing. Delilah sounds the same: direct, passionate, persuasive. I struggle to focus on her words instead of the looming shadow of our disturbing past. It's not easy, considering the fact that I still think about her on a daily basis.

"—so the dispatcher *actually* told me to call back when I can be polite. Do you believe that shit? Fucking government employees," Lilah rattles on. "She'd better hope she's off the clock when I get to that station."

I rub my temple, massaging the dangerous thud that reverberates there. I cannot go down this road, not with Lilah Campbell riding shotgun. We've always been combustible together, like napalm and a blowtorch. It sounds dramatic, I realize, but make no mistake: Alaska's no longer big enough for the both of us.

"I'm all the way down in Sterling, Lie. Just go on up to True. Half the town can probably brief you." I sound firm, but don't feel it. Well, *part* of me feels firm—rock-hard, as a matter of fact—but he has a mind of his own and is usually best ignored.

"I need more than information, Connor," she huffs, and I can practically feel her breath in my ear. I tell myself it's my nightcap affecting my inhibitions, and not the layers of unspoken urges I hear when she utters my name.

I have needs too, I want to tell her. Ones that are readily apparent by the painful pressure behind my zipper.

"I can pay you," she presses, sounding reasonable...logical. The Delilah I know is neither of these things.

"I don't want your money, Lie." I'm proud of how

bored I sound at her suggestion.

"Come on, Garrett." Her proposition sounds all throaty and soft. I lick my parched lips, which burn like a mother, thanks to my half glass of scotch. She's scorching, and I'm a recovering pyromaniac. "I *dare* you."

I swallow hard, my throat like sandpaper, despite the lubrication in my glass. Her challenge harkens back to a time when we could've convinced one another of anything. A bygone era when we were more concerned with each other's opinions than anyone else's. It's her Hail Mary pass, and until she says those three words, I'm actually considering it.

"Don't start that shit, Delilah. We're not kids anymore." Wrath is the only weapon in my arsenal against her, so I lock and load.

"But—"

"No."

"Con—"

"I said no and that's final. We're not doing this. Not again. You're on your own."

"I'm gonna find her, Connor." Lilah blunders on, and as exasperating as she is, I admire her tenacity. "The news says they'll suspend the search within the next seventy-two hours. If we...if they still haven't found her, I'll need a guide."

I cover my eyes with my hand. Fearless as she is, Lilah's been away from the bush a long time. She's always had wilderness skills, mad ones. Hell, her sense of direction puts mine to shame. Experienced or not, the Alaskan wilderness is no place to wander by yourself. Even well equipped and seasoned, dangers are plentiful, and I'm not just talking about the wildlife or the terrain. This time of year, people are a real concern.

Realization dawns that she's just double-talked me, and the ease with which she's done it is laughable. She appealed to my ego…my area of expertise…my loyalty to Lu. Lie's a master manipulator, but her request is warranted. I stay silent as I debate with myself.

There are a few guides I trust, guys I recommend for overflow business, but do I want any of them taking Lilah into the bush? Hunters and trappers currently litter the countryside. Then there's the Aurora 10 treasure hunters, a cutthroat lot in their own right, but their numbers have dwindled significantly since I'd left for the military. Alaska is the final frontier, and it can turn deadly in an instant. And when a woman looks like Lie does…

My wandering thoughts are lost in her long, curly hair and that unbelievable body. One thing is painfully clear. I still have no self-control when it comes to Delilah, and she probably has more to fear from me than just about anyone. I weigh the danger to my sanity against any hazards she might face in the wild. It's no contest. Someone has to look out for me.

"You'll have to find someone else." My tone is non-negotiable, but that has never stopped her before.

"But…" She sounds very young, and the boy in me who loved her once wants to agree to anything she asks. "I need someone who knows their shit."

I say nothing, because the things I want to say don't pertain to searching for her mother at all.

"Fine." Her rich alto voice sounds way too close for comfort. Against all reason, her dismissive response stings like ocean water in a gaping wound. "Recommend someone. Anyone."

We're back to the problem of who I trust alone in the woods with Lilah. I draw a blank.

"I need a name, Connor. While we're still young." Her tone is stone cold.

I'm pacing again. Runt looks up at me, concerned eyebrows twitching at my obvious agitation. "I don't know. I don't trust—"

"I know you don't trust me. Jesus, you've made that very clear. I figured you might try to get past that for Mom's sake, but I guess I was wrong." Her sharp resonance slices through me. "Sorry I interrupted your evening."

"Lie—" I start, but I've no idea what I plan to say. As it turns out, it doesn't matter. The line is already dead.

CHAPTER TWO

LILAH

HOMECOMING

I'M THE CURATOR of my own destiny, which wouldn't even be a footnote if I were a man. Since I'm not, everyone has a theory about why I'm defective. Daddy issues: check. Absent mother: double check. Something to prove: triple check underlined in bold. Whatever.

My ex-husband, Josh, used to claim I had an overdeveloped sense of adventure. I say one person's "overdeveloped" is another person's healthy. Regardless, I never put much stock in other people's opinions, whether or not we were sleeping together, and being an oddity never bothered me much.

My mom's people were settled here before Alaska was even officially a state. She's a commercial supply pilot, delivering groceries and other necessities to people who live far enough out that driving or boating into town isn't a practical option. She's also a director for the Ninety-Nines, the International Organization of Women Pilots. In her spare time, she takes wannabes up for lessons. LuAnn Campbell is a living legend in her remote little corner of the world, and fear isn't even in her vocabulary.

She has a reputation for always making the right call, and she always, *always* finds her way home. Until now.

I haven't slept much since receiving a strange phone call from my mother on the morning she was reported missing. Wherever she'd been when she called me that sweltering morning, she'd had piss-poor reception and I only managed to catch a few words amidst the stuttering transmission.

"Li—found—Aurora.—your father."

"Mom?" I covered my ear to block out the sounds in the bustling hangar. She'd called while I was doing my morning inspection of one of the company's birds, and the echoing acoustics only enhanced our communication issues.

"—low. Don't—home."

"Mom? I can't understand you. You're breaking up!" One of the mechanics bumped into me. I ignored him, covering my free ear and straining to hear her.

"I—Connor. Connor—you. D—home."

"What? What the hell, Mom?" Mom hadn't mentioned Connor to me since Claire's funeral. She damn well knew better.

"Don't trust anyone!" For that one sentence she was clear as crystal. I froze mid-step. The *way* she said those words chilled me.

She was slurring. I was used to that from Dad, but never from Mom.

There was something more though. Beyond that, she

sounded off...*afraid*, maybe?

After the call dropped, which was seconds later, I tried to call her back several times and finally resorted to texting her, insisting she call me back, ASAFP. She hadn't, and I got swamped with work and sidetracked. I blew it off.

Two nights later, my younger sister Andi called me with the news.

"Check your email." That's all she said before hanging up. Andi's call rivaled Mom's in its weirdness quotient, and half-asleep, I stumbled to my laptop and logged on. I glanced at the clock in the lower corner of my screen and discovered it was 1:00 a.m. I immediately saw an email from Boone, my unofficial brother, who worked for Search and Rescue back home in the Anchorage area. His email contained a bunch of links to news stories about my mother and her missing plane. Since then, I've been on the phone, in an airport, or on a flight.

"Would you like a luxury car? We have one available." The perky rental clerk's bubbly voice rips me out of my headspace. Her flawless hair and starched white shirt have me yearning to wash the desperation of coach class off of myself.

"I need something with four-wheel drive," I tell her, knowing there's no telling what I'll put the sorry rental through. Better to be prepared for anything, since Connor shot me down, as expected. *Fucking Connor.*

I can't spare another second to dwell on him. Based on his reaction to my call, I see no reason to tell him that Mom had mentioned him before she vanished. With or without him, I'll be searching for her in some pretty remote places. Some roads here crack from the pressure of a hard freeze or under the weight of all the snow and ice. Plus, they're rarely serviced. Some places I'll likely be traveling will have no roads at all.

By the time I make it out of the airport, it's nearly 8:30 p.m. and still not dark outside. The wind nips at my ears, and I hurry to put up my hood. Nighttime back in Vegas can get chilly, but I've lost any real cold tolerance over the years since I moved away. As I turn the key in the ignition, I glance at the temperature on the dash: forty-five degrees. I'm comforted by the fact that Mom shouldn't have to worry about hypothermia. At least, not yet.

My phone rings and when I see Connor's name on the screen, I don't answer. I don't have the energy to deal with his negativity or listen to any insults he's come up with since I hung up on him. If he's thought of a guide for me, he can leave me a voice mail.

I hope Mom still keeps a spare key under the flowerpot on the porch. There's no telling how long it might take to find her, and since I can't search and work at the same time, I'm not making money. My savings might have to last me a while, so staying in my childhood home isn't optional.

As I turn north toward my hometown, I meditate on Mom's bizarre phone call. It came just hours before she'd been reported missing, and my suspicious mind jumps directly to foul play.

Don't—home.

Was it part of a sentence? Like, "if you don't come home I'm going to kill your father" or "if you don't come home I'm going to lose the business"?

Or had I just done exactly what she'd told me not to do?

Crossing into the city limits of True, I marvel at how little the place has changed over the years. Same old main street, same old cobbled-together buildings, same nosy-ass people gawking at me as they loiter outside the shitty little dive bar on Main. I don't miss it. For eighteen years, I hated everyone knowing everything about me, or thinking they did.

Turning west toward Knik Arm and Mom and Dad's place, my sense of dread grows with every passing mile. I maneuver the untended road, laser focused on avoiding any hazards, such as downed trees or nocturnal wildlife crossings.

As I pull into the driveway, the sight of Dad's dented-up car parked haphazardly near the ramp to the boathouse makes me groan aloud. I'm thrilled that the windows are dark down there. He's likely passed out for the night, and I'll have a chance to get some sleep before sifting through his verbal garbage.

Mom's key is stashed where it always is. Inside, the house has that stuffy feeling of a cabin that's been sealed up for the winter. I open a couple of windows to let the breeze roll in off the water. Tossing my coat on a hook near the door, I search for Mom's laptop. As I approach her desk, I spy an unfamiliar photo of Mom and Connor's mother,

Claire. I gather from the scarf on Claire's head and the forced smile on Mom's lips that this picture was taken shortly before Claire's death. A lump forms in my throat, and I set the frame aside.

Though our moms had been friends since elementary school, they couldn't have been more different. I'm still baffled about how two such different women were so inseparable. Claire was all sugar and spice; Mom was straight-up rock salt and WD40. The only thing they seemed to have in common was their bad taste in husbands.

Coming up empty-handed in my hunt for Mom's computer, I succumb to my growling stomach and peek inside the fridge, expecting decayed produce and rotting leftovers. I should know better. Mom's fridge is empty, except for condiments and beer.

"Thanks, Mom," I murmur, snagging a can. Beer isn't my thing, but alcohol always makes me drowsy, and I just can't go another night without sleep. I take my first sip, pleased to discover it's palatable, unlike the skunky stuff my father guzzles by the barrel.

My bag has gained fifty pounds since I packed it, and hefting it up over my shoulder, I wander into my old bedroom and flip on the light. It looks the same as it did the day I left, except for a few random items piled in the corner. Though I fight valiantly, my eyes fall on the framed picture above the dresser. The pressure in my chest sky-rockets, and I rub at it pointlessly. There we were, Connor Garrett and me, on the cover of *People* magazine. Smug sixteen-year-old delinquents, forever immortalized sharing a secretive glance.

We'd had reason to be smug. We'd accomplished what so many professional treasure hunters before us had failed to. We were the youngest people who'd found the ninth of the ten missing pallets of Aurora Corporation's gold dropped during an infamous hijacking. We were the toast of True for a while, bringing new tourist dollars into our sleepy little town, as our find reignited the hunt for the final pallet. Not modest by nature, Connor and I were the first in line to believe our own press. We'd thought that we were hot shit and completely untouchable.

I drop my bags and pull the picture off of the wall. Carrying it into the bathroom with me, I draw a hot bath, and I catch a glimpse of my frizzy hair and the dark circles under my eyes, then dismiss them. I've got bigger problems than my haggard appearance and no one to impress. What I need is sleep. Booze and a bath might make that happen.

Scalding water steams up the mirrors, and as I wait for the tub to fill, my gaze wanders back to the magazine cover. Unable to resist, I rub the steam off of the glass over Connor's image. Seeing his face again crushes me. That strong jaw, his thick, careless hair, those devilish eyes, and that cocky-ass grin.

Memories rush through me, like refusing to come out of my room for a week when Connor's dad got transferred and he had to move away in fourth grade. My joy when they moved back to Ft. Richardson when we were starting junior high. How he and Claire showed on our doorstep weeks later, her with a black eye, and Connor looking like he'd gone three rounds with Mike Tyson. The way his sixteen-year-old eyes flashed when he cornered me in the cockpit of my mother's plane, informing me that he'd made up his mind and he wanted us to be "more than friends."

The summer after graduation, I'd abandoned my life here. The sprawling forests reminded me too much of Connor's mossy eyes, and the jagged glaciers served as a sharp reminder of his vicious rejection.

Bombarded with flashes of what we'd once been, and everything that loving him had taken from me, the urge to chuck the frame into the bathtub almost overwhelms me. I resist. I've already destroyed every other picture of us that ever existed, and it would be disrespectful to destroy the one relic Mom managed to salvage after my youthful tirade. I hurry into the guest room and drop the picture onto the bed where it's theoretically safe from me.

Stripping unceremoniously, I sink into the scalding water, anxious to wash away Connor, and the pain he still inflicts on me. He made his choices, and I made mine. My jaw clenches tight as I replay our last few conversations, and ruminate over the shrapnel I carried as a result of our final showdown before he joined up. It's good that he refused to help me. Neither of us needs to excavate all that ancient history.

I fucking *dared* him.

Like he dared me to pinch the Camp Fire counselor's behind when we were six.

Like I dared him to compete in the Reindeer Run wearing nothing but his swim trunks when we were twelve.

Like he dared me to stop fighting and be his girl not long after we found the gold.

My eyes sting and I clench my teeth defiantly. I will not cry. Not for him. If Connor's not with me, he's against me, and I'm better off.

I swallow more beer, already feeling the buzz. I file Connor Garrett under "Shit To Think About Another Day." Finding Mom and her plane is front and center where it belongs, and I quickly come to the conclusion that I'll need to rent a plane. Mine's long gone and Mom's isn't an option since it's wherever she is. A plane will liberate me from Search and Rescue's constraints.

The pervasive quiet of the empty house is starting to get to me, so I climb out of the tub. I pop in earbuds and start up a playlist for some white noise. Tossing on something to sleep in, I wander out to shut the windows. The sun is finally setting over the dark water of Knik Arm, and I'm mesmerized for some time by the dappled pastel sky. Finally, I make my way back into the kitchen, and I notice something odiferous emanating from the sink. It turns out to be a dirty plate and cup. Mom probably tossed them there, figuring she'd just wash them when she got home from her workday. The thought chills me more than the brisk night air had moments before.

I'm hand-drying them when I feel that tickle...the sensation of being watched. I tell myself it's just fatigue and an active imagination. I catch the reflection of something moving behind me in the window over the sink, and I spin around, ready to brawl.

An abnormally large figure hovers in the darkened doorway. My heart's in my throat strangling me. Long hair and an overgrown beard make the hulking man look like he's part Sasquatch. I'm ready to spring for the knives on the counter nearby when he steps forward out of the shadows, and his brutally gorgeous gaze pins mine. I freeze. The heat behind those eyes flusters me, and I immediately understand why his sinewy movements are so painfully familiar.

The man glaring across the room at me is Connor.

CHAPTER THREE

CONNOR

FEVER

AFTER ARGUING WITH myself for thirty minutes, I call Lilah back. I get her voice mail, and when she introduces herself as Delilah Andrews, I want to throw my phone into the river and pour myself another drink.

Grumbling to myself, I toss my camping gear and jump back into my Jeep and whistle for Runt. He lopes over and hops in, and we start the two-and-a-half-hour drive north. It kills me to admit it, but I can't let her stubborn ass wander into the bush alone. I owe it to LuAnn to keep her daughter safe, from herself, if nothing else. After all, Lu looked out for me after the army, especially when she had plenty of reasons not to.

The tall tales I spin about loyalty and altruism are all well and good, but underneath my rationalizing, I hear my father whispering, "A hard dick has no conscience." As I come to a crossroads, I pause, considering my motivation. I have no choice but to do what I can for LuAnn. That's a given. But Lu's not the reason I've had the pedal to the floor. There is no one around for miles, so I take a long moment to decide whether to whip a U-turn back to my comfortable, misanthropic life or to press on and mix it up in the lion's den.

"Son of a bitch!" I smack the steering wheel and rake my hands through my hair to get it the hell out of my face. Runt whines sympathetically, and feeling like a lunatic, I whip the steering wheel of my Jeep in Lilah's direction. No one else can hear my thoughts, and there's no use lying to myself. It's no longer a question of want. I *need* to see Lilah, and the sooner the better.

She'll be at LuAnn's. It's where I'd start, and after years of plotting alongside her, I know her strategies like they're my own. We'd hunted treasure together before, after all. More importantly, we'd managed to sneak around for months without anyone finding out in a town the size of a postage stamp.

I pass through Anchorage, unable to ignore the exit that would've taken me to Dad's place. I consider calling his nurse, Cyndi, just to make sure he's still alive. Considering the way I snuck out of her apartment that last time we hooked up, it's probably better to leave well enough alone.

Don't get me wrong; Cyndi's still as easy on the eyes as she was back in high school, and I'm no monk. She just isn't the type to settle for friends with benefits. She's already been divorced twice, and probably has her sights set on me as husband number three. That isn't happening. We have virtually nothing in common, and Delilah taught me early in life that all relationships, even those built on friendship and history, are slow-acting poison.

Finally, I pass the "Welcome to True, Alaska" sign and wave to the familiar faces having a smoke outside of The Corner Tap before I slip down Old Knik Road and skid into Lu's driveway, like I had hundreds of times before. Gooseflesh breaks out on my upper arms. LuAnn's presence is everywhere…in every board of the aging fence she stubbornly mended every spring and every single blade of grass in the large, neglected yard.

An SUV with rental plates is parked neatly near the house and I know it's Delilah's. I throw the door open and hop out of the Jeep before I can change my mind. Runt leaps out too, and he takes off toward the muddy dunes behind the house. I'd like to join him…to just run and keep on running.

I knock, and when no one answers, I peek in the window. Lilah's standing at the sink with her back to me. Black boy-short panties showcase her voluptuous heart-shaped ass, and her little black shirt leaves no doubt that she's braless. Spellbound, I stare with slack-jawed appreciation.

She's put on some weight through the hips and the chest, her formerly gentle curves now a full-blown hourglass. Even in the dimly lit kitchen, my eyes feast on her naturally dark skin. Her bushy hair tumbles down to the middle of her back, darker at the roots, the ends bleached auburn by the Nevada sun. She's an exaggerated version of her former self, and seeing her half-naked is pure torture. People are sometimes described as aging like a fine wine. Delilah's aged like a finely crafted scotch. Full and complex, pure satin over the palate and intoxicating with plenty of after spice.

I try the knob and I'm not surprised to find it unlocked. She still has more guts than good sense. Lilah doesn't turn around, even when a board creaks beneath my boot. I catch the gleam of her white earbuds just before she whips her head in my direction.

Her face goes stone cold, and I can tell her hackles are up. Complete calm settles over her features, but she rips the earbuds unceremoniously from their rightful place, and based on her stance, she's ready for a fight. I step into the room, and her expression shifts. Her eyes darken, and the air grows turgid and charged around us, like the gulf before a tempest rolls in off the water. I can tell by the rise and fall of Delilah's chest that she feels it too.

"Connor." Her golden eyes dart over the scar splitting my eyebrow, and the thick beard and long hair I'd grown out since last we met. "You scared the shit out of me."

"Sorry." I'm not and she knows it.

"Since when do *you* move so quietly?" Her raspy voice has a serrated edge. She hates being caught off guard, and I'm delighted to have thrown a wrench into her evening.

"Since Special Forces training." I take another step toward her, my eyes roving over her as if they have a mind of their own. "If you're going to walk around dressed like that you should really lock the door."

Her frown deepens and she reflexively backs against the sink. Despite our last ugly encounter after Mom died, I'm surprised by this. Ashamed, too. I stuff my hands in my pockets, holding my ground.

"Are you camouflaging your face?" Her tone is just this side of bitchy as her eyes sweep over my long beard again.

"Making up for all those army-mandated barber visits," I joke, unable to suppress a smirk. Always with an opinion, this one.

"You look…" The tilt of her delicate chin lets me know she's deliberating.

I feel my lips twitch, anticipating an insult. "What?"

Her face remains impossibly neutral. Predictably un-predictable. "You don't look like *you*."

I shrug and my shaking hands remain in my pockets. "You look…"

Her spine goes board straight, her chin up. She's brac-ing for me to insult her. I'd like to, since jabbing her ego might release venom from my festering wounds. The truth is, she looks amazing. I stick to the simplest observation and spare us both more awkwardness.

"Tired," I finish. She releases a breath and nods curtly.

"Being back here is harder than I thought."

"I'm sorry," I say. It's automatic, a pointless platitude. She looks at the floor as if gathering strength from the scuffed wood planks beneath her feet. "You know how I felt about LuAnn."

She bristles.

"How you *feel* about LuAnn." Her penetrating eyes are a caution sign that I'm careening forward at one hundred miles per hour.

I tilt my head. "Lie…"

"Pilots walk out of the bush all the time," she declares.

I nod, but I'm sure she sees how skeptical I am. While pilots *have* turned up weeks after vanishing due to mechanical failures or emergency landings, it isn't the norm. "If anyone could, it'd be Lu."

The silence that hangs between us is sadly familiar, and I want desperately to fill it.

"I cleared my schedule for the week." I arrange my face into a neutral mask. "So if you still need a guide…"

She tucks a strand of hair behind her ear and turns back to the sink. Reaching for her lotion, she flips her long curls over one shoulder. As she slathers on the sweet concoction, I notice a tattoo on her right shoulder blade.

I move a little closer, curious.

"This is new." I reach out to brush her tiny strap aside for a better look at the ink. The tattoo is an antique compass rose, the figure that displays the orientation of the cardinal directions on old maps. The design is actually really nice; a couple of roses and some leaves give the outer circle a wreath-like quality.

"Not really. I got it a long time ago." Her voice is husky as my fingertip glides across her silky skin. Gooseflesh appears on her upper arm, and that gives me a thrill. "When I was like…twenty… maybe twenty-one."

She turns around, and her hip brushes against the front of my zipper. I'd say the contact made me hard, but I was halfway there watching her from outside. She looks up at me, and though she's had to crane her neck to meet my eyes since we were in middle school, it's always felt as if *she* were the one looking down on *me*.

"I was dating the tattoo artist. I guess you could call it 'dating.'" Her tiny eye roll implies it wasn't one of her finer moments.

I tilt my head, my blood pumping something fierce between my jealousy at the idea that anyone else has ever touched her and her sheer nearness in this moment. "Oh yeah?"

She nods, and a macabre smile flits across her face. "He was tall. And a major know-it-all. Totally *my type*."

I feel an appreciative smile working at my lips.

"Why didn't you marry *him*?" It's a bold and weighty statement and her mouth drops open. She searches me, and for a rare, candid moment, I allow it.

"*He* was mean." I see something flicker behind those liquid amber eyes.

"Sounds like a match made in heaven." My voice is gruff, but I'm glad I spoke the truth. I'm even gladder for how solidly the blow lands, based on the way her perfect bow of a mouth turns down at the edges. In a surprising move, she lifts herself easily onto the counter so she's sitting on it, and I struggle to keep my eyes off of her well-defined arms and that gravity-defying chest. "This doesn't have to be ugly, Connor. Let's have a beer. Catch up. Talk about old times."

I say nothing, and her lips form a slanted smile. "We did have some good times, didn't we?"

That's for fucking sure.

I could step between her legs right now. Slip her panties

aside and bury myself in her tight, wet heat. It would be as easy as breathing, and three-quarters of me is ready to take the easy route. I move to the far cabinets away from her, putting temptation at arm's length. From there, I have an even better view, so I force myself to look away, grabbing a beer from the fridge. "No."

"No we didn't have good times, or no we can't talk about them?" She sounds entertained.

I crack my beer and lock eyes with her. "We're not talking about us."

She's completely unreadable now, and that puts me on edge. "Why not?"

I lean against the cabinet, sipping from my beer. "Because I'm not done being mad at you."

She blasts an incredulous laugh and when I don't respond in kind, her laughter dies, and she gives me another thorough once-over.

"*You're* mad at *me*? You've got to be kidding."

I tip back my can in response.

She lets out a sardonic chuckle, but she's obviously pissed. "That's rich."

I wait for her to convince me that I shouldn't hate her. She seems to be waiting on something too. Her smile, the one that isn't really a smile at all, fades.

"You *promised* me, Connor. You *promised* we'd always be friends." It's nearly imperceptible, but her lip quivers. Most people wouldn't have noticed, but most people aren't me.

I wrinkle my brow, squinting at her in amazement.

"You were very clear, Lie. You said I should never contact you again. How'd you put it? Oh, yeah. You said, 'Have a nice life.'"

Her shining eyes narrow into dangerous slits. Then, in a classic Lilah move, she wipes her expression blank, closing the shutters, blocking out any hope of peeping inside. "Fair enough."

I should be glad we're on the same page. That we're slamming the door on all of that shit. Instead, I want to roar. Frustrated, I chug my beer. By the time I'm done, she's chewing on her bottom lip. It's a quirk of hers that I've always found sexy as hell, so it's like a metaphorical kick in the nuts.

"I'm staying in my old room." She's either blushing, or she's still coming down from the crisp night air. "Take any of the other beds you like."

My treacherous mind recalls the handful of times I snuck in her bedroom window, and I know exactly which bed I want to slip into. I hurry to grab my bag from where I'd dropped it in the entryway. I'm startled when she speaks again.

"Connor?"

"Yeah?" I turn, hopeful that I've finally gotten through her armor in some minute way. Maybe she'll cry. Crying would be excellent.

"Thank you." Her earnest eyes tug at my worn and frayed heartstrings. "For coming to help me."

I drop my bags and stride toward her. Instead of flinching away, she leans forward in anticipation. Though we don't touch, we still clash like two storm fronts, me dark and ominous, her all lightning and show. I'm close enough to kiss her, and she bats those long lashes, which used to be my undoing. The challenge in her smoldering gaze elicits a deep ache in my groin. I grip the countertop on either side of her thighs until my knuckles turn white.

"I'm not here for *you*," I growl. She stares into my eyes, unflinching, and turning, I stalk out to my Jeep for the rest of my gear, whistling for Runt, who appears with whirlwind speed that belies his years.

When I come back inside, Lilah's no longer in the kitchen. I put out some food and water for Runt and debate about where to sleep. The thought of Lu's bed creeps me out more than a little. Andi's old room creeps me out a whole lot. That leaves me in Boone's former room, just down the hall from Lilah. For the first time since arriving, I wonder where her husband is.

As I undress, I notice something on the bed. It's our *People* cover. I force myself to take a good hard look at it, then collapse on the bed, pulling up the archived story on my phone just to twist the knife like the total masochist I am. As I review the redacted version of events we gave during our press conference, the real events monopolize my taxed brain.

Before Delilah and I were even born, an infamous hijacking occurred in our remote neck of the woods. Two men had attempted to steal a large air shipment of gold pallets owned by Aurora, a local mining and assaying corporation. Almost all of the gold, which they tossed out of the plane before plummeting to their deaths, had been lost to the Alaska wilderness. In the decades since, treasure hunters had recovered eight of the ten pallets.

Lie and I had obsessed over the missing gold for as long as I could remember. Hell, in elementary school, we wandered the woods at my place on the river, hoping to randomly stumble upon our fortune. We spent our tweens devouring everything we could find about the incident, poring over countless books and articles and staring at maps every weekend like it was our job. Shortly after my sixteenth birthday, Lie called me, waking me from a dead sleep.

"I found a pattern to the drops." Lie sounded giddy, and out of breath. I sat straight up in bed. It couldn't be true. Without knowing the order in which the drops occurred or the integrity of the existing facts, everything Aurora related was guesswork.

When I met her at the bakery the following morning, she'd been in a booth near the back, chugging coffee, her knee going a million miles a minute. I made her wait until I had my bear claw, an apple fritter, and a bucket of coffee in front of me before I allowed her to speak.

She unfurled her map and I saw the Xs, same as always.

"What do you see?" She folded her hands in front of her, and I wanted to strangle her.

"It's way too early for games, Lie."

"They used forks."

She stared at me as if her words should mean something. I glanced down at the silverware, hoping that seeing a fork would assist my sleep-deprived brain to decipher what she was babbling about.

"The drops, Connor." She shot a suspicious glance at the counter lady, who was fastidiously ignoring us. Lilah leaned in and whispered, "The drops are where two rivers meet. Every single one of them. From a bird's-eye view."

My addled mind slipped into gear, and I snatched the map from her, zoning in on the Xs. She was right, of course. Eyeballing it, I couldn't believe we hadn't seen it before. The hijackers had used river forks as landmarks, and all the previous drops had been recovered within five miles of the water.

Lilah speculated that one of the drops was where the Deshka River meets the Sustina River northwest of us. Thanks to Dad indulging my paratrooping questions, I worked the math to see where the trajectory might have carried it, based on recorded weather conditions at the time of the hijacking and the new information regarding the pilot's account of the weight. We narrowed things down to a five-mile stretch north of the river.

After a flyover, it was clear that Delilah didn't have decent conditions for a water landing, and the closest place with a clearing was a few miles upstream from where we suspected the gold had landed.

"So now what?" I asked.

"We'll go land here and raft down. I can borrow one of Dad's. He'll never notice it's gone."

I frowned. "Rafting?"

She nodded, all nonchalant like we did that all the time. "Here's hoping the gold didn't land in the water, or we're just chasing our tails."

"Lie…" I was about to list all of the reasons that this might be a bad idea. We'd spent time on the water, but mostly on the lake. We'd be dealing with currents, in a pretty remote area, so we'd be operating without a safety net.

She tilted her head coyly and narrowed her eyes. That was the moment I realized my longtime pal had gone from tomboy cute to drop-dead gorgeous. "Chicken?"

"No…but—"

"I dare you." Her impish grin gave me no choice but to agree.

As we paddled down the river, Lilah looked over her shoulder at me. "If we find the gold, we need to keep the location a secret."

My forehead wrinkled as I steered toward the left bank where we'd agreed to start our foot search. "Why?"

"Because we'll have an edge finding the last Aurora." Her devilish smile made me grin in response.

"You're an evil genius, Lie. It's our secret," I said, with no clue that I'd just made a pact with the devil.

We found the gold one mile from the riverbank, on our third trip out, camouflaged by a thin, circular cropping of spruce trees. The fractured pallet was half buried in mud and leaves and still partially wrapped in dark tarps with the Aurora logo printed on them. Lilah bounded into my arms, and wrapped her legs around me. The next thing I knew, her lips were on mine, her grip fierce around my neck. As quickly as it started, she released me and dropped to the ground.

I was on fire, and grateful my sweatshirt covered the bulge in my pants. Between her rubbing against me and the sight of those solid gold bars, I was hard as a rock.

"Now what do we do?" I asked, though I had a few ideas and none of them were P.G.

"We count it." She was already moving toward the tarp.

Later that day, as we packed up the last of the bars, Lilah wore a sullen, un-Lilah-like expression.

"What's wrong?"

"What are we gonna do now?" She seemed genuinely lost.

"I could sex you up." I was only partially kidding.

Lilah sniffed and rocked her shoulder into mine.

"We'll find Aurora 10," I told her confidently, ruffling her hair in an attempt to break the tension. She slugged me in the arm, and a bemused smile had overpowered her gloom and doom. When the last of the gold was packed up, we carried the pallet to the riverbank and after weighing it down with rocks, we flung it in. The tarp was close behind, and we both watched as the Aurora logo disappeared into the murky depths.

WHEN WE GOT back to her place, no one was home. We headed straight to her bedroom. Sadly, all we did was hide forty-two gold bars under her mattress. We waited a full ten days before calling a press conference. During that time, Lie and I took her mom's plane out three times, just in case anyone was paying any attention to our flight plans.

Our pact to keep Aurora 9's coordinates a secret seemed so clever at the time, but that naïve decision had a ripple effect we hadn't been prepared for. An irrational part of me—the part that's missing his nightly Valium—still thinks that fucking gold was cursed.

Thoroughly spent from my trip down memory lane, I sit up on the bed and turn the *People* cover facedown on the bedside table. I cross to the door, pressing my ear to it. I can hear faint music from Lie's room, and sighing heavily, I lock the door before I do something I'll regret.

CHAPTER FOUR

LILAH

DARE

I KNOW CONNOR'S talking. I can see his lips moving behind that monstrosity he calls a beard. I remember all too well what's concealed beneath, and those recollections make it hard for me to focus. His strong, squared jaw. His full lips, the gatekeepers of a beautiful smile and a sharp and talented tongue. I force myself to meet his eyes and nod absently at whatever he's just said. Mesmerized by the scar that slices his left eyebrow, I recall how raw it looked at his mother's funeral, when it was still fresh. Retreating from that arduous memory, my eyes drop again to his powerfully distracting mouth.

My plan had been for us to have breakfast at a nearby diner, figuring neutral ground was our best bet to keep things congenial. Then he came into the kitchen looking like the hero of some Viking movie, and I was derailed, stumbling over my words. I finally managed to string the suggestion together, but he was already wearing his bemused smirk. Connor's resting face looks like he's up to no good. His new lumbersexual image just makes it more pronounced.

"With everyone in town listening in on us?" His naturally arched eyebrows elevate, and his point hits home. Lilah Campbell and Connor Garrett doing breakfast would be front-page news in Podunk True. Our reunion is destined to be difficult and awkward enough without an audience. Connor brushes his long hair out of his face with both hands, putting the top half back in a knot.

"Let's just eat here," I suggest. He shrugs.

"I called some contacts on the way up last night. I just checked my email and I have some of the search details."

As he pulls his computer from its bag and plugs it in, I scramble to get a meal together. I'm jittery. I haven't cooked for anyone since I used to keep Boone and Andi alive with ramen noodles and PB and J, I want to be out there now looking, but I'm not stupid. Tempting as it is, we can't run off half-cocked. Distracted, I wreck the eggs, which Connor prefers sunny side up. He gets them half scrambled, and the toast a little overdone because Mom's toaster is evidently set on cremation mode.

I set his plate down beside him, careful to avoid his computer. He glances up from the screen, and his eyes are level with my chest. After a discernible pause, he drags his gaze to mine. He's brimming with anger and a light dusting of lust. For a second, I think he'll grab me, and clear the table with one sweep of his powerful arm. The air between us practically crackles, but he turns away and picks up his plate.

"Sorry, it's nothing fancy. It's all Mom had that doesn't

need to thaw." My hardening nipples humiliate me, and I'm thankful for Connor's dismissiveness.

"This isn't a social call." His gruff response stings like a slap, but it's the truth, so I hurry away gripping the handle of the coffeepot.

"Cream and sugar?"

"I'd better not." His eyes wander over me more thoroughly, as if I'd just invited him to my room for a nightcap. He wears a distasteful frown and I suspect he's judging me for using cream and sugar when I'm still carrying ten extra pounds.

Asshole.

Turning my back on him, I pour my own cupful, dumping plenty of half-and-half and sugar into it with flourish.

His disapproving "she's let herself go" expression infuriates me. It shouldn't matter, but there was a time that Connor couldn't take his eyes off of me. Breathing deeply, I put the half-and-half back in the fridge door and gather my wits. Silently, I give myself some tough love.

How many times are you going to let this man hurt you?

Squaring my shoulders, I return to the table. I slide his cup of black coffee over to him, deciding to skip breakfast.

Seated at the same table where we'd planned our childhood adventures, we sip in uncomfortable silence. So many topics are off-limits that filling said silence is completely impossible. Connor's broody expression and the uncomfortable way he shifts in his seat tells me he's having similar thoughts.

Luckily coffee fills the gaping crevasse in our conversation. Finally, Connor nudges past the elephant in the room and pulls up the maps of the search grids. I come around to read over his shoulder, standing close enough to smell him, and the musky scent of his cologne unleashes a memory so vivid that tears spring to my eyes.

Prom night. The two of us, pulled over in the middle of nowhere, bickering. His lips on my neck as he untied the straps of my gown. My face burns, and I thrust the memory aside through sheer willpower.

Connor doesn't seem remotely fazed by my nearness, and soon we're too immersed in the data for me to care. "What's with these holes in the search grid?" Pointing out three small gaps, I frown. "Who's in charge of the air search? Do you know?"

"I'm not sure." Connor keeps clicking through screens until he finds scanned lists of volunteers. "Half the town showed up for the ground search."

"Well, Mom's a pillar of the community, just ask her." That earns me a reluctant grin from Connor, and it's disarming to see he's still capable of one. I place my fingers on my temples, trying to ignore the throb starting there.

"Looks like Reece Warren is in charge." Connor sounds amused, and I suppress an eye roll. "You ought to be able to get what information your little heart desires out of *him*."

Leaning over Connor's shoulder, I whip out my cell phone and dial Reece's number, which he'd scrawled so boldly on the sign-up sheet. Reece picks up on the second ring.

"Reece. It's Delilah."

"Lilah!" I can hear his smile over the phone.

I glanced at the clock and grimace. "Oh my God, it's only six a.m. I'm so sorry."

He chuckles dismissively. "I can't think of a better way to wake up. You back in Anchorage? Do you need me to come pick you up?"

After the shade Connor's thrown my way, Reece's sweetness is like an electric blanket on a January night.

Such a nice guy.

Connor's kicked back in his chair, his long legs resting where I'd been sitting a few minutes before. He lifts his mug to his lips, unwarranted accusation written all over him.

Too bad nice guys don't do anything for me.

"Thanks, but I'm already in True."

"I'm so sorry about all this stuff with your mom."

His words land like a punch in the gut. "Me too."

"I just saw her that morning. She told me you and your husband are separated."

Well, now. That's quite the non-sequitur.

And an inaccurate one.

"I'm divorced," I correct him. "Hey, listen. Connor and I were just reviewing the search grids and he mentioned that you were in charge—"

"You're with *Connor*." I can practically hear him deflating. Reece made a play for me after Connor and I broke up shortly before senior prom. He obviously remembers how calamitous the results of that play were. Connor watches me over his tipped coffee cup, and I can see he's on the same trip down memory lane. I haven't had enough caffeine yet to juggle both their egos, so I take my mug out onto the back deck.

"I saw a few holes in the air search and need to know what ground you've already covered," I say into the phone, skating any further discussion of Connor entirely.

"It should all be on the grids. I made a couple of passes up by Willow. It was a long shot, but I figured it couldn't hurt. I helped with traffic control the day Lu's plane went missing. A storm rolled in while she was out on her daily runs and I advised her to wait things out up there. She said it wasn't bad enough to divert. I thought once she'd had a taste of the downdrafts…" He trails off.

The name Willow jolts me, and I remember Mom's call. She might have mentioned Willow.

She definitely mentioned Connor.

And goddam Aurora.

Mom cringed and left the room every time Connor and I talked about Aurora. Dad said it was because her friend, Hank, had been flying the hijacked plane. Hank Brown killed himself a few weeks after the incident.

The one time Connor and I did get Mom talking about Hank Brown was the day that redefined our search strategy. I mentioned Hank's suicide, and she went ballistic, ranting about how Aurora smeared Hank's name in the press, since he stuck to his story that they had only one double pallet on the plane, instead of the two they listed on their original manifest. He'd called them out for over reporting to their insurance company, so they painted him like a pill-popping drunk in the court of public opinion. Mom's conviction that Hank was telling the truth made us focus on his version of the story, and eventually that approach led us to Aurora 9.

"Lilah? Are you there?" Reece's soothing voice lures me back into the here and now.

"I have a favor to ask." I stare out at the water, but I'm not really seeing it. If Mom's disappearance has anything to do with Aurora, I'm going to lose what is left of my mind.

"Anything." He means it, and I'm grateful to have someone to rely on.

"I need to rent a plane. Know where I can get one?" In my peripheral vision, I see something large moving down on the lawn. I spin, worried that it might be a wolf or a bear heading my way. I squint against the glare off of the water and realize an Alaskan malamute is bounding toward me.

"Runt?" The puppy I'd spent weeks bottle-feeding and nursing to health has grown into a cheerful drooling monster. I'd never have believed it possible that this was the same dog, but his malformed ear and parti-colored eyes are a dead giveaway. The slobbering mongrel doesn't slow his approach when he jumps up on me.

"Ahhh!" My phone skitters away from me and luke-warm coffee flies everywhere. Runt shakes off the coffee that landed on him onto me with unbridled enthusiasm.

"Lilah? Is everything all right?" Reece's concerned tone

emanates from the tiny speaker of my phone.

"Yeah." I snatch up my unharmed smartphone, scrunching my face as the dog licks at the coffee I'm wearing on my cheek. "Just getting reacquainted with an old friend."

"Why don't you just come down to the airport and use your plane?" he suggests.

"What?" My voice sounds flat.

"Your floatplane. Your mom still stores it here at the airport."

"Cherry?" I huff out the word, gently pushing Runt's face away from mine.

"Well, yeah." Reece laughs and, delirious with joy, I want to jump through the phone and hug him. "I thought you knew."

I'm speechless, trying to make sense of the information. Cherry's the floatplane I'd bought with my reward money from Aurora 9. I love her like most kids love their first car. After I got engaged to Josh, I told Mom to sell her. It'd damn near killed me, but I'd finally made peace with the fact that I was never moving back to Alaska, and it seemed like the sensible thing to do.

"I let my float rating lapse, Reece." I'm practically pouting. "Think you can get me something with wheels?"

"I can re-certify you. Come on down. We'll take her out for a spin."

A massive smile overtakes me. "When?"

"How about tomorrow at 0900? I assume you'll be at the ground search today, since Connor's around."

Connor.

I look back through the screen door. Connor's still in the kitchen scrolling on his smartphone. His nonchalance is such a glaring contrast to Reece's support that I curse my younger self for being so dismissive of Reece. "Yeah. We'll be at the ground search."

"Be careful out there. They've had a couple of bear encounters already. I'll meet you at the front desk tomorrow." Reece sounds eager. "Maybe we can do breakfast before your check ride?"

Mentally, I'm already settled in behind Cherry's controls. "You've got yourself a date."

As I hang up, I realize I never got any hard details on the unexplained gaps in the grid. They weren't far from Willow, so Reece probably covered them on one of his passes and hadn't documented it. I try to text him for clarification, but the text is kicked back. Apparently I'd reached him on a landline.

Connor stands when I open the screen door. Runt pads along beside me and promptly sits obediently at Connor's feet.

"Ready?" He ruffles Runt's fur without looking up from his phone.

"Thanks to your old pal here, I need to change." I yank my sweater off over my head. I have a cami on underneath, but Connor reacts like I'm a naked leper. Whipping his head away, he exhales deeply before he violently rips his laptop cord out of the wall.

"I'm checking into a hotel." Red-faced, he refuses to

look my way as he packs his stuff. "I'll meet you at the launch point. I texted the coordinates to you."

"You don't need to do that." Frowning, my hand is on his forearm without consciously deciding to touch him.

Connor makes me immediately regret it. His face goes crimson, and he yanks his arm away as if I've scalded him. He's all angry skies, glaring at my upraised hand as if it's a cobra.

He's hostile again, and I'm clueless as to what I've done to set him off. I used to be great at poking his buttons, but since he joined up, I don't know him at all. With this newly evolved Connor, the rests are often more telling than the melody. His glare is scathing as he slings his bag over his shoulder. I have no idea what to make of this sudden outburst.

"Name one hotel that allows ninety-pound dogs," I chide, then unable to resist another jab, "Or you could just leave him with me. He is *my dog*, after all."

"I should have known not to give you something that needed to be cared for." His incredulous eyes fixate on me. I've seen this disquieting expression once before, after his Mom's funeral service. Though I want to slap him unconscious and call him a hypocrite, Connor's imposing presence magnifies in Mom's tiny kitchen, and my instincts tell me to stay silent. Fear and desire war within me for the second time since he's arrived, and I brace for whatever's headed my way before I speak again.

"This is a four-bedroom house. You won't even know I'm here."

Connor's acrid eyes ease up and his jaw visibly relaxes. Dropping his gaze, he gives another terse shake of his head.

"I'll see you in the woods." Without another word, he's out the door, Runt trailing behind him.

CHAPTER FIVE

CONNOR

MADNESS

SITTING BEHIND THE wheel of my Jeep in the parking lot of the Northern Lights Bed and Breakfast, I focus on breathing techniques I learned from the V.A. shrink. I'd always felt like a fraud, walking in to group therapy. The others had been wounded in real combat: gunshot wounds, major burns, missing limbs. I had to down a couple of shots before I'd dragged myself to the first session. Turns out I needed that group, probably more than they needed me. Their stories reminded me how lucky I was. I kept going; even after my court-ordered time was up. I had to be there, taking inventory…counting my fucking blessings.

Recluse that I am, I'd missed the fact that RunFest is in full swing, so every running enthusiast in Alaska has descended on Anchorage and the surrounding area. After trying three different hotels, it's clear that I'm not going to find a vacancy. Now I'm trying to decide whether to drive all the way back home or deal with Andi Campbell's shit.

Or…you could just go back and stay with Lilah.

The images that thought conjures are phenomenally Xrated, and I close my eyes wearily.

Her scent's the same. I could smell her sugary fragrance wafting off of her as we looked over the grids. Sadly, I can still recall her ritual, slathering lotion over her hands and elbows, then smoothing what was left on her hands over her hair. She claimed it helped tame the static her natural curls attracted. From the second I got a whiff of her, I'd been struggling to keep my cool. Being that close together after what we'd put each other through was hellish, but we managed, because mysteries are what we do.

All was tolerable until she called Reece Warren. My blood started to boil as she worked that sorry excuse over, telling him she was divorced, creeping away to talk to him in private. Then she just flounces back like nothing happened and invites me to stay. When she dared to touch me, I noticed she wasn't wearing her wedding ring.

What the hell happened to her husband?

Spending another night under the same roof with Lilah is unthinkable.

Still…

"No." I shake the idea off like it's a bad case of fleas and force myself out of the vehicle.

I enter the B&B, welcomed by boisterous laughter and clinking silverware. Before I can enter the communal dining room, I spot Boone lurking behind the ornate counter, like a jeans-and-flannel version of the butler from *The Addams Family*.

A clean-cut, decent-looking dude, Boone is the best tracker I know. Give the guy a screwdriver, and he can fix just about anything. But around True, Boone's known as the village idiot. It's complete and total bullshit. Small towns breeding small minds. Boone's as sharp as a tack. His only issue is that he doesn't talk.

Like…ever.

I've known him since I was five years old, and I've heard him say a grand total of a hundred words. And that's probably a hundred more than most of True has ever heard out of him.

Seeing him at the carved oak counter, you'd think he was just the guy next door. Until you tried to check in.

I raised a hand in greeting. "Hey, Boone."

Though he looks sleep-deprived, the corners of his mouth turn upward and his watchful gaze encourages me to continue.

"I'm in town helping Lilah and I need a room."

Boone's features express everything his mouth doesn't, and his shock and confusion startle me. I exhale audibly, frowning.

"I take it you didn't know she was here," I acknowledge.

He shakes his head.

"Sorry." I silently curse Lilah. No matter what their issues, her family should know she's back, and Boone's been an honorary Campbell since he turned up in True. "She's hell-bent on finding Lu."

Boone's sapphire eyes mist over, but he nods definitively. He knows as well as I do that Delilah won't rest until Lu is located. His attention suddenly shifts over my shoulder, and I turn to see Andi Campbell standing between me and the door.

"Andi." I greet her with an awkward nod, my face flushing as I recall our last encounter. From the looks of Andi's blotchy skin and fidgeting hands, she's right back there with me.

"Connor." Her clipped response makes it clear she isn't interested in grabbing coffee anytime soon. This dynamic isn't new for us. Since all hell broke loose between Lie and me at the end of our senior year, Andi's been Lie's hostile first line of defense. The only exception was Mom's funeral, and I'm fairly sure I liked things better when Andi hated me.

Seeing her again while actually sober and in the light of day, I can forgive myself a little for my drunken antics after Mom died. The resemblance between the Campbell sisters is uncanny, though Andi has ivory skin and blue eyes. But after a few generous pours of hard liquor, and by the light of a roaring fire…she's the spitting image of her older sister, especially when she's glaring me down like this.

My cheeks are on fire, and I remind myself to call the pharmacy for my refills the minute I get the hell out of here.

"I'm helping with the search and I need a room," I manage.

"They haven't called that off yet?" Andi folds her arms, just like her sister did the night before. My eyes widen involuntarily. Lu and Andi have never been tight, but her lack of concern makes no sense to me at all.

I glance at Boone, and his eyes are trained on Andi, as always. I'm unfazed by his deference. Boone adores LuAnn, but he has been Andi's shadow since the first night Lu brought him home and announced that he was staying. Lilah always wanted a brother, and one who wouldn't talk back was her dream come true. Four-year-old Andi immediately claimed him as "her Boone." The name stuck, and so did Andi's claim.

Turning back to re-evaluate her, I try to ignore the scar marring Andi's alabaster cheek, but my eyes betray me. I'm not directly responsible for her disfigurement, but I still feel guilty about it anyhow. Had I not been so drunk that night, I'd have insisted on driving her home.

An older couple breezes into the parlor from the dining room, conversing merrily. The frosty atmosphere surrounding the three of us silences them immediately. They side-eye us, and hurry out the front door. The ironically cheerful tinkle of bells would have made me laugh any other time. Instead, I heave a long-suffering sigh. "Look. Lilah asked me to help and I totally forgot about RunFest. Got any vacancies or not?"

"We're completely booked, Connor." Andi toys with her flashy necklace and stares at the polished wood floor.

I nod and make like a bandit for the exit.

"If my sister's so concerned about Mom, why didn't she come herself?"

I laugh before I can contain it. "She's already here."

Andi whirls my way, and her aghast expression tells me I've just stepped in some serious shit. That's my cue to get out of Dodge.

"Gotta go." I hurry toward the door. I do not miss all this Campbell drama. Not one tiny bit.

"Wait!" I barely recognize Boone's voice, I've heard it so infrequently. I stop and slowly turn in his direction. I can tell by her wide eyes that Andi's as shocked by Boone as I am.

"Coming," Boone states definitively, and without looking in Andi's direction, he hurries out ahead of me. Andi glares at his back all the way out the door.

BY THE TIME we arrive at search headquarters, vehicles of all shapes and sizes clog the surrounding area.

Swarms of volunteers mill around the Red Cross tent, and I feel a small swell of pride at the turnout. We get to makeshift HQ in time to catch Senator Junior Franz shaking hands with several random constituents. The assembled crowd claps politely as he steps up to address the assembled crowd. Bred for politics since birth, Franz artfully directs his good side and his comments to the nearby news cameras.

"Your determination and perseverance makes me prouder than ever to be from the great state of Alaska. Let's get back out there and bring LuAnn Campbell home." He smiles, all manufactured humbleness and ultra-white veneers. Everyone applauds, this time like he's carrying the Olympic torch or he's the second coming of Christ. Boone and I exchange a side-glance, and I see Boone roll his eyes. Lu would be rolling hers, too. Always vocal about her opinions—political or otherwise—LuAnn sure as hell hadn't voted for Franz. I can't help but notice how quickly his entourage ushers him away and into a waiting SUV after his sound bite has been delivered. I guess he'd been using the royal we, since he evidently had more important matters to attend to.

"Remember people. Buddy system. We don't need this search for one turning into a search for two or more." My skin crawls when I recognize Merle Jones's voice over the bullhorn. Sure enough, I catch sight of him, holding a clipboard against his mammoth gut in an official capacity. I look around for Lilah, wondering what she'll have to say about the Aurora Alumni's involvement in her mother's search party.

Back when we were still trying to find the first Aurora drop, we'd spent weeks listening to every word Merle Jones and Stephen Williams had to say. They were the only locals to find Aurora gold, and had the distinction of claiming Aurora 2 and 3. They hung out at a diner near the airport, swapping stories every Thursday night, amassing a loyal crowd of Aurora enthusiasts over the years. Lie and I figured they must know something about something, and it couldn't hurt to spend some time listening in.

It didn't take long before Lie decided they were useless to us, since she'd found a police report detailing how Merle and Stephen were witnesses when Hank came into the bar immediately after the hijacking. Lilah called them out on it in front of their fanboys, stating at the top of her lungs that they were just drinking at the right place at the right time.

Things were a bit of a blur after that, but I recall Merle telling me to get my bitch back on her leash. Next thing I knew, Lilah was on her feet, her finger jabbed into Merle's gut.

"I'm nobody's bitch, bitch."

Stephen stepped in, threatening Lilah to shut her mouth before he took her out back and gave her something else to do with it. Stephen was a tattooed ex con, not the kind of guy I'd want to meet in a dark alley. I was scared, not of him, but of what I'd do to him if he laid a finger on Delilah, so I dragged her out of the diner, Stephen and Merle happily dismissing her to the gathered crowd as a "loudmouthed piece of tail."

Boone puts a hand on my shoulder now, nodding in the direction of the Red Cross awning. I follow his gesture and spot Lilah about thirty yards away. She wears blue flannel and faded jeans like a Hollywood bombshell. Her dark hair is pinned up, crowning her serious face. She's nodding decisively, and the person she's agreeing with is Stephen Williams.

My stomach twists. All I can think about is the way he talked to her when she was just an opinionated young girl. My protective urges awaken, and the adrenaline surge is incredibly unpleasant. As reluctant as I am to spend time with Lilah, I won't be far from her side while Steve-O's around.

Lilah had expected the Aurora Alumni to eat their

words after we found Aurora 9. She thought they owed us an apology, or at least an ounce of respect. When we got neither from them, she said some pretty embarrassing shit about them to the *New York Times*. After that article was published, Lilah started receiving prank calls—heavy breathing…ugly threats. One night, someone told her to keep her "hole shut" or her father would find her "floating in one of his fishing nets."

I pleaded with her to tone it down, but Lie said she didn't negotiate with terrorists.

Then someone spray painted the word "cunt" onto her windshield in the middle of the night. She was furious, but I hoped she'd learn from it.

Instead, she doubled down live on the air at a radio show in Juneau. The D.J. got Lilah all riled up, bringing up the *Times* article, and she pretty much accused Steve and Merle of targeting her without naming names.

My less-than-stellar memories stoke my temper, and when I appear at Stephen Williams's side, I'm itching for a fight. His rosy face contorts in surprise when he recognizes me.

"Garrett. Nice of you to join us." His steely eyes shift to Boone, but he doesn't bother to acknowledge him.

My teeth clench so tightly I'll probably need a dentist. "Stephen."

Runt growls at Stephen, and I scratch him behind the ear reassuringly.

"Are you going out with our group?" Stephen ignores my dog, too busy sizing me up. Even into his fifties, he's not the kind of dude you simply dismiss.

"Yep." I have no idea if I've been assigned to a group, but I don't care.

"In that case, I'll pack some extra provisions." His lips twitch slyly, and he wanders away. I watch him go, unwilling to turn my back on him even in a crowd of people. When I finally pivot back to Boone, Lilah has him in a bear hug.

"Damn, Bro! Look at you!" Lilah beams. It's unlike her to be so demonstrative, but Boone's always been a special case.

Lilah was in first grade when Lu found Boone digging in the dumpster behind Johnson's Grocery. Next thing everyone knew, the Campbells' den was Boone's bedroom. Dick Campbell was at a loss. His wife had taken in an odd, dirty little vagrant child, without even consulting him. He didn't dare argue, though. The inseam on the family pants was perfectly tailored for Lu, not Dick.

Lilah grips Boone's large biceps. "You've been working out!"

Boone grins abashedly and shakes his head. He looks incredibly happy to see Lie, regardless of whether he can find the words to say so.

One of my earliest memories is when my mom examined Boone at our river house down on the Kenai, not long after Lu had taken him in. She'd seen no anatomical reason why he couldn't speak, and since Boone passed a hearing test with flying colors, she'd deduced it was his choice. Selective mutism, she called it.

"He'll talk when he wants to," Mom assured Lu. "I just wish we knew if someone out there was looking for him."

Evidently they weren't, because here he is, twenty-five years later.

"It's so good to see you," Lilah's saying to Boone, but as the words are leaving her mouth, her smile slowly melts. The cause of their reunion creeps back into focus for them, and somber expressions win out. "Are you on our team, too?"

Boone shrugs, and Lilah's curious eyes slide to mine.

"We didn't check in. Who's on your team besides Stephen Fucking Williams?" I demand. The lift of her eyebrows reminds me how out of line I am and how little I give a flying rat's ass.

"Those two." She nods to a couple of townies nearby. "There aren't enough people for us to have a full team."

"There are now." I slip my pack off my back so I can pull out a dog treat for Runt. He deserves a reward for recognizing Stephen for the scumbag he is.

Boone claps me on the back and points to the water bottles, then to Runt.

"Yeah, he gets thirsty. Thanks, buddy," I say. Boone wanders off. Lilah turns to me like she's about to fill the silence.

"I couldn't find a hotel because of RunFest," I blurt. "Even the B&B's full."

"So you went to see Andi." Her face is surprisingly placid, unlike when she walked in on me making out with her sister.

"I—" I'm not certain what I intended to say in response, but luckily she interrupts me.

"Listen." She goes to touch my arm again. Something in my expression makes her reconsider. "You can go on home now. Reece offered to help me."

"Reece?" I can't contain my amusement.

Her honey eyes darken with suspicion. "Yeah."

I raise my eyebrows. "You lose your pilot's license or something?"

She shoots me her best "bitch, please" look, very much like old times.

"Then what's he gonna do for you? Give you a foot rub?" The comment is beneath me, but flying over the bush in the comfort of an airplane and traveling through it on foot are two very different things.

"He's taking me out for a check-ride. I'll be able to use Cherry if the search gets called off. Stephen said he'd be my guide, so you're off the hook."

"If you think I'm letting you go anywhere alone with Stephen Williams, you're even crazier than I thought." The words are out before my brain is fully engaged.

Lilah brushes off my declaration without a fight, which is more of a slap in the face than if she'd actually slapped me.

"He's qualified if that's what you're worried about."

"You know *exactly* what I'm worried about," I seethe in a hushed whisper, glancing around to see who's in earshot.

Delilah blushes, her eyes darting back and forth as she looks up into mine. She's obviously recalling Stephen's inappropriate comments back in the day, maybe for the first time. In a place like Alaska, where men outnumber women seven to one, it's amazing what a girl can get used to.

"I heard you loud and clear last night." She breaks away from our staring contest, smashing a divot of grass back in place with the toe of her boot. "This was a terrible idea, and you were right to tell me no from the beginning."

I take a step toward her, and dangerous lines appear between her brows. She doesn't back away this time, but I freeze, rooted to the spot. Not because her look would kill a lesser man, but because the challenge in her eyes is nearly more temptation than I can resist. I'd only intended to put a hand on her shoulder. Now I want to drag her off into the trees by her thick, fragrant hair.

"Do you want my help or not, Lie?" It's all I can manage under the circumstances.

She weighs the question for an infuriating amount of time considering that *she* approached *me*. She seems to be assessing my motives. I wish her luck, since I'm not sure what the hell I'm doing here besides torturing myself.

"All right," she finally concedes, like I'm twisting her arm.

CHAPTER SIX

Lilah

Off the Beaten Path

I'M DESPERATE FOR my caffeine fix, but I'm at a dead stop in the middle of Main Street. Three moose block my turn as they meander around the center line, forming a living wall between me and my beloved coffee cart. I resist the urge to blast my horn, since I know it will just piss them off. They can be pretty damn dangerous creatures, and these wheels aren't mine to gamble with.

This entire day has been a shit show. From the second I arrived at search headquarters, it was obvious that I was the only one who still believed this was a rescue operation. Ten men were gathered in a circle prepping cadaver dogs to do their thing. Watching the enthusiastic canines jumping all over each other to sniff my mom's jacket wasn't exactly the best part of waking up.

I wanted to throw a tantrum, but I managed to just keep walking. Approaching the tent for the Alaska Mountain Rescue Group, the first people I saw were Merle Jones and Stephen Williams. The two former Aurora hunters barked orders while three young volunteers scurried around to do their bidding. Both men looked up and spotted me in unison. I squared my shoulders, ready for whatever B.S. they planned to dish out.

"Delilah." Merle's smile wasn't genuine, but at least it was civil. After all these years, he still looks like a pissed-off Santa Claus.

"I'm here to help." None of us like each other, so there was no need to pretend otherwise with social niceties or bullshit platitudes.

"Ummm..." Merle looked over his clipboard in mock concentration. I prepared for him to stonewall me or condescend.

"I'll take her out," Stephen offered, and I turned to him in surprise. It seemed like a genuine invitation, shocking from a guy who'd always dismissed my accomplishments as beginner's luck, and referred to me publicly as "primo jailbait."

"We've got a whole lot of well-meaning amateurs and we're just trying to disperse the babysitting evenly. You can obviously handle yourself."

True to his word, Stephen introduced me to several key Search and Rescue operators, who explained the assignment for the day. Though I kept waiting for a caveat of some kind, Stephen was respectful, which was a big change from what I'd come to expect from him. By the time Connor made his over-the-top entrance, I felt fairly comfortable with the situation, and had even asked if he'd be my guide if the search was called off, which he agreed to without a moment's hesitation.

Connor's always been the diplomat, the voice of reason in our double act, but today he was purposely poking the bear with every word that came out of his mouth. All puffed up like a peacock, he seemed to have lost his sense of humor entirely. I pulled him aside shortly after we'd begun, and asked him to play it cool with Stephen, but he snapped at me and walked away mid-sentence. His capacity for holding a grudge is impressive.

Connor and Steve spent the first two hours of the search in a spectacular pissing contest. They argued over every decision that came up, causing our group to lag behind all the others. I felt sorry for the guys in the group who didn't understand their history, but I felt sorrier for my mother, who was out there in need of assistance. I played Switzerland initially, but when Stephen suggested Boone lead and Connor argued the point, I'd had enough. He was wasting precious time playing King of the Hill, and Boone was hands down the best man for the job.

"For fuck's sake!" I exclaimed, but Boone placed a gentle hand on my shoulder, cautioning me to stay out of it.

Once I fell silent, Connor put Boone in front and Steve in the rear. For all the drama, Connor had always been a natural leader. Without Stephen's armchair quarterbacking, Connor played on everyone's strengths, and by the time we got rained out for the day, even Stephen was deferring to him without pushback.

Unfortunately, the search produced nothing. None of the teams found a trace of Mom or her plane.

On our way back to base camp, I fell in next to Boone.

"Thank you," I said to him. When he tilted his head and frowned, I went on to elaborate. "For keeping me in line out there. Orange jumpsuits aren't a good look for me. And thank you for making Andi contact me. I know she wouldn't have called if it wasn't for you."

He ran a hand over his damp sandy hair and nodded, looking off into the woods. He seemed embarrassed that I knew he'd pressed Andi to tell me about Mom.

"Andi." I could tell he wanted to say a whole lot more, but the devil that's been riding his shoulder since childhood wouldn't allow it.

I paused for a long moment, trying to decide what I wanted to know. "Should I go see her?"

Boone's dark blue eyes shone with something elusive, and he shrugged his massive shoulders. I wasn't sure what to make of it, but it wasn't a hard no.

Now, as I sip my coffee on my way to the bed and breakfast, I'm second-guessing.

Andi and I are less than a year apart in age, and Mom always referred to us as her "Irish twins." I know a lot of girls fight with their sisters, but Andi and I had always been tight. My little sister was my best friend even before Connor, and my most trusted confidante since before she could do more than listen. Now whenever I look at her, I see a stranger wearing my sister's skin.

I enter the Northern Lights B&B, rattled and soaked from the earlier downpour. Andi is behind the front desk, her spa music and scented candles going.

She looks up from her computer with her customer service smile in place. It vanishes the second she realizes it's me.

"You look like shit." Her gaze returns to the screen of her Mac.

"You look great," I respond, and it's the truth. Andi has always had a fantastic sense of style. Today her makeup is picture-perfect. Her long, sleek, highlighted hair falls around her shoulders in expertly crafted waves. Even though her hair was never as naturally curly as mine, I knew it took a lot of time and product to get the look down. "I love your hair."

She ignores my flattery and clicks away on her mouse. "If you're looking for a room, I already told your boyfriend we're booked solid. He and his dog will have to stay at the campgrounds."

The backhanded reference to Connor sets my teeth on edge.

"He didn't look much like my boyfriend with your tongue down his throat." Bitterness creeps into every syllable, and I know I've lost both the battle and the war.

Andi blinks as she turns to face me head-on. "So you finally want to talk about that?"

"Not really." I toss my purse onto her counter. She glares at it like it's a dead skunk.

"You were *engaged, Lilah*. To someone else, I might add." She emphasizes each word as if I'm hard of hearing.

I fold my arms, and then unfold them. I can see them still, Andi straddling Connor on Claire's couch the night he'd buried his mother. He'd had nothing but hate for me earlier that evening, chasing me away hours earlier. I guess he'd been saving all his sugar for her. I lost a heel, sprinting across the lawn away from the two of them, peeling away in my sister's car, pedal to the metal. Breathless at the memories, I brush my damp hair away from my flushed face. "I know."

We fall silent, serenaded by the placid tones that serve as the soundtrack to our harrowing reunion.

"Did you find Mom's plane?" Andi lifts her mug to her burgundy lips. Her quick sweep of my damp hiking attire is remarkably non-judgmental.

I inch closer to the counter. "Not yet."

"Have you seen Dad?" She glances at her perfect French manicure, then back up at me.

I exhale deeply, feeling like a failure. "No."

"You need to." She stands, and we're eye to eye. "He's so far off the wagon that he may as well be in orbit."

"He needs rehab." I must sound like a song on repeat. What he really needs is to stumble off the end of the dock, but I know better than to say so out loud.

"I can't keep these plates spinning by myself, ya know?" Andi's outraged, like I'd blamed her for Dad's lack of coping skills.

"I know. I'm sorry." She rewards my apology with a wan smile.

"For what? Ditching me here with this poor excuse for a family or for freezing me out of your life?"

My eyes drift to the scar marring her otherwise flawless face. I hate how that scar permanently punctuates the chasm between us. If I'd known then what I know now, would I change things? Of course. As mad as I was that night, she'll always be my baby sister. "For not being able to forgive you."

"Yeah. I'm sorry about that too." I recognize the stoic mask she slips into place. I've seen it in the mirror a thousand times.

CHAPTER SEVEN

CONNOR

HARD

I MAKE MY way back to LuAnn's place, wondering what I'll say to Lilah when I get there. Her irritation during the search efforts was obvious. I'm still fluent in her body language, having been an apt pupil.

When I pull into the driveway and Lilah isn't home, I wander down to the boathouse. Ignoring the empty bottles cluttering up the dock, I rap loudly on the door. Dick Campbell answers, looking like the floor of a taxicab and smelling ten times worse. He squints bloodshot eyes at me and graces me with a bleary smile.

"Connor Garrett! How the hell are ya?" I can smell his rank breath from two feet away.

"Surviving." I eye the man who fathered both Lilah and Andi Campbell, wondering how he contributed genetic material to either of them. The notion had been at least plausible when we were kids. Dick used to be a cheerful, chummy "good time" guy with a true gift for gab.

Some men thrive with a strong woman at their side. Some men crumble. Dick wasted away in Lu's shadow, but now, in her absence, he's dismantling himself entirely.

"Where's your daughter?"

"Which one?" His knowing barb makes my cheeks ignite.

"Touché." *He may be a drunk, but he's one observant old bastard.* "I meant Delilah."

"Haven't seen her, but Andi called ranting and raving about her being in town. My guess is she's over at the B&B and they're having it out." He frowns at me. "You wouldn't know anything about that, would you?"

And all these years I thought Lilah got her sharp tongue from her mother.

Dick notices the shame on my face, and his pinched expression slides away, replaced with his usual barfly grin.

"Looks like you could use a drink." He shuffles inside, opening a grubby cooler beside his ragged La-Z-Boy. Both the cooler and the recliner have been generously patched with duct tape.

My icy feelings toward Dick thaw as I realize how lost he must be without LuAnn. He's a waste of space, but without Lu to cattle prod him through life, he'll likely be dead in a few months. He's the poster child for absent fathers, especially when you consider that he's always lived on the property. Once when we were in middle school, he famously took Andi and her best friend Sura to the movies in Anchorage, wandered off to a bar, then drove all the way back to True without them.

Though they'd been separated for years, LuAnn kept Dick eating and working semi-regularly. With her gone, there is no one at the helm.

I'm struck by an idea that will keep me out of trouble and make sure Dick gets something in his belly. "Tell you what. I have an errand to run, but I'll buy you dinner afterward and we'll throw one back."

Dick grins, and I notice he's missing one of his front teeth. I wonder if someone knocked it out for him or if he just fell on his face. Neither would surprise me.

"It's ladies' night at the Damn Beaver." For a moment, Dick looks like the man he used to be. "They make a great elk burger."

"That'll be...interesting." I picture the run-down road-house and its sticky floors, but Dick's gaunt face alarms me. I wonder when he last ingested solids. I'm buying him a meal, regardless of where he chooses to order it. "How about six?"

He claps my back, like he didn't threaten to cut off my dick and shove it up my ass not long ago. "Don't be late! The wet T-shirt contest starts at eight, and we want a clear tabletop, if you know what I mean."

I want to grab him by the collar and scream in his face, "Your wife is missing, you piece of shit." Instead, I smile and nod. Wet T-shirts in a seedy bar or suppressing the urge to toss Lilah onto her bed and screw her until we both can't see straight. The decision isn't as hard as I am thinking about it.

As I crest the incline heading for my Jeep, I notice a tall black man peeking into LuAnn's windows. He looks out of place in True, which other than a few native families is so white it's Wonder Bread. He has to be in his late fifties now, graying a touch up top, but I recognize him immediately.

"Mr. Garrett? Is that you?" Dixon's bright smile hasn't dulled over the years, but still falls short of his caustic eyes.

"It is." Memories of this man's relentless questions after we surrendered Aurora 9 have me slogging forward as if through three feet of snow.

"I'm not sure if you remember me. I'm—"

"Marcus Dixon!" I grip his outstretched hand, shaking it firmly. I produce the smile I perfected back when my father paraded me in front of his army cronies. Faking is a way of life when you're beaten and berated in private and bragged about in mixed company. "Of course I remember you. From Anderson and Hart—the insurance investigators—right?"

"You've got a keen memory, son." Dixon's laying it on thick, but that was always his strategy.

"Please." I try to think six steps ahead. "Call me Connor."

"You've certainly grown up, Connor." He eyes me with caution, and I note that he's not as large as I remember. Then again, I'm 6'4" and about 240 pounds now... harder to intimidate than your average Joe. I'm nothing like the clean-cut kid he'd encountered all those years ago, when he'd come calling to question Delilah and me about where we found Aurora 9, and whether we'd kept some bars back for ourselves. It's unlikely that he recognized me from memory.

He's been watching me…maybe keeping tabs all along.

"It's been a while." I stuff my hands into my pockets. "What brings you back to True?"

"I pass through from time to time. I heard LuAnn Campbell's gone missing." He's conversational, but his predatory eyes gauge my response, taking me in all at once. The sensation is unnerving. "I thought I'd drop by and offer Mr. Campbell my condolences."

His turn of phrase rubs me the wrong way, and I understand why Lie's so salty about Lu being spoken about in the past tense. Condolences aren't in order yet, and LuAnn had greeted this guy with a loaded shotgun when he'd come calling on Lie. "This is still a rescue operation, so don't let Delilah hear you talk like that. If you're looking for Dick, he's down in the boathouse."

"Delilah's in town? Why don't I treat you both to lunch tomorrow? The salad bar at the Great Northerner isn't half bad. Maybe we can exchange some theories on where Mrs. Campbell might be."

"I do love the Great Northerner." I force a pleasant smile, but my mind spins like a misbalanced top, grasping for some hint of what his real motives are for being in True. "But I'm helping with the search party. If the weather cooperates, we'll be in the bush tomorrow."

"Not out hunting for the last Aurora?" Dixon's smile seems to have extra teeth.

I grin, genuinely amused that this guy's singing his same old tune. "I gave that up a long time ago. I hunt bears now. Sometimes moose."

"Or your girlfriend's mother when she goes astray." A flicker of something intangible crosses his features. I don't respond—I'm not sure how to—and that doesn't seem to rattle him. "I'm gonna give you my card, son. Just in case you and your lady friend find the time to squeeze me in to your busy schedule."

As he moves forward, I see the butt of his gun peeking out from under his overcoat. I'm not too concerned by it. Alaskans love their firearms, and if I had Dixon's occupation or his disposition, I wouldn't leave home without one.

I TEND TO get into trouble in bars these days, so I take time to properly prepare. I'd stopped by several motels, but even the worst of them were full. Disappointed and defeated, I hurried here to meet Dick, stressing the whole way. Unless I crashed on Dick's unspeakable couch, I'd be spending another night with Lilah just down the hall.

She'd better have one hell of a dead bolt on her door.

The interior of the Damn Beaver hasn't been remodeled since it was built, and the worn Naugahyde booths remind me of a Bangkok gay bar my army buddies and I wandered into once by accident.

"Connor!" Dick has showered and shaved since I last saw him, which is to everyone's benefit. "We get to be judges for the contest!"

"A dream come true," I mumble dryly as I take a seat across from him.

"I texted Boone to get his ass over here, but that kid doesn't text any more than he talks." Dick chugs the rest of his pint.

I nod to his glass. "How many of those have you had?"

"Since I've been here?" His eyes go wide like a kid caught in the cookie jar. I nod. "This is my second one."

"I'd better catch up, then." I wave the waitress over.

We stick to local gossip, agilely dodging the topic of LuAnn. We've just received our burgers when Dick pivots the subject to Lilah.

"You're a good man, Connor. Looking out for Delilah like this." He claps me on the arm, ignoring his dinner for his freshly filled glass. "That girl will kill herself out there trying to find Lu."

"It's the least I can do. Lu always had my back, so…" I scrunch my face as the past tense slips out. Dick doesn't seem to notice.

"Lilah should've waited for you when you went to basic. Rotten kid. I knew I should have spanked her more when she was little." He rolls his eyes and makes a sound with the back of his throat. "And Jesus…that snooty shit she winded up married to. Gold cufflinks and fifty-dollar ties… Boy did he pick the wrong girl."

I empty my glass in one long swallow. If we're talking about Lie's husband, I'm gonna need a lot more lubrication.

"You know, the first time he met me, he called me 'Dad.' Me! Thank God they split up." Dick shudders, but I'm too curious to muster a polite laugh.

"When did that happen?" I pick at my coaster casually, gesturing to the waitress for another draft.

"The divorce? A few months back. But he moved out a long time ago."

My lips are numb, and it's not from the beer. They were still engaged at Mom's funeral, and that was only three years ago. Lie wasn't married for long. I see the light bulb go on over Dick's head. "Hey! You're single...she's single... Lu wants her bac—"

All at once, he seems to remember his wife's missing. Unable to stand the wretched look on his face, I change the subject.

"I'm pretty sure Lie's done with me, Dick. Especially after the shit that went down in Mom's kitchen and...after... You weren't very happy with me either, as I recall." That night Dick put his "dad" hat on and swung on me. Not that I can blame him. I hadn't meant to hurt Lilah, not really, but things went sideways with her like they always do.

I can see him playing the same scene over in his mind. He makes a halfhearted pass at a smile, as the houselights dim around us.

"I don't care what bullshit she's feeding you. Lilah won't ever be done with you."

As the unfortunate wet T-shirt contest begins, I consider Dick's words. Mom said something similar about Lilah, just days before she died, and I ride my beer buzz like a wave back to that conversation, and the bedlam that followed.

When Mom's cancer came back three years ago, she chose hospice over chemo. I was stationed in Germany at the time, but I was immediately granted emergency leave. Still recovering from one of the worst battles of my career, I skipped several follow-ups and got on the first flight home that the army could line up. By the time I landed, my brother Quinn was back from California, and already had Mom down at the place on the Kenai.

While Quinn, a celebrated pastry chef, baked her every sinful concoction she craved, I wasted precious time badgering Mom about seeking treatment rather than throwing in the towel.

"Connor, I'd give anything to see at least one grandbaby from you boys, but I've done chemo and it made me sicker than the cancer did. Please, honey. Have a cream puff. Tell me stories. Let's enjoy this time together. Please."

Mom wore me down instead of the other way around.

Two days into our sugar coma, Quinn ran into Sterling to stock up on supplies. Mom was in the recliner, watching old camcorder footage, while I fixed her a banana split I knew she'd barely touch.

"Connor, get in here!" Panicked, I hurried out of the kitchen, ice cream scoop in hand, and Mom was sitting forward, rewinding with the remote. Grainy footage of Lilah and me shooting hoops appeared on the screen. Lilah was up on my shoulders so she could dunk a basket. It had been nearly seven years since I had seen Lie or spoken to her, and there she was. Her laughter emanating from the surround sound gave me chills. As I approached Mom's recliner, I watched as Lilah bent down and kissed my mouth.

"*Look at the two of you. You were such a gorgeous couple. The way she looked at you—*"

"We were idiots," I replied mirthlessly, handing Mom her dessert.

"Beautiful idiots." She patted my arm. I tried to ignore the tremor in her fingers and the predominant appearance of her veins. "I've never seen you care about anything like you did that girl."

"Quit digging up bones, Mom," I said, and then cringed at my callousness. She was in the act of dying. The least I could do was humor her.

Mom brushed my comment aside. "Life's so short, Connor. Too short to hold grudges. Especially against someone who looks at you like that."

Her last few days were intense, but incredible. LuAnn came by every single day and she and Mom ganged up on me, giving me a hard time about my childish exploits. Quinn was an enthusiastic audience for their two-woman comedy act, and they regaled him with tales of my juvenile delinquency, since Dad kicked him out of the house before I was old enough to get up to much. Most stories involved Lilah, since she was typically the mastermind. Quinn's hysterical laughter egged them on, and the barrage of memories combined with the morbid reason behind our reunion made me an emotional live wire.

Quinn cornered me after Lu left and Mom was fast asleep.

"Are you two still in touch?" I knew right away he meant Delilah.

"I haven't seen her since I left for basic training."

He was all attitude instantly. "Why the hell not?"

The thought of getting into that ugly shit made me tired.

"It's a long story."

He cocked a sardonic eyebrow. "This whole week has been one long story after another."

"What do you want to know, Quinn? I hurt her. She hurt me." I sipped my scotch, shaking my head. "The whole thing's fucking ridiculous. Who falls in love at sixteen, anyway? Stupid kids with zero perspective, that's who."

"Sounds like a tough act to follow…" Quinn's weighty gaze pinned mine over the rim of his wineglass.

I bristled at the idea, because he was right. It was unfair that Lie still meant so much to me, but she was always present, like an out-of-reach itch.

Mom passed away in her sleep that night. I was useless, so Lu called the funeral home and helped Quinn make decisions. I sat by, blankly nodding at random times. We wouldn't have gotten through it without LuAnn, but thankfully we didn't have to.

After, LuAnn patted my back reassuringly. "It'll be a beautiful service, Connor. Lilah just texted me. She's catching a flight back as we speak."

This news shocked me from my grief. After watching Mom slowly unwind like a clock, seeing Delilah again after so many years seemed like a gift. I felt like the universe owed me a solid. Obsessing about what I'd say to her allowed me to brush aside the fact that I was about to plant my mother in the ground.

When Delilah showed up at the funeral home, decked out in elegant slacks and a string of pearls, I barely recognized her. Her hair was board straight and she looked like she belonged on the cover of a fashion magazine. It was her confident strut that gave her away. Some GQ businessman type with a butt *chin was at her side, and had his hand permanently glued to her back.*

I couldn't even look in her direction during the service, but I couldn't focus on anything else either. My anger bubbled until it was a rolling boil. I burned with shame and rage, and it took all of my self-control to keep from storming out and dragging Lilah along with me.

She showed up at the gathering at Mom's house afterward, and I said things. Terrible things. I've blocked most of it out, but I'll never forget her red-stained cheeks and bruised, angry eyes. Never one to take shit lying down, Lilah fired back with hateful words of her own, and that's when I hurt her. I hadn't planned to, hadn't meant it, but none of that matters. Had I had my gun that night, I'd have put it in my mouth.

COLD WATER RICOCHETS off the latest wet T-shirt contestant, dousing my overwhelming memories. Between my charged flashbacks and all the tits on stage, I drink way more than I should. By the time Dick and I finally pick a winner, I'm long past buzzed.

"We're gonna need a cab." My tongue feels oversized.

Dick shakes his head, his eyes still on the contestants. "We're good. I called Delilah while you were settling the tab. She's on her way."

Shit.

Lilah. Here. And me, not operating on all cylinders. Considering the way I've been obsessing about her all night, it's not just a recipe for disaster: it's the entire fucking cookbook.

"Hey there, big boy." Our winner strolls over and in an impressive display of flexibility, she straddles my chair.

"Hi." I scan her spectacular rack, unsure how to remove her from my lap without touching her inappropriately. I'm not entirely sure I want to.

Somewhere nearby, Dick chuckles. The girl's baby blues lift from my face and grow three sizes like there's something terrifying behind me. I don't even have to turn around to know it's Delilah.

"Are you riding with us or are you riding *her* home?" Lilah sounds like she doesn't give a shit one way or the other, but I extract myself from the girl like she's on fire.

"Is that your wife?" Wet T-shirt Champ whispers a lot louder than she probably meant to.

"Not even close," I slur, and my eyes shift to Lie, hoping to witness the sting of my response. Lilah gives me a sardonic double thumbs-up, and her indifference leaves me reeling. By the time I claim my coat and down my beer, she and Dick are already halfway to the door. I catch up just in time to see Lilah gesture for the bartender. He looks her up and down and saunters in her direction with a slow grin.

Lilah moves in and gestures to him, like she's going to whisper in his ear. Instead, she grips his hair with vigor, fixing him with a deadly glare.

"Serve my father again and I'll staple your balls to that tree in town square."

"Hey!" the bouncer bellows, charging in her direction. I step between him and Lie. Drunk or not, I could dismantle him in seconds. He freezes at the sight of me, clearly rethinking his career choice. I shake my head at the bouncer, confirmation that he doesn't want to choose the path he's considering.

"It's cool," the bartender calls out. He's grinning ear to ear, even though Lilah still has a handful of his hair, and seems even more into her than before she turned on him. I can sympathize. Her brutality gets a real rise out of risk-takers, adrenaline junkies, and the criminally insane. Lilah releases him with a disdainful side-glance at the bouncer, which implies he was never a threat, with or without my interference.

I follow her out the door, and the cold air hits me hard, since my jeans are sopping wet from the tipsy contestant's visit to my lap.

Lilah herds her dad in the direction of her parking spot, which is right next to mine. "Take your jacket off and sit on it. This is a rental."

"She was on my lap, Lie, not my ass," I fire back, pulling my laptop case and jump bag from my Jeep.

Lilah turns on her dad. "Do you always go out drinking without a designated driver?"

"God will provide, Delilah Anne," Dick responds.

"Like he provided you an open tab tonight?" Lilah's eyes slant in my direction.

"Lie…" I fall into the role of peacemaker out of habit. "He called you. If he hadn't, I would have called a cab."

"In True?" She pulls her chin back sharply. Her expression floods me with déjà vu.

"You two make a charming couple," Dick observes at the top of his lungs, rattling me out of my wet daydream. "You're perfect for each other. You should really give it another go."

"Thanks, Dr. Phil." Lie's voice is flat. I feel my jaw buckle. I know Lilah's sharpest edges, and can tell when she's spoiling for a fight. I'm mellowed from drink and I'll be damned if I'm getting pulled into her torrent.

"Don't have kids, though. Kids ruin everything."

"Wow, Dad." Lilah's affectless as she refuses to look my way. My adrenaline spikes, and I consider sleeping it off in my Jeep. I'm far too sober all of a sudden.

Dick looks serious. "Your mom and I would still be together if we never had you."

Blanching, Lilah unceremoniously stuffs him into the passenger side, like a cop shoving a perp into her back seat. As she circles the SUV, her eyes flit to me, still standing by the back of the car, debating on whether or not to pull the rip cord. She comes around to open her door, and for a long moment, we wage a silent debate about whether to let what he just said incite a feud or just wave the white flag for the evening. A line appears between her eyebrows, and I realize she's pleading with me to forget what Dick just said. I'm not sure if it's the booze mellowing me or Mom's words haunting me, but I'm in a forgiving mood.

As we pull onto the highway, Dick drones on about how Lu had never given him the time of day until one night when they'd left the bar together and ended up doing it in a lifeboat. I play third wheel during this private exchange, feeling like an involuntary voyeur. Understandably mortified, Lie tries to change the subject, but Dick's oblivious. He raves about how LuAnn glowed on their wedding day, but they later found out it was because she was knocked up with Delilah.

"…and now she won't even speak to me. I watch her every night through the bay window. She just sits in the living room staring at that damn map on the wall."

"That's not creepy at all," Lilah blurts, and I laugh before I can stop myself.

"You'll never find her, Delilah Anne," Dick slurs, his eyelids heavy as I glimpse him in the rearview mirror. "Your mother…she doesn't want to be found."

CHAPTER EIGHT

LILAH

WRECKED

ONCE WE'RE HOME, Connor carries Dad to the boathouse, but being drunk himself, he nearly falls off of the dock, tripping over some of Dad's empties. I fiddle with the key ring, only to discover Dad never locked up in the first place.

On our way back up to Mom's house, Runt launches himself out of the darkness and sidelines Connor. I see it coming and grab his arm when he stumbles, but he's like a toppling redwood tree. We both end up on the ground with me on top of him. Connor snickers as Runt licks both of our faces. As he playfully elbows Runt away, his other arm slips around my waist. That sets off every alarm I've got.

"Seriously?" I scramble to my feet and rush off, leaving Connor to fend for himself. Face aflame, I hurry for the porch, cursing Dad for shooting off his big fat mouth and cursing the universe for putting me in the vicinity of Connor Garrett, who will forever be my goddam Kryptonite. I'm spitting mad and working myself into a froth, when

I notice the door's standing ajar. I inch forward and spot the splintered frame. Someone's kicked it in.

Rushing forward, I grab Mom's shotgun from its stand behind the door. Seeing red, I blaze through the kitchen, cocking my weapon so I can unload it into the sorry son of a bitch who decided to help themselves to my mother's things.

I round the corner, and someone rushes me, knocking me flat on my back. The shotgun goes off as I hit the ground, blasting a hole in the plaster directly above me. I'm pelted by debris, choking and coughing on dust and residual gunpowder. I turn my head in time to see the intruder's boots as he vanishes out the back door.

"Are you hurt?" Connor sounds miles away since my ears are still ringing.

I shake my head, thankful for Mom's thick carpet. Connor leans in closer, and his beard tickles my ear.

"How many?" His voice is full of deadly promise.

"One," I sputter.

"Where?"

"Out the back."

He snatches the shotgun and by the time I sit up, he's clearing the blind spots before advancing out onto the deck and into the darkness.

He's gone long enough that I get nervous. Finally, I see him approaching the deck. Once back inside, he discards the gun and takes my face into his hands.

"Are you sure you're okay?" There's enough moonlight for me to see his fuse is lit. Anger radiates off of him.

"I'm fine." I try to mask my surprise at his concern, and for several seconds he searches me like I'll spontaneously bleed out. His hands drop away, and then he's gone, retreating toward the broken back door. I follow.

"Did you see anyone?"

"Did you hear the gun go off?" he snaps back, not breaking his stride as he disappears into the kitchen.

I shake my head and flip on the light in the living room. Mom's place looks like it's been hit by a tornado. Moving down the hall, I see the guest room mattress is slightly off-kilter, but otherwise, it seems the intruder bypassed that room. Andi's bedroom seems untouched too. I probably interrupted him before he could get to it.

My room is trashed. My mattress leans against the wall, shredded. I can see the springs poking out like molested Slinkies. The contents of my suitcase and dresser are scattered all over the room.

I hear pounding and when I investigate, Connor's securing the broken door with a hammer and nails.

"Here's hoping we don't have a fire," I quip. Connor doesn't even crack a smile, so I move on to assess the damage from our unwelcome guest.

The drawers of Mom's bedside tables are upside down on the bed, their contents fanned out on her quilt like someone was sifting through them. I scour the items, finding nothing remarkable, besides an extremely large, anatomically correct purple vibrator.

I hear rustling and see Connor in the doorway. His large arms bulge as he crosses them, leaning against the doorframe for support. I brandish the giant sex toy at him like a sword, and Connor smiles with just his eyes. It's a talent of his, and in the current context, it's disconcerting. His layered expression makes me tingle, or maybe I'm having a stroke from all the stress. I toss the vibrator onto the bed and crack my knuckles nervously.

"Notice anything missing?" Connor's deep voice compels me to look his way.

"Nothing obvious. There's a layer of dust on Mom's jewelry box, so it hasn't been touched. I'll have to ask Andi and Boone to look to be sure."

"We need to call the police," he informs me.

"Yeah. Because they've been so helpful." My tone is unnecessarily harsh, but I've reached the end of my patience.

Stacks of mail draw my attention. I cross the room for a closer look. Someone opened every single envelope, most of which I'd brought in from the mailbox when I'd first arrived. *What kind of thief leaves your jewelry and reads your mail?*

What the hell has Mom gotten herself into?

"We shouldn't stay here," I say, more to myself than Connor.

"All the hotels and motels are booked," he reminds me. He changes his position now that I'm near him, his black T-shirt creeping up so I can see the trail of dark hair from below his rippling abs, disappearing behind the button of his fly. I scold myself for noticing.

"I need to figure out who was here and what they were

looking for." I gesture to the piles of junk. "I can't do that from a hotel anyway."

"Don't you have a breakfast date with Reece in the morning?" His tone is light, but his eyes don't match.

I chew my lip. Connor's smoldering eyes are getting to me, so I turn back to the mess on the bed. He's always been too much to take in big bites, and it's worse now that he's all ripped and rugged. He's the only one who was ever enough for me. Handsome enough, smart enough, strong enough. And that was before he became a seasoned warrior. Now...well, Connor 2.0 is nearly irresistible.

Except he doesn't want you anymore.

He'd been clear about that since basic training.

I never should have let him kiss me. I should have clocked him in the mouth when he did. I shouldn't have allowed him inside my walls...convinced my dumb-ass self we were something special. I'd gambled for the grand prize and come away heartbroken and empty-handed. Connor had ruined me—my body, my mind, and my spirit—and now that I'm back here, I just get to marinate in my misery.

I swallow the pain, so cloying and bittersweet. It's easy to romanticize the past under this kind of stress, and his savage good looks make it even easier. I'd made sound decisions way back then, and almost every one of them holds up under the scrutiny of hindsight.

"Let's just get some rest and I'll call Andi in the morning." I move toward my room and he grips my arm.

"You can't sleep on your mattress without a tetanus

shot, babe." His face develops a rosy glow at the unintended pet name, and his eyes shift away. I flush too, but it's not from embarrassment.

"Sleep is pretty far from my mind." My voice is husky, and Connor's features take on a sharp ferocity. Raw emotion shines in his eyes, and I smell bald-faced lust all over him. I'm startled and incredibly turned on as he pushes off the doorframe, straightening to his full height. A weaker woman would cave right there and then.

But weak isn't in my résumé anymore, and when it comes to Connor, there's always something to prove. I recall the way he looked at me earlier that morning, like I was something he'd trim off of his steak. The only difference now is that he's drunk. I can only see his eyes, since his face is covered under that outrageous mask of hair, but those hazel eyes are on fire. He takes a step in my direction, backing me against the closet door. The memory of him slamming me against the wall surfaces with sudden clarity.

"I…I need to prepare for my oral exam," I stammer.

Connor smolders, and I realize I've just made things worse with that choice of words. I have to douse him fast before I succumb to his eye-fucking and beg him to do me.

"For my floatplane test. With Reece."

Connor's features stiffen at Reece's name, his demeanor suddenly tense and rigid. "You need a good night's sleep."

He turns and stomps out of the room. Or he tries to, anyway. I hear him nearly slip on all the shit cluttering the hall. This strikes me as hilarious, and I have to stifle nervous laughter.

I end up in Andi's bed, but my racing thoughts make it hard to fall asleep. I toss and turn, obsessing over the intruder, some stranger riffling through our private things. I've only felt violated like this once before, when the strangers came for me at the school.

It was winter of our senior year, and Connor and I had just started dating a couple of months before. Andi was the only one who knew about us, and Connor and I had been arguing about that a lot. He wanted to go public, but I told him our parents wouldn't let us out of their sight if they knew something more was going on between us, and our alone time would come to a screeching halt.

The truth was a bit more complicated. I've always been good with patterns, and I knew Connor was going to get bored with me like he had all the others. If we broke up, I wanted it to be in private. It was the only way we could stay friends when this infatuation played itself out, and he'd promised me that no matter what happened, we'd stay friends.

I was thinking about our situation as I crossed the sloppy parking lot after leaving the school. The temperature had plummeted, and I hurried for the sanctuary of my car.

As I climbed behind the wheel, I wrinkled my nose. My car smelled like cigarettes. I didn't smoke, but Andi dabbled. She'd probably snuck out over lunch with her latest bad decision. If that was the case, she was going to shampoo the upholstery of my back seat. I tried to start my car, and nothing happened.

"Dammit, Andi!" I smacked the steering wheel. She must have used the spare key for the radio and killed my battery.

I got out and looked around like some solution might appear in the fresh fallen snow. The parking lot was a frozen ghost town, since I'd stayed behind to argue about my grade on my research paper. I decided I'd go ask the janitor to give me a jump. If he wouldn't, I'd wait for Connor and his pack of miscreants to get out of detention.

I zipped my coat up all the way past my chin and headed back toward the school. My breath escaped in visible clouds, and the crunch of my boots sounded thunderous.

A dark SUV rounded the corner at the end of the street, catching my attention with its sheer speed on the sketchy roads. The driver hung a sharp right and trundled into the parking lot, slowing as he drew near. I assumed they were waiting for me to cross. Instead, they came to a halt directly between me and the school. I took a couple of steps like I was going to cross behind them and the SUV inched backward, blocking my path. I stopped again. The window came down on the passenger side, and a young man with a pale blond crew cut smiled at me in an embarrassed manner.

"Hi!" His expression was self-deprecating. "We seem to be lost. Can you help us?"

The driver was twice the size of his smiley companion, and stared straight ahead, puffing on a cigarette. He wore no smile, embarrassed or otherwise. This triggered my silent alarm, but maybe they'd been arguing about directions. Based on my experience with Connor, men truly did hate to ask.

"I can try. Where are you headed?" I stepped closer to the vehicle.

Smiley's grin widened. His chill surfer vibe clashed with his military-style hair and our frigid surroundings. Something seemed familiar about him, but I hadn't met him before, I was certain of that. He was kicked back in his seat as if in the midst of a long road trip. "We're looking for the Campbell residence. There's a girl there we've been dying to meet."

The back door opened and a man climbed out. He was stocky, like Sly Stallone in the Rocky movies. Judging from his crooked nose, he'd taken his share of punches, and his heavy brow resembled a hawk's. His eyes homed in on me, and I took an instinctual step back.

Smiley laughed. "You think you can help us with that, Delilah?"

That's when I knew why he was so familiar: Smiley was the one who'd been calling me.

I SIT UP on the side of the bed, running shaking hands through my hair. If it weren't for Connor's good timing and quick thinking that afternoon, I'd probably be dead. I couldn't sleep right for weeks after the incident, and Connor insisted on getting me a guard dog for protection. He was irritated when I picked out the runt of the litter, and told me not to even bother naming him, because he wouldn't live through the night.

Agitated I pounce out of bed and tiptoe down to the kitchen to grab a glass of water. I pause when I hear Connor roll over in bed, and wish I could climb in next to him and have him hold me like he used to. Then I wonder if he still sleeps in the nude, and remember the other side of the Connor coin, and why he's such a slippery slope. I close my eyes against the image, and wandering back into the living room, I snap my fingers. Runt hops down from Mom's sofa he's not supposed to be lying on, and comes to sleep at the foot of my bed.

"You sure showed him, you big galoot," I murmur, reaching down to stroke the malamute's thick coat. "Never underestimate the underdog."

Just as I'm ready to drift off, I picture my mom out in the cold wilderness. Soon this won't be a rescue mission, it'll be recovery. I'll be alone with my inability to quit lost causes. We need answers, and soon.

I CHUG MY oversized coffee as I run through my preflight check for the second time. I confirm the water rudders move as intended, and I try to ignore my trembling hands. My plane appears flawless, but that doesn't stop me from wanting a triple check.

I refuse to cave. Fear is wasteful, and circular thinking leads to inaction.

I run my fingers along Cherry's fiery red paint with a contented sigh. I was just sixteen years old when I got my pilot's license, and Cherry was my reward to myself after finding the treasure. She was an investment in my future. I'd planned to be a bush pilot like Mom since I was old enough to remember my dreams.

In fact, my earliest memory is being buckled into her copilot's seat. The lake below us was clear and placid, the calm surface reflecting the pinks and oranges of the magnificent dappled sky.

"Pretty!" I exclaimed.

"It sure is. But glassy water is dangerous to land on, Delilah," Mom explained. "It's so peaceful you'd never guess it, but it's practically impossible to tell how high up you are. You look down and just see sky."

"You can do it, right, Mommy?" I frowned.

"You bet." Grinning from ear to ear, Mom touched down, skimming the sparkling lake as effortlessly as breathing. I clapped like crazy and Mom just laughed. She was ten feet tall and bulletproof, as far as I was concerned. I wanted to be exactly like her.

Mom's taken excellent care of Cherry. After I fled to Vegas, I'd sent her money for maintenance, hangar space, and inspections. It all got done. From the looks of things, she'd taken her out to stretch her wings every once in a while, too.

When I married Josh, I asked Mom to sell Cherry for me. Though she initially objected, Mom sent me a check a few months later, so I assumed the plane was long gone. I have no idea where that money came from, but I'm already weaving theories.

Mom had always been a free-range parent, but from the moment I relocated, she made no secret that she hoped I'd come to my senses and move home. Since I told her Josh and I had separated, she'd pressured me incessantly, saying I should come home so she could groom me to take over the business. "I can't keep this up forever, Delilah Anne."

That's why she kept her. If I returned, I'd need my plane. My insides twist as I glance at the empty spot where Mom's plane should be. Grief sweeps over me, but I thrust it aside as if it were an unwanted groper in a seedy bar.

Knowing when to fly and when not to was a critical lesson Mom taught me straight out of the gate. "You'd rather be on the ground wishing you were in the air than vice versa, kiddo," she always said. It was the best advice she'd ever given me. Mom was a much more conservative pilot than I was, so I couldn't understand why she'd played so fast and loose with the weather.

"Lilah, are we leaving today or…" Reece softens his jab with that dimpled grin of his.

"Yep." I sound a lot more confident than I feel. Shaking off all the whys and what-ifs, I focus on getting this shit handled so I can bring Mom home.

It hadn't been hard to spot Reece when I arrived. He's very tall and lanky, like someone you'd see shooting three-pointers on ESPN. He's always been handsome, but he's really settled into his angular features over the years. He's always worn his chestnut hair a bit long, and it still falls into his gentle eyes.

When I arrived at the airport, Reece was going off on someone on the phone. He sounded incensed. "Got it. I want it done right so I guess I'll just have to handle it myself."

He turned to some scruffy guy in a ball cap who had been listening in, murmured something, and pointed to a clipboard. I waited patiently for Reece to notice me. When he did, his face bloomed.

"Delilah!" He shoved the paperwork at his companion and hopped over the counter. Sweeping me into a hug, he held me way longer than was appropriate. He smelled great though, like leather and musk.

"Damn! You're a sight for sore eyes." He scanned me with blatant admiration.

"Who's your friend, Reece?" the surfer reject he'd been talking to chimed in. I'm too taken with Reece's lopsided grin and his penetrating blue-green eyes to acknowledge his companion.

"Lilah, Patrick, Patrick, Lilah," Reece replied as he took me by the hand and led me away toward the lounge. "Don't get any bright ideas, P—I saw her first."

Reece Warren's dad ran the flight school in Anchorage while I was growing up. Since Mom was with the Ninety-Nines and I was her mascot, Reece and I ran into each other all the time.

A couple years older than me, Reece had worked part time as a line boy to earn fuel money and save up for his own plane back when I was still taking classes for my license. He'd often marshaled us in when Mom had the wheels on and we were using a traditional runway.

Reece had always been sweet on me and being the little shit that I was, I hadn't exactly discouraged him. I felt a little sorry for him, since his mom had died when he was really little and his dad was always such a grouch.

One time, when I couldn't have been much older than thirteen, Reece nearly killed himself flirting with me. He'd been on a stepladder fueling a plane and I'd called out to him. He tried to wave back and got his thumb stuck in the fuel nozzle. Jet-A spilled out onto the wing. Panicked, Reece flung the fuel hose halfway across the ramp, spraying himself in the face with fuel. He's damn lucky he didn't go blind. The nozzle landed with a thud a few feet from my mother, who dodged it easily, and fixed Reece with a homicidal glare. Then she called 911.

Seeing him now, it's hard to reconcile that awkward boy with the competent man he's become. Reece took me on a quick tour, making introductions and showing me recent renovations. Eventually, we came to his father's office.

Ronald Warren's hairline is a little higher and his body a little thicker, but otherwise he looks the same. Though he's no taller than I am, he has the same patronizing way about him that he always did. Ronald never liked me, probably because I wasn't exactly the kind of girl you bring home to momma, and Reece couldn't disguise how much he was into me.

Ronald made platitudes about my mother...conciliatory words about my loss that I'm not ready to hear. Plenty perceptive, Reece quickly made excuses for us to leave, his hand resting conspicuously around my shoulders on our way out the door.

I tolerated Reece's hands-on approach, but I'm rehearsing what I'll say if he makes a serious pass. His attempts at eye magic make two things clear: he still wants me, and he really needs to get laid.

Take off is like riding a bike, and while I demonstrate basic techniques through the lush valleys, Reece peppers me with questions like we're speed dating.

"So, you're single now," he asks, finally getting down to brass tacks.

"Yes. Since March first." My gaze doesn't stray from the windshield. I can feel his hopeful eyes boring into me, and inside I groan.

"Cool. I mean…sorry, that was rude," he blurts, and I spare him a glance.

"Don't be sorry. It's been almost six months, but it was over long before that. I'm just not wife material. That whole 'obey' vow just doesn't sit well with me."

"Same old Lilah." His dimples make another appearance. "Lu mentioned you were thinking about moving back."

I shake my head and then adjust my headset.

"My mother says a lot of things, Reece. That one is mostly wishful thinking."

"I hope not," he replies.

"Why do you think she went back up that day?" I peek at him and see his jaw twitch. His eyes narrow as he scans the landscape.

"Go ahead and land there." Reece points out a familiar lake that isn't much more than an oversized pond. I remember that it's notorious for having several rocky spots. After plotting my course, I descend, coming in at an angle and landing on one float before leveling the plane.

"Nice." Reece draws out the word, and the sensual undertone is unmistakable. I'm too elated to care. I'd forgotten the rush of a water landing, and it's like fuel for my battered spirits. I circle and prepare to take off again. Reece puts his hand over mine on the control and mimes for me to turn the engine off. I do as he instructs, frustrated that we're burning daylight. With every passing minute the chance of rescue dwindles.

When the propeller dies, the silence is deafening. It's just us and the gentle thump of the waves against the floats.

Reece turns toward me, which takes effort, since his height requires him to practically fold himself into the small cockpit.

His hand comes down on my knee, and the walls of the plane seem to close in on us. His eyes are like cobwebs I can't shake off, and I pray he won't ask me out.

I brought this unrelenting infatuation on myself, so I need to just own it. I used Reece to get back at Connor, when he asked Cyndi Mallory to the prom so soon after we broke up. Cyndi and I had been rivals since elementary school, and I couldn't let it go. I asked Reece to escort me like I was ordering drive thru. When I saw his absolute joy, I should have pumped the brakes, but all's fair in love and war, and Reece was destined to be collateral damage from friendly fire.

Karma evidently has a long memory.

I'm exhausted from worrying, full up on Connor drama, and I just don't have the energy for the "I-think-of-you-like-a-brother" talk. Especially when Reece isn't that boy anymore, and right now I don't think of him that way, which means I need to get laid as badly as he does.

"Lilah, I'm so sorry about your mom. I really am. Fact is, she made a risky judgment call. It wasn't like her. She should have diverted to Willow like we advised her to."

"To Willow Lake?"

"No. Willow Airport. She was flying the amphibious."

I turn, confused. "What amphibious…"

"She bought one a while back. Said she needed more flexibility to keep up with demand. Her old rickety piece of shit was on its last leg. After your dad lost the boat, she said she needed to up her earning potential."

"New or used?" I interrupt, uncomfortable with the topic of my parents and their finances. An amphibious complicated matters. If Mom could land and take off from both water and traditional runways, it meant more ground to cover. Like pretty much anywhere she had the fuel to reach.

"Used. Two thousand and four. White." He rattles off more details and sits back, thankfully removing his hand from my leg. I file the information away for research purposes. Fuel capacity, known issues with the model. I turn to Reece, and it's not puppy love I see in his eyes this time; it's sexual aggression and tactical assessment. I'm suddenly uneasy that we're alone in the middle of nowhere.

I take a breath and blow my hair out of my eyes. I'm being ridiculous. Reece is as threatening as a kitten in a barrel of cotton candy. I exhale, and another question occurs to me.

"What did she do with the De Havilland?" Reece may

think her old plane was shit, but I remember her fondly. I'd cut my teeth on that plane, and it was hard to imagine Mom getting rid of it without mentioning it.

Reece's lips press into a flat pale line. "She sold it."

I just shake my head. I'm a jerk-off for knowing so little about what's happening with my family. His comments about Dad's boat confirm my long-held suspicions about how bad things were for them financially. My father been a worthless fisherman my whole life…but he loved the water like I love the sky, and the thought of him landlocked crushes me. It's hard not to see how much that money Mom sent me hurt them, since it obviously didn't come from the sale of my plane.

Reece's face transforms with some misguided desire, and he reaches out to touch me again. My patience is gone in a puff of smoke.

"Is this inappropriate touching required for me to pass my test?" I sound colder than I meant to, but my aggression has never been the passive variety.

He reacts as if I've kicked him, and the puppy dog eyes are back with a vengeance. Reece has never been good at hiding his emotions, but the new, improved Reece gathers himself with surprising deftness.

"Of course not, Lilah. You can outfly me with both your hands tied behind your back. I would never…" He trails off and I can see him reprocess the day from my point of view. Heaving a weary sigh, he turns to me. "I'm sorry I made you uncomfortable. I like you, Lilah. I always have. And I loved your mom."

"Don't talk about her like she's dead," I blurt.

He nods, but his knowing expression reminds me of Connor's. "I just want you to know I'm here for you. I want to help…however I can."

We're back at the airport tying down the plane when my phone rings. I pull it out of my pocket.

"Hello?"

"Lie." I can tell by Connor's voice that something's up.

"What's wrong?" I demand.

"I've been calling you for a half hour." Connor's words rush from him.

"We've been in the air," I explain, feeling more anxious than ever.

"One of the pilots spotted your mom's plane. The ground crews haven't been able to get to it yet, but we're about two miles out."

My gut clenches and I can barely breathe. "Land or water?"

"What?" Connor seems thrown by my response.

"Was it a land or water landing? Where did she crash?" I demand.

He pauses, and I hear him murmuring in hushed tones. I feel a hand on my shoulder. I look up at Reece, who has gone pale. After what seems like an eternity, Connor finally responds.

"Land. The plane they spotted it from is too big to touch down anywhere close. They're calling the choppers back, but it'll take them a bit to get here. They're in the middle of refueling."

"Text me the coordinates." A calm comes over me, and I grip Reece's arm. "We're on our way."

"Li—" I hang up before Connor can say another syllable.

"We'll take my plane," Reece says in a rush. "It's gassed up and the wheels are on."

"All right, but I'm flying."

He hesitates and I'm taken aback by it. This same boy has done colossally stupid things to make an impression on me over the years. Part of me is glad to see he's grown some balls. Most of me isn't.

"Dammit, Reece! Connor says it's in an awkward spot. I need to get there first."

He stares into my eyes, debating. If he refuses, I'll burst into tears like some silly girl. Thankfully, he gives a decisive nod. "Okay."

We sprint to the airstrip and hurry into Reece's plane. I flip on switches with shaking hands. Mom…crash landing. I close my eyes and take a couple of deep breaths as Reece quickly charts the coordinates.

"That's…bizarre." Reece frowns. "We've searched that area more than once. The canopy's pretty thick up there. It must be hard to see."

I don't remember flying to the crash site. My imagination works overtime, playing out scenarios as if I'm rehearsing for a play that I don't have the last half of the script for. I must do okay, because Reece doesn't show any signs of distress. At least, not until we circle around and spot the wreckage.

"Is that it?" I've lost all semblance of my cool.

Reece lifts his binoculars and rattles off numbers and a letter. "I can only read the last three. But they're a perfect match."

From our initial vantage point, all but the mid-section of the plane is hidden by a large bank of bushes and overgrown pines canopying a riverbank. I can see how it could be missed during a flyover. Surrounding the wreck site are the shallows of a small river that's split by a narrow gravel bar.

A group of about twenty people are crossing a clearing below heading for the fuselage. I see Runt running ahead of the group, so I know Connor has to be among them. I'll risk their safety if I land on that side of the river, so I press on.

"Put her down in there." Reece points to a broader, flatter clearing west of the wreckage. Just as he says it, a Search and Rescue helicopter crests the hill from the opposite direction and starts to land. There's still room for me if I circle around again, but I don't want to take the time. I need to get to her first.

I shake my head. "I'll land on the gravel bar."

"It's way too short." Reece's concern is etched on his chiseled face. "You can't decelerate enough."

Ignoring him, I begin my descent. Under normal circumstances, Reece would be right. But I'm not using conventional methods. I plan to lower the wheels into the river to slow the plane.

"Lilah." Reece has deduced my plan. "This isn't a race."

"Shhh." I narrow my eyes. "I got this."

In my peripheral vision, I see Reece grab ahold of his seat belt, groping at the ceiling as if to brace himself. "Shit."

I've never actually landed this way, but I've seen Mom do the maneuver on two separate occasions. If I manage my airspeed perfectly, we'll come to a stop at the end of the gravel bar. Too fast, I'll sheer off Reece's landing gear. Too slow, I'll flip the plane end over end.

I tap the wheels down decisively, and water tunnels up around the plane like a ride at a waterpark. We come to a stop with plenty of sandbar to spare. Reece sounds like he just ran a marathon when I jump from the plane and run full force in the direction of the wreckage.

"Lie!" Connor's voice echoes behind me, but I don't slow down. I can see how banged up Mom's plane is. One of the wings looks like a broken appendage. I sprint down the gravel beach and moments later I'm in the river, attempting to wade across it.

It's a big mistake. Though the water isn't more than a couple feet deep, it's moving at a pretty good clip and I struggle to keep my footing. I get about halfway across before the current takes me, spilling me over and carrying me downstream away from the crippled plane. I'm sputtering cold water when I crash into something hard. The impact knocks the wind out of me. I go under, tangled up in the branches of a fallen tree. Thankfully, I'm aware enough to keep my mouth closed.

Then I feel myself being lifted and I'm staring down at

Connor's muscular ass. Even through an oxygen-deprived haze, I'm aware that he's flung me over his shoulder. By the time he wades to the other side, I've managed to recover enough to take a shallow breath. He sets me on my feet, and I bolt for the plane, ignoring the splitting pain in my side.

"Lie! Wait!" He sounds a thousand miles away.

"Mom!" My voice is strident, like the shriek of a scared child. I don't care. I don't give a shit what anyone here thinks of me. "Mommy!"

Connor grips my shoulder, and I wrench away. I stumble, but I continue on my path. I'm within twenty feet of the plane before he grabs me around the waist. Pain radiates from my rib cage, but I buck and fight anyhow. It's no use. Connor outweighs me by over a hundred pounds and all of it seems to be muscle. I sob and struggle, but it's a waste of time. He's too familiar with my tricks. Runt barks and jumps up on me, knocking me back into Connor.

"Lilah." Connor spins me so I'm facing him. His grip on my upper arms is firm, as are his eyes. I wriggle, trying to escape his clutches, but he doesn't ease up.

"Let me go!" My feral and hysterical voice sounds foreign even to me.

"Lie, baby...listen to me." His eyes match the color of the trees behind him, and they snare me, pleading with me to hear him out. Runt nudges against the back of my leg, bumping me into Connor's chest. His arms come around me, and I'm incapable of moving.

"You might not want to see what's inside." His gentle tone matches his expression.

The certainty in his eyes undoes me. He believes we're too late.

Tears follow, and I don't even brush them away. I've been so focused on the finish line that I'm not prepared for what the reward might be. I haven't allowed myself to entertain the idea that Mom's dead. I open my mouth to tell him he's wrong, but what comes out is a gasping sob.

"N—" I can't even finish the word. Connor leans down, his big hands cradling my face. His forehead touches mine, and that simple contact steals what's left of my courage. I go limp in his arms, and he holds me for a full minute while I try to breathe. Connor wipes away my tears and I feel remarkably unjudged, even though it's obvious he's seeing into me.

"Stay here," he urges in a hypnotic way that brings me down a notch. His calloused hands are warm against my cheeks. My heart hammers, and my teeth chatter, but I barely notice, cocooned in Connor, and the dying embers of our feelings for one another. "I'll go check it out. All right?"

CHAPTER NINE

CONNOR

FALLING

TEN FEET AWAY from the plane, I know I'm not going to find a dead body. In both of my careers, I've encountered my share of rotting corpses. Decay has a very distinct smell, and the absence of it is a huge relief.

Runt stands at attention between Delilah and me. The old malamute seems to understand that I want her to stay away, and acts as my enforcer. Lie's dripping onto the rocky sand and trembling all over, but she watches my every move intently.

She'd nearly wrecked me when she went into the river. Everyone occupying space between us had the good sense to part like the Red Sea. My heart seized when I heard that terrible smack as she connected with the downed tree trunk. I was sure she'd split her skull open.

Imagine my surprise when I sat her down and she bolted away from me. She's resilient as hell, and even at a full sprint, I just barely caught up to her. Luckily she wasn't clear-headed enough to fight me effectively. That sobbing, though…Christ. She ripped my heart in half. Powerless against her raw anguish and those real tears, I nearly let her have her way. Lilah stripped of her war paint was equal parts terrible and beautiful.

Reece Warren, Human Beanpole and Lilah's long-time stalker, races in her direction. While I was saving her from drowning, he'd taken the time to put on hip waders before braving the river, farther upstream where it was maneuverable. He unfurls a thick blanket, which he wraps around his fair maiden's shoulders.

I turn back to the plane before rolling my eyes.

How fortunate. Prince Charming's here to save the day.

With Lilah contained, I turn my focus back to the wreckage. I wrench open the dented door of the outer fuselage, rewarded with exactly what I expect to see. An empty cockpit.

There's no visible blood, no abandoned cargo, and no obvious signs of a struggle. The only damage to the interior of the plane is to the windshield, which looks like someone took a crowbar to it.

A chorus of distant barking signals the arrival of the cadaver dogs. Search and Rescue, the Red Cross, and the Coast Guard surely aren't far behind, so I take several pictures of the cockpit before anyone can stop me. I'm backing out of the plane, when something shiny catches my eye.

A silver cell phone, wedged underneath the pilot's seat.

I struggle to free it from the tight space, snagging the device just as I hear huffing and puffing behind me. Slipping the phone up into my sleeve and praying that the case is waterproof, I pretend to gander around at the empty cockpit.

"Son. I'm going to have to ask you to step aside." I turn and Lieutenant Colonel Floyd stares me down. He's been a trooper in True for as long as I can remember, but he's a good five years past retirement age. He seems pretty proud he's gotten the jump on me.

I level a curious gaze at him, which he takes as a personal affront.

"I said 'step aside.'" His hand inches toward his sidearm.

Though I could disarm him, break his neck, and shoot everyone present in the amount of time it would take him to draw, I surrender. He's lucky I have less ego and more patience than he does. "Hey, no problem."

"Did you touch anything?"

"No, sir," I lie effortlessly.

"You shouldn't have opened the door." He regards me like I'm a special kind of stupid. "This could be a crime scene."

I cock an eyebrow, though visions of violence still dance in my head. Crime scene? An odd statement for someone who still hasn't looked inside the plane. "Just making sure Mrs. Campbell wasn't inside in need of medical attention."

He clicks his tongue at me like I'm an idiot and practically body checks me as he grunts his way into Lu's empty plane. I'm surprised to see that several troopers I recognize from True are right on top of me. We're miles from their detachment area, yet they've arrived on the scene before Search and Rescue or the Coast Guard.

As I back away (snapping a couple more pictures of the outside and surrounding trees), I consider mentioning the break-in at Lu's to one of them. Something tells me I shouldn't. Cadaver dogs rush past me, and not one of them heads off in any direction. They simply circle the plane, sniffing and waggling their tails.

I'm roused by angry shouts, and I hurry through the gathering crowd toward Lilah's vicious diatribe. I jostle and shoulder people aside, no longer questioning my motives. When the rubber hits the road, my default is Team Lilah.

"You misunderstand me, Mrs. Andrews." I recognize the droll tone of Investigator Dixon before I see his vulturous grin.

"Miss. *Campbell.*" Lilah's abrasive edge is all too familiar. Though I'm not the focus of her outrage, her bite makes me tense. "And I understand you perfectly well. There's no gold here, so just leave me alone and stay out of the way."

Dixon moves toward Lilah. He's either very brave, or very foolish. "Delilah, hear me out."

I don't see a trace of the adversary I'd sparred with earlier when I encountered Dixon. That's peculiar; he's always wanted the same thing from Lilah he wanted from me. Perhaps he's offering her sympathy. If so, he's barking up the wrong tree. Lie's nowhere near acceptance yet, but she's got anger to spare.

Whatever his motives, Lie isn't biting. Her deadly glare

tells me shit is about to get real.

I take my place beside her. "Everything okay, Lie?"

"Fan-fucking-tastic," she responds without glancing my way. "Mr. Dixon was just leaving."

Dixon's face transforms with genuine amusement. "You're not in charge here, little lady."

"Neither are you," Lilah says, like he's the worst kind of trash...the opportunistic kind. She swivels on the troopers nearby. "Why the hell are you guys even here? Is there a neon warm donuts sign somewhere nearby?"

Dixon laughs, a deep sound that echoes. "Does that moxie get you far in Vegas?"

Lie's overinflated glare tells me she's going to jail if I don't intervene.

"Whoa. You need to stop talking. Now." I step forward without a trace of humor. Dixon isn't fazed, but the nearby troopers are at attention, hands hovering near guns. They don't concern me. I'm testy and ready to rumble.

Dixon's eyes flit to Delilah, and then back to me. "Mr. Garrett, again. Constant as the northern star, I see."

I crinkle my brow at his out-of-left-field comment. I glance at Lilah and see something complex brewing in her eyes as she studies the investigator.

She turns on her heel and hobbles off toward the Red Cross chopper. It's the last reaction I expect, and I blink at her retreating form in disbelief. Once the initial shock wears off, I turn to Dixon.

"Why *are* you here?" I demand, done playing his games.

He seems taken aback by my frankness, but quickly slips into his diplomatic mask. "I'm just here to help."

"Bullshit." I'm not screwing around and I can tell he knows it. "If you have something helpful to say, spit it out."

"*Not here.*" His grave expression and low tones pique my interest. Many members of law enforcement or local searchers lurk close by, some of whom are taking selfies with the wreckage. "Lunch tomorrow. Bring Delilah."

"She won't come."

He glances around and lowers his voice. "This wasn't an accident."

A shallow smirk bleeds through my bravado. "No shit."

He pulls me aside, casting watchful eyes about for eavesdroppers. "LuAnn and I were corresponding before she disappeared. She'd learned something about the Aurora hijacking. Something huge."

I gape at him in disbelief. "Lu's disappearance has something to do with Aurora?"

He shakes his head. "I can't say anything more. Talk to Delilah. Get her to come. She'll listen to you."

I rake a hand through my hair, knowing what it'll take to get Lilah within five miles of this man. "I'll do my best."

Dixon smiles genuinely for the first time since the day we met.

"I have faith in you, Mr. Garrett."

CHAPTER TEN

LILAH

SECRETS AND LIES

THE FEMALE PARAMEDIC hands me a towel and a set of scrubs, then she ushers me over to the helicopter.

"Delilah, I'm Bernice. Come find me when you're done changing so I can assess your injuries."

I peel off my soaked flannel shirt, and my hand shoots to my side. Gritting through the pain, I inch out of my wet jeans and underwear. Drying off, I wriggle into the scrub pants and cinch them tight with the drawstring. I've already made an ass out of myself today, no need to moon the entire search party for an encore.

I pop the back fastening of my bra and toss it into the plastic bag with the rest of my wet things. I'm about to slip the scrub top over my head when the chopper door swings wide and Connor thrusts his head inside. His eyes widen at the extreme close-up of my breasts.

"Connor!" Scowling, I pull the material tight across my chest.

Connor's frozen, except his eyes, which seem to be having a field day exploring my exposed flesh.

"Go away!" I seethe, hoping he didn't see the tiny stretchmarks peppering my belly and hips.

"I just wanted—"

"Shut the damn door!" I bellow.

"Calm down, Lie. I've seen you a hell of a lot more naked than that." He's wearing an amused smirk, and I want to kick him in the mouth. He whips around, leaving the door wide open to the elements.

I mutter a long string of four-letter words as I toss the shirt over my head and hurry to slip my feet into dry socks. They have pompoms on the backs of them, but beggars shouldn't bitch. As I scoot to the open door, I suck in a sharp breath. I need a couple Tylenol, but I'm otherwise ready to roll.

I seek out Merle for a stilted update on the perimeter search. The teams fan out, covering a two-mile radius in every direction. Law enforcement guards the fuselage, which they've decorated with police tape. I try to get a look inside, but a sanctimonious officer standing guard says I can't go near it until the NTS completes their investigation. I'm not blind, though. Something doesn't add up. I don't see how Mom broke off the wing. Where was the damage in the surrounding trees?

I wander to the riverbank looking for collision damage, anything that might explain the state of the plane. I spot some worn tracks, but they run parallel to the crash site, and they're badly smudged.

With one last beseeching glance at the grizzly wreck, and the only major clue we have, I turn away from the wreckage to seek out my teammates. Reece is with them.

I stride over to the group of men, ready to take the reins. I'm no longer content with playing second fiddle to Stephen or Connor.

"What do we know?" I scrutinize my team, planting my hands on my hips. Reece's eyes drop to my chest and he flushes crimson. He's suddenly very interested in the clouds above us.

"Uh…um…n…no one's found any sign of her," he responds, and I turn to Stephen to ask what Reece has been huffing. Stephen's stroking his red mustache to cover a devilish grin. Connor sighs heavily and takes off his jacket, holding it out to me. His eyes sparkle, and his face is artificially composed.

"Thanks, I'm good." I don't even reach for his jacket. I'm still not happy with him for barging in on me.

"You're cold," he responds patiently, thrusting the jacket at me in an insistent manner.

I must be giving him my crazy eyes, because he blinks pointedly, and his gaze drops to my chest, then returns to mine. Conner and I are capable of complete conversations in the matter of a blink, and I get his message.

No bra. Thin scrubs. And the weather's just chilly enough…

I can feel my resting bitch face click into place as I take Connor's jacket. I put it on, marveling that the human race hasn't died off when a set of erect nipples can bring competent men to a screeching halt.

How am I not the ruler of this planet already?

"Focus, guys," I manage. "What do we know?"

"No one's found her trail yet." Now that the girls are out of sight, Stephen's a pro again. "The dogs picked up her scent in the plane…but nowhere else."

"Well, what are we waiting for?" I ask.

"You're done for the day," Stephen informs me and turns to one of the other team members. "Why don't you two find Merle and see where you can fill in?"

"E…excuse me?" It's my turn to stammer. "Who the hell do you think you are?"

"The one calling the shots, that's who." He stands up straighter, ready to mix it up. "Right now you're a liability."

"Why? Because I have boobs?" I cross my arms to take the offending body parts off the negotiating table. "That's your problem, not mine."

His face goes so red that he looks like a human thermometer. "No, smart-ass. Because you don't listen."

Though my side is killing me, I take a step toward him.

Connor slips between us and turns my way. "They think you're dangerous, Lilah."

His calm delivery takes the wind out of my sails. I turn to the team, and they're watching me like I'm an unexploded bomb.

I take a breath. "You worry about yourselves. I'll worry about me."

"That's not how this works, Lie. I just dragged you out of the river. Now you're wasting everybody's time arguing. If you don't fall in, we aren't efficient. There's a pecking order for a reason."

I scan the group again. They've been discussing me behind my back, all right. I'm about to cuss them all out when Bernice, the paramedic, appears at my side.

"Miss Campbell? I need to examine you. Now."

"I'm fine." I glare at Connor like we're about to box. "I just need a couple of aspirin."

"Lilah. Are you sure?" Reece's concern implores me to reconsider.

"She's *not* fine," Connor interjects. "She needs X-rays. We're not taking her anywhere until you medically clear her, Bernice."

"Con—" He holds up a hand to silence me.

"End of discussion."

I look from Connor to Stephen. They cross their arms like oversized obstinate bookends. I turn to Reece for sympathy.

"You know he's right, Lilah," Reece says delicately. "Let me fly you back to town so you can get checked out."

"I'll come with you," Connor insists, and Reece shoots him an annoyed glance, like he finds the prospect distasteful.

"With all due respect, gentlemen, she's riding with us." Bernice sounds done with everybody. "We'll fly her directly to the hospital helipad. She could be bleeding internally while you're all banging your chests and comparing penis sizes."

My eyes gleam with admiration as she jumps into the fray, and I bite my inner cheek to suppress laughter at the way their collective jaws work in response to her uncompromising command.

The flight crew snaps to when they see us coming. Bernice insists I lie down on a portable gurney in the back of the chopper, and I'm too humiliated to argue. I'm supposed to be pushing all of these assholes to find Mom and I've taken focus off of that objective. The truth of Connor's statement weighs on me, and I'm so mad at myself I'm afraid I'll cry.

"You're guarding your left side. Is that the only place it hurts?"

I nod, blinking back the unwelcome tears.

"I'm gonna take a look," Bernice says. "I'll be gentle, I promise."

I lift the top so she can see my midsection and her lips purse slightly, her eyes grave. She probes carefully, asking a series of questions.

"You've got some swelling and what's shaping up to be an ugly bruise. You may have cracked ribs. We need to ice it until we can do some imaging, all right?"

"All right."

The pilots run through their preflight check, and I listen with envy. I wonder if Reece will have enough runway to clear the tree line when he tries to leave. I know I could do it.

I close my eyes and feel a tear escape. The search is going on all around us, and I'm completely useless. Worse than useless; I'm a fucking hindrance. If my ribs are broken, I'll be no help at all.

"You need to step back," Bernice barks, and I flinch at her sharp tone. She's arguing with someone outside the chopper door. Connor's voice carries from beyond her, and she lurches back over to me with a dramatic eye roll that says it's long past beer-thirty.

"Connor Garrett's demanding to ride along."

My throat narrows and I'm nauseated. If I have to listen to him say "I told you so" all the way back to Anchorage, I *will* cry. Crying in front of Connor is a fate worse than drowning.

Bernice softens as she watches my indecision. She places a hand on my arm, an act of solidarity. "I have no problem telling him to piss off, Delilah. It's totally up to you. There's room for him in here, but just barely."

I don't want to cause more drama for these poor people who are just trying to do their jobs. Connor probably saved my life today. If he needs to gloat, I deserve it.

"It's okay," I croak past the frog in my throat. "Let him in."

Seconds later, Connor's boarding the chopper. Bernice thrusts a headset at him and carefully places one on me. She points a finger in the direction of the tail and Connor wedges himself as far back as he can, considering his monstrous size. I'm surprised that she didn't stick him up by the pilots, but then she hands him an ice pack as the propeller deafens me.

"Make yourself useful," I hear her tell him through the headsets, and she nods toward me. Connor kneels down next to me, his long hair spilling onto the gurney as he adjusts the padding under his knees. He's so close that I smell his familiar earthy scent. I'm swept away by nostalgia, the way he shushed me when I'd finally mustered up the courage to break up with him before he left for basic, kissing the tears from my face, then tormenting my ravenous body with possessive hands and demanding lips. After, when I needed him the most, his cold dismissal taught me the most important life lesson I'd ever learned. A girl can only rely on one person in this world: herself.

Choked up on these memories, I steal a glance at Connor, who looks up from his spot beside the gurney. Our eyes lock for a long moment. He's unreadable, though I do my damnedest. He reaches out and smooths my hair back, and God help me, I sigh.

He removes his hand like I've shocked him, and he wears an uncomfortable expression like he doesn't want to touch me, even with the ice pack as a barrier. We lift off, and I turn away, staring at the metal hull to my right. It's been a long time since I felt this low, and Connor was the source of my blues back then, too.

As we lift off, he presses the cold pack to my side. The pressure's not bad, but I scrunch my face in response to the searing cold.

"Am I hurting you?" Connor's deep voice sounds artificial, synthesized through the headphones and the thunderous sounds of the propeller. I shake my head, but I can't look at him. These tight quarters are way too intimate, and he *is* hurting me.

Just not the way he thinks.

CHAPTER ELEVEN

CONNOR

DRINKING AND DRIVING

As I PACE the waiting room, I review my behavior in the field today. What it boils down to is this: I'm screwed. Even though Lie went into the river, I'm the one who's drowning. Addiction's funny like that. I'm jonesing for a hit, and I'm not alone.

If we're together much longer, things will get out of hand. She's chipping away at me...breaking me down whether she knows it or not. Whether she means to or not. I wish I put up more of a fight or that I could say I'm caving to comfort her. That would make me sound so much nobler than I am. Truth is, Delilah can be very persuasive on a normal day, and today had not been anywhere close to normal.

I can't resist her.

Okay, that's an exaggeration.

I don't want to resist her.

I should be on the road right now, driving as far the hell away from this circus as a tank of gas can get me. Yet here I sit, not only letting it happen, but looking forward to it too.

She's infected me with her inexhaustible faith and her insatiable curiosity—two things I haven't felt in a very long time.

I force myself to choke down some terrible cafeteria coffee, and honestly analyze our breakup, hoping the hurt will help reel me back in.

We'd snuck down to the Kenai, both telling our parents we were spending the weekend at a friend's. The weather turned on us partway down, and nearly got stuck trying to get down the lane to the river house. Opting for plan B, we cut back and went down the secondary road to the original homestead cabin, which Mom's father's father had built with his own two hands back when he first settled here. That cabin had been our hangout when we were little, where we used empties for target practice and played cards when it rained.

Lie had been unusually quiet on the ride down, while I babbled about how I'd aced the ASVAB, I droned on about my projected career path, unable to wipe the smile from my face. This was what I'd always wanted; I was going to be a Green Beret.

The cabin was freezing when we arrived, so we hurriedly built a fire and buried ourselves under the covers. I joked how we'd have to put in a better heater if we were going to live there someday.

"And an indoor bathroom, since that outhouse was frightening," I insisted.

"What? No white picket fence?" I could feel her eyelashes tickle my cheek in the darkness.

"Obviously." I kissed her tenderly, my hand slipping up her shirt. "How can you live happily ever after without one of those?"

On the way home she ended things. She said it would be easier to do it then, not wait until I shipped out in June.

"You're not gonna wait for me?" I'd known Lie was working up to something…whatever it was had been in the cab of the truck with us all the way down to the Kenai, but I was driving in snowy weather, so I couldn't properly defend myself.

"For how long?" She was intentionally abrasive, like she wanted things to escalate. "From the sound of things, you'll be gone for years. Maybe forever."

"Then come with me." I glanced at her for as long as I dared in those conditions. I didn't like what I saw. Game Face Lilah was waiting for me, and she was raring to go.

"And do what? Join up?" An aborted laugh escaped her. "Come on, Connor…authority and I don't mix."

"We should get married." It's not how I pictured proposing, but the words were out and I meant them.

She didn't smile or tear up. She did none of the things you always see in the movies, and who could blame her?

Her face remained as calm as a glassy lake. "So—what? I can knit and watch soap operas while you're somewhere you can't tell me about on missions you can't discuss?"

Good old Lie. She'd been doing her homework. And there I was, unprepared and unarmed.

I reached for her hand. "You've always known this was what I was gonna do."

"You're right." She pulled away from my grasp. She sounded frustrated...furious. "That's on me."

I was gutted by the hurt I saw in her eyes. "Come with me, Lie. You can fly anywhere."

"You can serve anywhere." Her voice sounded thick with emotion. "Be a cop. Search and Rescue—"

I ran a hand over my shorn hair. "You know it's not the same."

She simply observed me as the reality of our situation came into focus for me as it obviously had for her long ago.

"Flying anywhere else wouldn't be the same for me either."

I swallowed, and it hurt my throat. Asking Lie to teach flying lessons to cocky doctors and bored housewives in the lower forty-eight was like asking Tiger Woods to settle for three holes of mini golf. I couldn't expect her to shelve her dream for mine.

"So what do we do now?" I asked. Lilah stared pensively into the dark.

"We end it."

And there it was. The rest of the conversation was all preamble. Knowing Lie, she'd been rehearsing this since I took the ASVAB weeks before, probably while I'd been trying to shave time off my five-mile morning run.

"CONNOR?" A NURSE calls my name, startling me out of my thoughts. I nearly spill my coffee and I scramble to my feet. She looks taken aback by my size or my frazzled state or muddy Carhartts.

"That's me."

"Miss Campbell's completed all of her tests. She said to tell you she's bored and that she needs a Diet Squirt and Chick-O-Sticks."

After a long beat I burst into laughter. The poor nurse waits until I spin down and pull myself together. "Of course she does. Know where I can find the vending machines?"

Forty-five minutes and a trip to Fred Meyer later, I knock on Lilah's hospital room door. She mumbles a greeting. When I enter, her back is to me, and she's gazing out at an impressive view of the Chugach Mountains. Her gown hangs open in back, but sadly, she's wearing scrub pants. Her abdomen's wrapped with a wide bandage.

"I come bearing gifts." I present her snacks, which I had to leave the hospital to track down. Picky little shit.

Genuine pleasure appears on her face, and she holds her hands out expectantly. I toss her the Chick-O-Stick, and even with a running IV as a handicap, she easily snags it out of the air.

I saunter over to hand her the bottle of soda. Close up, I note her puffy eyes. Lilah's not just stoic by nature, she's chiseled out of diamond, or maybe even something harder. Her tear-stained cheeks pit me against the battered boy within who'd once been her willing slave.

Our fingers graze as she takes her drink. Sparks fly, and her hair toss and darkening eyes tells me they're not one-sided. She moves away and I clear my throat. "They didn't have diet, so you'll have to settle for the real stuff."

"Ah, well. I didn't get this way overnight. Can't fix it in a day." She twists the lid and takes a long drink. When she comes up for air, she notices my disdain and sighs. "Aging happens to the best of us. Maybe not you…but every-fucking-body else."

"Am I missing something?" I blatantly scan her body, which is unfortunately masked in a shapeless gown.

She looks down at herself disparagingly and toddles over to the bed. "I'm pretty hard to miss. You can see my ass from space."

I regard her for a long moment and decide she's not kidding. "You've never looked better, Lie."

She eyes me with wounding doubt. I refuse to look away, but it's like digging a splinter out of my soul. I remind myself how hard she was to be in love with, but as her ruthless eyes devour me, I realize she's still impossible not to love.

She finally looks away to unwrap her candy, holding a piece out to me.

"I'm sorry I lost it out there today." Her bleak gaze meets mine again. "Stephen was right to send me away."

I struggle to hide my surprise. Introspection has never been her strong suit, and apologies are unheard of. Seeing the stain of defeat all over her is a knife in the gut.

"You've got nothing to be sorry about. Remember how I was when I lost my mom?"

Her eyes widen, whether because I'm comparing Mom's death to Lu's disappearance or because I'm bringing up *that* night I laid hands on her, I'm not sure. She fidgets with the crisp bedsheet.

"This is going to sound sick, but when I saw that wreckage...I was relieved. To have closure, I mean." She looks exhausted, but phenomenally beautiful. "Now we're back to square one. It's driving me crazy. I don't know where to go from here."

"I don't think she wrecked her plane." I sit down beside her, pulling up the pictures I took of Lu's cockpit. I hand my phone to Lilah.

"You got pictures!" Something akin to relief washes over her face. It's a gorgeous sight...one I could easily get accustomed to. Her amber eyes meet mine, overflowing with gratitude, which I lap up like a thirsty dog.

Delilah zooms in, turning the phone to get a better look. The further she gets into the collection of snapshots, the more her brows draw together.

"Anything jump out at you?" I wait for her to see what I've seen.

"There's not a drop of blood anywhere."

I nod.

"The primer nob is unlocked. That doesn't make sense. And the controls...the levers are in the wrong position. Like the pilot was taxiing, not trying to touch down. And here..."

She scrolls to one of the close-ups I took of the outer fuselage. "This is really minor, but you see this tie eyelet? It's busted. Like someone used a winch to push the plane. I mean...maybe it's always been like that. But..."

"But what?" I ask, and her eyes whip back to me. She's

looking at me, but she's back out there with that plane.

"Mom would have replaced it." She shifts in the bed and her knee brushes my thigh. Warmth shoots through me and I try to ignore it. "I saw tracks. They were faint and they weren't running along the same heading but…"

"ATV tracks?" I'm considering how someone would get a vehicle all the way out there, all terrain or otherwise.

"No." She's certain. "Like the wheels of a plane."

"You think someone knew where she crashed and tampered with the evidence?"

"I doubt it. It's so remote. The closest paved road is what? Twenty miles away?" She frowns. "There's something else that's been bugging me. The damage to the nose…it's crumpled, but not enough. Same with the wing, broken at the base like that? Like she was in a fender bender versus hitting a brick wall at high speed. And the lack of damage to the trees along the trajectory…it just doesn't gel with the impact. I'd expect a serious trail of destruction with a crash landing like that."

"So what are you saying?" I'm buzzing, just like when Reynolds and I are hunting and we find tracks or when Runt catches the scent. "Someone landed the plane, towed it into place, and staged the crash?"

Lilah's lustrous eyes scan mine, and I see she's trying to remain calm. "That's exactly what I think. Any aviation investigator will come to the same conclusion within ten minutes of arriving on the scene."

I nod slowly, organizing my thoughts. "Floyd called the crash site a 'crime scene.' It smelled rotten to him, too. And

Dixon…he claims he's been talking to your mom. Says she was onto something before she disappeared, and he wants us to meet him tomorrow to discuss it."

Before she can respond, the nurse bustles in. She takes Lilah's vitals and asks about her pain level. I ask about the test results, and the nurse claims the doctor will be in soon. Then she hurries off.

"Dixon and Mom?" She's clarifying more than asking.

I nod. "He said that Lu was looking into Aurora. Something big."

Lie chews her lip, but she looks a lot less surprised than I expected. "She called me before she went missing. She kept cutting out and the call dropped, but she mentioned Aurora. She also said to trust no one and not to come home."

I sit back and fold my arms. "You don't listen for shit, do you?"

Her lip curls, and she's so sexy I can't help but smile back. Then her brow furrows.

"What Dixon said about you? Constant as the northern star? Mom described you to me just like that."

I take some time to consider, finding the characterization condescending, not to mention embarrassing. I try to focus on Lilah's point, which is that Lu probably said this to Dixon, proof he's been talking to her.

I lean forward. "What else did she say on the phone?"

She shakes her head. "The reception was total shit. I could barely understand her."

"Maybe she found Aurora 10," I offer. "And someone

else found out."

Lilah says nothing. She sips her soda thoughtfully.

"We should meet Dixon," she says. "See what he knows."

"Yeah." I don't doubt it's the right move.

"Goddam fucking Aurora." Lilah's venomous, bank-shotting her now empty bottle into the trash can. "If everyone who hunted that shit all these years panned for gold instead, they'd all be rich."

I'm speechless. Finding the missing Auroras had been Lie's obsession; she'd been willing to sever ties with me once when she thought I was hunting for it behind her back.

"Why bother staging a plane wreck if you're going to do such a half-assed job?" Lie's staring out the window. "I mean at least make it a challenge...set it on fire...something..."

"Rush job?" I offer with a shrug.

Lie purses her lips. "Distraction? To keep us focused on the right hand so we don't notice what the left hand's doing."

I nod slowly. "Watching the plane when we should be...looking at...what?"

She seems uncomfortable, and it hits me. She thinks we should be investigating LuAnn. Lilah needs the evidence to support the outcome she wants. That LuAnn's alive out there, even if it means Lu faked the crash.

"If your mom faked that crash—"

"She would never—" She's seconds from lunging at

me, and I put a hand on her thigh.

"I know, Lie. Because if she did, she would have faked the shit out of it. Nothing lame like this." I sit back, digging through my coat pockets. I keep the rest of my theory to myself. Because if Lu found the gold, and someone found out…

"I have something else you need to see." I pull the silver cell phone out of my pocket and hold it up. Recognition blazes in her eyes. "I found this under the pilot's seat."

Lie reaches for it. "I bought Mom that case three years ago. She really needs an upgrade."

"It needs a charge." I lean in conspiratorially. "But if she didn't crash—"

"She didn't." Lie sits forward, then collapses with a wince. A lush tendril of her ruddy hair falls into her face.

"Okay." I brush the strand away so I can meet her gaze directly. The warm color of her exotic eyes contrasts with the cool, measured control I witness her mustering. "*Since* she didn't crash, we have to assume someone put that plane there. Her call history…who she was texting—"

"Special delivery." Reece knocks as he enters, and Lilah drops Lu's phone onto the bed like it's a hot potato. I flip her sheet over it, elated by her response to Reece. There's no denying her reaction. The phone is our secret, which means she trusts me more than him.

Reece strolls in with a large bouquet of pink roses. Judging by his shiny boy band hair, he's been home to shower. He's all smiles until he sees me.

"You shouldn't have." Lilah's saccharine grin is one I'm

not familiar with.

He thrusts the flowers at her. She takes them with an obligatory sniff. "Are they keeping you overnight?"

"We're still waiting on results," I say. Reece's jaw tightens and I struggle to keep my laughter at bay.

"Your car's outside." He dangles her keys in front of her. "Your purse is locked in the trunk. You left it in my plane."

She remains as sweet as syrup. "You're too good to me."

Reece glows, and I've got serious sympathy for him. Then he turns contemptuous eyes on me and any pity evaporates. "Boone is headed back to True with your truck and your dog."

I nod stiffly, feeling like an asshole for abandoning Runt and imposing on Boone. If I don't get my shit together, my one-track mind will be as much of a detriment as Lie's knee-jerk reactions.

My shame fresh and miserable, I pull my phone out to text Boone while Lilah flirts shamelessly with Reece. Uncomfortable, I stand to leave just before the doctor strides in. He gives us the *Reader's Digest* version: Lilah has no breaks or fractures. When she denies any breathing problems, he tells the nurse to cut her loose.

"Take it easy," he demands and turns to me, as if I'm her keeper. "No white water rafting or rock climbing for at least a couple of weeks."

"Got it," I reply, as if I have any control over Delilah. Her blistering eyes capture mine, and her undivided attention awakens a needfulness that's disturbing in mixed company.

Reece and I wait outside while Lilah dresses. The atmosphere is hostile, worse than when we first met, and that time we'd nearly come to blows. I wish we had, and I get the impression he does too. Neither of us got closure.

"I'll drive her home." Reece sounds firm, like a man who's never been afraid a day in his life.

"That won't be necessary." I lean casually against the wall. "I'm staying with her."

Reece grows ashen at the notion that I'm sleeping so close to Delilah. Good. He narrows his eyes. "Why are you here?"

I cross to the other side of the hall. It's too tempting to backhand him otherwise. "She asked me to come."

He smiles, and it's a decidedly unfriendly one. "And this time you actually came through. I guess we should throw you a parade."

I inhale through my nose and blow out through my mouth. "You got something to say to me, Reece?"

"You should go crawl back to whatever hole she found you in before shit gets real."

My eyebrows shoot up in surprise. "You've got balls, Warren. No brains, but balls."

He ignores me, pressing onward. "When we find Lu-Ann, Lilah's gonna take it hard. You saw how she was today. She's strong, but she's still gonna need someone with staying power."

I feel my blood pressure climbing. "Don't talk about things you don't understand."

He pushes off the wall suddenly and points a finger in my face. "You broke her when you ditched out to play soldier. She tried to move on, but she bolted, ditched her dreams about living and flying out on Kodiak. She deserves more and you fucking know it. It's why you left her here in the first place. Do the noble thing again. Leave her to someone who won't bolt when things get tough."

My face feels like an inferno and my teeth clench hard enough to ache. I don't want to hear what Delilah did to forget me, and I sure as hell don't need a lecture from her rebound guy.

Staring him down, I recognize my own kind. We both know the agony when the ride with Lilah is over and the payment comes due. You'd think I'd feel some kinship with him, but I don't. I'm possessive and outraged that he's even sampled what's mine. I take a step toward him and we're nearly nose to nose.

Delilah breezes through the door and we whip our heads in her direction. Her eyes boomerang between Reece and me and we step apart.

Shockingly, Lilah refuses to leave in a wheelchair. I'm opening the passenger side door for her when Reece reappears again.

"You forgot these." He's all bashful dimples as he thrusts the roses at her a second time.

She's up on her tiptoes, kissing his cheek. "Thank you, Reece."

As I shut her door for her, I give Reece a sardonic salute and he furrows his predominant brow. I hurry around into the driver's seat, and Lie's already trying to plug her mom's phone into the charger, but hers is not the right adapter.

"You shouldn't mess with him like that," I say, buckling my seat belt.

"Huh?" She flips down her mirror and preens, assessing her reflection.

"Stringing him along," I say. "He was ready to fight me."

"Half the people in Alaska want to give you a beatdown," she chirps. "You can't blame that on me."

CHAPTER TWELVE

LILAH

ONE FROM THE VAULTS

ONNOR'S EYES ARE glued to the two-lane highway in front of us. He hasn't said much since we left the hospital, other than when I asked him to buy a charger for Mom's phone. His silence suits me just fine.

I'm perturbed by his comments about me stringing Reece along. First of all, he forfeited the right to say anything about my love life more than a decade ago when he went off and married the U.S. Army. Reece has shown me nothing but kindness. Granted, his brand of kindness can be a lot to take, but at least he's consistent. Thanking someone who just brought me my purse, my car, and remembered flowers too, isn't disingenuous.

Connor's fastidiously ignoring me, so I shoot off a text to Reece.

Thanks again for being so thoughtful, Reece. Sorry Connor started shit. Not sure what that was.

He responds immediately.

Be careful around him. I've heard things. Remem-

ber, I'm a phone call away if you need me.

I read the message three times and chalking his cryptic warning up to their rivalry, I decide not to respond. Retrieving Mom's phone from the center console, I power it up, impatiently waiting through the glowing Apple screen. The display fills with scores of missed texts and phone calls. I start with voice mails, putting it on speaker so I don't have to regurgitate the info for Connor.

The automated voice declares the date and the time of the message, which happens to be the morning of Mom's disappearance. A familiar male voice starts to speak.

"Hey, LuLu. Honey, I appreciate the help, I really do, but I've chased these leads down and nothing comes of it. I'm in Denver now, but I'll be there by Thursday night. I'll email you my itinerary. I'm booked at the usual place. Wear that little blue thing I bought you." The call ends and the robotic female voice asks if we'd like to delete it.

"Whoa…" Connor's eyes are wide. "Dixon…and—"

"My mother…" I sigh, not half as surprised as I should be.

Connor's leery when he glances at me. "Lie, I'm sorry. That's one hell of a way to find something like that out."

"Mom and Dad have been apart for years. Divorce costs a fortune," I repeat the excuse Mom has offered up for most of my childhood. Truth is, I'm deeply disappointed, mostly because Dixon is an ambulance-chasing snake oil salesman.

Connor's expression darkens. "What if he's responsible for her disappearance?"

I find the idea morbidly amusing. "Dad?"

"No." Connor's answer blasts forth as if he's been holding his breath. "Dixon."

I pull a face. "He wasn't in town."

"Or so he says…"

I nod and shrug simultaneously, scrolling through recent calls. Missed calls from Andi…me…

My scrolling comes to an abrupt halt when Connor's number appears in the outgoing log. My chest tightens.

"What's wrong?" Connor narrows his eyes, and I struggle to keep my composure.

"What did she say to you?" I'm watching his every move.

"Who?" He acts like I'm speaking Greek and I feel like I have a boulder on my chest.

"She called you, Connor. Right after she called me."

"Lu?" He reaches for the phone but I hold it out of his reach. I'm trying to see past that stupid beard, looking for his tells. "When?"

"Don't play dumb, Connor. The call lasted for four minutes."

"I'm not playing at anything." His exasperation is blatant as he pulls into Mom's driveway. "I didn't talk to Lu."

I flip to the texts and see there are many unread. I see no text conversations with Connor at all.

Just because he says the phone was dead when he found it doesn't mean it's the truth. Maybe he deleted the texts and forgot about the call log.

My sister and Boone wave from Mom's porch. Boone's

fixing the doorframe, and Andi's supervising, beer in hand. I'd texted her right before I went up in the plane with Reece, but I'd forgotten that since she'd neglected to text me back.

"Lie—" Connor's expressive hazel eyes plead with me.

Be careful around him.

Don't trust anybody.

I'm too confused and infuriated to deal with him, so I open the door and climb out of the vehicle.

Runt jumps up on me, and I cry out. Connor whistles, and Runt drops and sits, wagging his tail.

My sister greets me with far less love and enthusiasm.

"What the hell happened to you?" She chuckles at my scrubs and muddy hair.

"We found Mom's plane," I murmur.

"Yeah, I heard," Andi says. "Sura's the editor in chief of the *Gazette*. If a tree falls in the forest, she's blogging about what color the roots are before it hits the ground."

"Sura?" Connor and I exchange one of our glances. We could do amazing things with her resources. "No shit?"

Andi's surprised. "She ran the school paper all four years of high school. What did you expect her to be doing?"

"Hard time?" I mumble, referring to Sura's side job selling her grandma's weed back when we were kids. Connor snickers and holds the door for me.

"Oh grow up, Lilah," Andi calls through the open kitchen window at us. "Everybody smokes pot nowadays."

With a headshake, I turn back to the ravaged kitchen. Connor has his hand out to me. I look at it and back at him.

"I want you on the couch," he informs me. My dirty mind kicks into overdrive, and I find it hard to form vowels.

"I…uhhhmmm…" He fixes me with a stare that dares me to argue. His commanding vibe takes me aback.

"You need to rest," he reminds me, oblivious to my rampant filthy thoughts. "Doctor's orders."

I reach out apprehensively, and he leads me by the hand through the trashed living room. I try to lower myself, but I'm stiff. Connor pulls me against his chest, his warm hands on my hips. The clinical smell of hospital soap does nothing to mask his underlying scent. I'm tempted to burrow into him, face to his firm chest and just stay put. Fortunately, one of us is thinking straight, and he lowers me to the couch, and then takes a decisive step back.

"Hello!" Andi nearly smacks into Connor as she hurries into the room. They practically lunge away from one another, and it's the most uncomfortable interaction I've witnessed since Mom forced me to go with Andi to the junior high dance. Andi turns to me. "Why are you wearing a hospital bracelet and walking like an old lady?"

"It's not important," I mumble. "Do you know what they took yet?"

"How the hell would I know? I just got here." She's defensive, like I've been riding her all day.

"I didn't know." I give Connor a look that says, "I'm going to bitch slap her."

"Zen the fuck up, Andi." Connor's reasonable delivery

contradicts his harsh words. "We need your eyes. Let's have a beer and figure out what they came for."

Andi's twisting her hair. "Mom's laptop's gone, but she might have had it on her."

"The laptop was the first thing I looked for," I tell him. "It wasn't here when I arrived."

After she retreats down the hall, Connor frowns. "The laptop wasn't in the plane either. We really should call the law. They need to come out and file a report. Lu's gonna want to make an insurance claim."

I look him over judiciously, measuring this behavior against the unexplained phone call. Connor didn't have to show me Mom's phone. If he's hiding something, he's being awfully sloppy about it.

Connor's involvement makes no sense to me, but I'm just not sure what to think. When it comes to Connor, things get jumbled in a way that never happens with anything or anyone else.

Andi returns, obviously pissed. "They tore up Mom's closet. Her photo albums are everywhere and pictures are scattered all over the place. I need another beer."

I hear the fridge open and close and Connor appears, popping the top of a cold one and handing it to her. Seeing them together again puts me on edge. Connor and I just found our mojo, and we're finally getting some useful leads about what's really going on with Mom. Throwing Andi into the mix may unravel all that, but she's a necessary evil for this piece of the puzzle.

Andi drinks deeply, then casts her eyes from me to

Connor.

"Just like old times." Her remark is drier than chardonnay. Before I take the low road and get snarky with her, I turn my attention to the couch cushions, which have been unzipped and tossed about. Magazines and books lie everywhere. Mom's wooden nesting dolls are scattered about, and Andi narrowly misses stepping on one. "Shit."

"Thanks for coming, Andi," I say, hoping to fake it till I feel it.

"Thank Boone." Andi flicks a dismissive glance my way, and her eyes return to Connor. "He guilted me into it."

"Good thing." Connor ramps up the charm, producing a panty-dropping smile. "Lilah's useless and I can't do this alone."

Andi twirls her hair with a flirtatious grin.

I can't watch Connor flirt with my little sister, so I slip away to the bathroom for a shower. My side throbs, and I turn Mom's medicine cabinet upside down looking for painkillers. She has nothing, not even a baby aspirin, but I stay there for a few minutes, pulling myself together. I notice Connor's jump bag on the hamper, and I unzip it, riffling through in hopes of finding a Tylenol. Instead, I find no less than five prescription bottles, all of which are empty. I google the drug names on my phone, disturbed to find that three of them are psych meds, anxiety, depression, sleeping pills…

I reemerge just in time to see Connor and Andi disappear into Mom's bedroom. Boone puts a hand on my arm, a silent question about my state of being or maybe my injury. I shrug, and he and I sift through the mess in the common space. Connor and Andi are yammering and laughing, so I assume they've managed to keep their clothes on.

About an hour later, Boone and I step outside for a break. He lights a cigarette, which is new. I refrain from commenting, figuring if I had to deal with my family on the regular, I'd need better living through chemistry too. Andi's cackle is audible even over the tide rolling in, and Boone shakes his cowlicked head. He descends the steps swiftly, heading for the boathouse. He's not crazy about Andi being in the bedroom with Connor either. No surprise there. Boone's carried a torch for Andi since the moment she hit puberty.

I watch after him, deeply concerned at the slump in his massive shoulders and his unusually tired eyes. He's always been close with Mom, and all of this has to be as confusing and upsetting to him as it is to me. The difference is, no one is bringing Boone flowers, or giving him premature condolences. Outsiders rarely bother to talk to Boone, which is absolutely heartbreaking, and it's their fucking loss.

Seeing Boone ready and willing to tend to Dad takes me back to Dad's accident, more fallout from my mishandling of the Aurora debacle. The memories chill me right along with the gulf breeze.

The night I broke up with Connor, he got a call from Mom. I wasn't supposed to be with him, but she was calling because I wasn't at Sura's house where I said I'd be.

"I'm sure I can track her down," I heard Connor say. His eyes widened before he pulled the receiver from his ear, staring at the tiny screen.

"Someone ran your dad off the road."

"Yeah, right," I snapped, and Connor's brows shot up. *"Just wait till they draw blood and see his alcohol level. He'll change his tune."*

TURNS OUT I was wrong. Not about the lab results. Dad was well above the legal limit. But there were witnesses, several of them, who saw a dark SUV purposely sideswipe him and knock him off the road.

The part none of them knew, not even Connor, was that Smiley had called me a couple of weeks before. I was freaked. I'd changed my number, so I had no idea how he got it. When I demanded to know, he'd laughed.

"My people know your people, Delilah. Aurora 10 is ours. You got your money for 9. That's a lot of cash for white trash like you. Hand over the coordinates to 9, and no one has to get hurt."

I'd slammed the phone down, telling myself he was full of shit. A small-time gangsta who couldn't even abduct one teenage girl with the help of two other men.

Visiting Dad in his hospital room was the reality check I needed. This shit was bigger than me and my stupid ego. He had a concussion, and three pins in his leg. His gray complexion and sunken eyes terrified me, and I couldn't walk outside without wondering if I was being watched or hunted.

When Dad came home from the hospital, I gave him my room and slept on the couch. I contacted the hospital, and used the remainder of my Aurora reward money to pay off his medical bills. He was a drunk before the accident, but the injury and chronic pain pushed him from functional alcoholic to full-blown professional day drinker. And these days I'm not around to help deal with that fallout. And that's all on me.

Breathing deeply as a lame defense against my vivid memories, I hurry back inside. Connor and Andi are toasting with fresh cans of beer, and I'm livid. Andi totally devolves when she drinks, a fact that Connor is well aware of since it's been true since high school. Remembering Connor's empty drug bottles, I wonder if he should be touching the stuff at all. How he can stand the smell of beer after his night out with Dad, I can't even imagine.

The image of Andi all over Connor the night of Claire's funeral festers inside me, and I turn away to stack Mom's magazines. Connor doesn't get to make me jealous, not ever, least of all with Andi. They can both go straight to hell.

When I turn back around, Connor's holding a beer out to me.

I pause and shake my head. We have no time for any of this, and I don't see why I have to say that out loud. I try to get up, but wince.

Connor offers me a hand. I take it and he lifts me like I weigh nothing. He's staring, his face just inches from mine, and I'm ensnared by his molten gaze.

In the silence that follows, I mourn our friendship. The bridges I nuked after prom haunt me, and it must show, because Connor's bright eyes soften. He reaches out like he'll touch my cheek, and I can actually feel the heat from his hand before he stops himself.

"Give the tough-girl act a rest for tonight." His tender tone guts me. "I know you didn't fill the pain meds the doctor offered you, and I know that side of yours has to hurt like hell. Have a beer with me."

"I can't, Connor. Someone has to stay sharp—"

"Mom's fire safe is missing. Her Kindle, too," Andi blurts as she enters with a couple photo albums. Connor's shrouded expression reemerges, and he meanders over to see what she's holding.

"What's that?" I'm suspicious of her impish expression.

"Pictures from high school." Andi's smile promises hours of embarrassment. "There are more where these came from. Did you know Mom still has roach clips and go-go boots? I shit you not."

Connor and I both snort. I almost mention the dildo I found the night before, but decide against it.

Boone returns through the back door, carrying a case of beer he's confiscated from Dad. He hoists it nonchalantly.

"Boone for the win." Connor smiles, arms straight up in the air like he scored a goal.

"How's Dad?" Andi asks. Boone shrugs in response,

but the innocuous expression he wears looks to mean "as good as he gets."

We all agree it's time to take a dinner break, and Boone fires up the grill out on Mom's deck. Andi and Connor busy themselves conjuring up sides from Mom's bare pantry. Connor demands I sit at the kitchen table and do nothing but "look pretty." When I protest, he threatens to tell Steve-O the doctor's recommendations/restrictions for me, so I cave, with great reluctance.

"Here." Andi pulls a beer from the case and thrusts it at me. "Help drink this before Dad comes looking for it."

I take the can from her, flipping open the photo album on the table in front of me. Four pages in, a picture of Reece and me takes me by surprise. We're out on the porch, dressed for prom. My fake smile is literally painful to behold, but not anywhere near as painful as the consequences of my actions later that night.

My past mistakes play like a cautionary propaganda film reel, coaching me against future poor life decisions.

"Find anything good?" Connor plops down beside me and I flip the photo album closed.

I purse my lips. "Nothing you'd be interested in."

"Bullshit." Andi's droll eyes land on me, and I can tell she's pretty sloshed. Connor snatches the album and when I try to take it back, he holds it out of my reach. Boone hands me a plate of food and Connor begins his colorful commentary on the photographs. Andi and Boone laugh like a studio audience, and I smile on occasion, having forgotten how animated Connor can be when he's playing to a crowd. I'm cutting a bite of steak when silence descends. He's found the prom pictures—I don't even have to look up to know it.

"That was a night," Andi murmurs. "Sura's date got pulled over for DWI and the cop let me wear his hat on the ride home. Didn't you go with Cyndi Mallory?"

"Umm hmm." Connor's mirthless as he turns pages. My appetite evaporates, and I stand, limping to the sink and rinsing off my plate. I grab another beer. I'm not as sore now that I've had a couple, and drinking seems the best course of action since it's evident that the blows will just keep coming.

I shamble down the hall to my bedroom and start to pick up my scattered clothes.

Seconds later, my sister is lurking in the doorway. Her glassy eyes telegraph that she's here to pick a fight.

"Nothing happened, you know," she says, as if I have a clue what she's talking about. I stare at her, waiting for an explanation. "With Connor and me."

Numb all over, I simply blink at her. "I don't care."

"The hell you don't." She's teetering on the cusp of level and falling-down drunk.

I exhale dramatically. "I don't need to hear this, Andi."

"That's too bad, because you're going to. We made out, okay? He stopped it before it went any further. It was three years ago, anyway—it's no reason to hate me."

I sigh as if the sound itself can unburden me. I clutch my anger close, even though I'm not entitled to it. "I don't hate you."

"Yeah you do." Her self-deprecating smile makes me tired.

"No. I just don't like you very much sometimes."

"The feeling's mutual." She flops down in the chair near my bed. "What's the appropriate waiting period before you nail your sister's ex, anyway? Have you consulted Emily Post?"

"It depends."

Andi's feline eyes study mine. "On?"

"How much history they have."

She huffs out a laugh. "So seven years past never." Her expression dims. "Jesus, Lilah. He was hurting. He just needed a friend."

I blink, an unfriendly smile twisting my lips. "You're a friendly gal."

"Screw you, Lilah!" Now that Andi feels justified to let loose, she does. She gestures to her ragged scar. "I've already paid my penance. Your Aurora buddies took care of that for you."

"Andi…" I hear a cautionary edge in Connor's tone that he typically reserves for me. He's in the doorway with Boone, and it's obvious they've been listening. "You can't blame Lilah for the scar. She wasn't even there."

"She was *never* there," she shouts at him, and then wheels around to face me again. "I always had your back. Even when I thought you were screwing yourself over. And you just took off and left me with this fucked-up excuse for a family. Do you know why I took so long to call you about Mom? Because I didn't even notice she was gone.

We don't talk much. We barely know each other. She never had time for *me*. I was just the run-off from her conciliation marriage."

Boone moves toward her like he's trying to talk her down, and she shrugs away from him.

"No, Boone. I'm done. No more keeping secrets." She steps past him to engage me. "You know why Dad moved out to squat in that boathouse like some forgotten Hemingway novel?"

"Andi…" Boone's seldom heard voice scares the shit out of me, but the sinister look in Andi's eyes terrifies me more.

"Because he found out that you weren't his." She looks triumphant, waiting for me to respond.

I blink slowly, waiting for my functioning brain cells to communicate with one another. I turn to Boone, whose hunched shoulders and apprehensive frown are impossible to misinterpret. What she's saying is true.

Afraid of what I'll do if I stay, I spin away and hurry out of my room and into Mom's walk-in closet. Andi's sobs carry through the walls, along with Connor's soothing tones. She's the victim here, naturally. That's the glory of being the baby of the family. My legs feel like they're going to give out, so I plop down amidst the memorabilia scattered all over the floor.

After all the whispers about Mom over the years, it's hardly a bombshell that I'm illegitimate. I'm hurt that Boone and Andi obviously knew and never told me. That neither of my parents bothered to clue me in. Hands on my temples, I apply pressure to keep my brain from exploding. I should be out canvassing the bush for my mother, not living a *Jerry Springer* episode, but I'm wounded and buzzing, and I have no idea where to even start.

Overwhelmed, I start to organize Mom's closet, keeping my hands busy so they don't find their way around my sister's neck. I find another photo album and open it to see what pile it belongs in. I freeze, mouth hanging open. It's full of photos of Connor and me, pictures I know I destroyed.

Mom and Claire must have kept the negatives. I lower myself to the floor, clutching the album to my chest like it might blow away. I'd ached for these pictures during my first days in Vegas. I'd missed Connor terribly then, despite my pain and rage, and without these mementos, I'd robbed myself of the chance to properly grieve.

Seeing our past exhumed guts me, but I have the masochistic need to inspect each and every photo. Toasting marshmallows with matching gapped-toothed grins. Hanging on as his father dragged us behind his boat on an inflatable. Compound bows drawn, our faces placid with concentration.

"Hey." I look up and Connor's there, taking up the doorway. "Up for some company?"

I shrug, returning my attention to our past. He proceeds with care through the land mine of Mom's keepsakes.

"Andi's settled down some," he offers.

I raise a casual shoulder, eyes on the snapshots. "I didn't ask."

His steps stutter, and I look up. Startled eyes search me in disbelief.

"What goes on between you and Andi is your business," I say, and I flip to the next page.

He hunkers down in front of me.

"Nothing goes on between us," he insists.

"I don't care," I lie right to his face, and we both know it.

He looms over me, as I sit cross-legged on the floor. The light bulb is completely masked behind him, surrounding him in a golden halo.

"I was in a dark place, Lie. I'd just lost my best friend in combat. Then Mom…"

"I know. My mom told me after…" I trail off, not sure how to continue. *After you told me to go back to Vegas with the other whores? After you pulled my hair and almost gave me a concussion?*

I tried to walk away that night, unable to wrestle the demons he was dealing with. He hurt me, and though I could see he hadn't meant to, I still had a goose egg three days later when I married Josh in Maui.

Connor drops down beside me and I flinch, still raw. He's at a total loss when he sees my reaction. When he finally speaks, his hushed tone is emphatic. "I was still in love with you, Lie."

I scowl and he looks dismal. "Funny way of showing it."

"I know." He rakes his hair out of his troubled eyes. "But it's the truth."

My resolution is faltering. Hope creeps into my patch-work heart though I want to beat it away with a stick. "That wasn't love, Connor. It was hormones and urges and lack of self-control."

He's contemplative, his candid eyes on mine. "Speak for yourself."

Surprised at his dauntlessness, I exhale carefully. I have no idea how to respond to his admission, so I hop topics. "Mom reproduced a bunch of our pictures."

Connor's eyes ignite with curiosity, and he shoves aside several caved-in boxes marked "tax returns" to make more room beside me. He holds his hands out palms up, and I pass the album over.

Tracing his super-sized fingers across the pages, Connor flips through eagerly, and I get why. These are a treasure trove neither of us expected.

We find a picture of Connor's dad's boat. I can't help but recall the day we took it up river to the lake, and Connor dared me to go skinny-dipping. That water is frigid on the warmest day, and people typically don't stick a toe in without a wet suit. I dove in stark naked, and as he was yanking me into the boat, two fishermen puttered by, gawking. Claiming I'd get hypothermia, Connor did his best to warm me up for the rest of the afternoon.

With an embarrassed chuckle, I cover my face. Connor arches an eyebrow. "Remember that time we took the boat out…"

His twinkling eyes answer before he can. "Vividly."

Overwhelmed, I fixate on the photos, not really seeing

them. Connor brushes my hair over my shoulder, and when I glance up, he's just inches away, assessing me with that dirty expression that no amount of scrubbing can wash off. It's a look that says, "I know what you taste like and I'm hungry for more."

His eyes drop to my mouth and silently asks permission. I nod without consciously deciding to do so. His hand finds the nape of my neck and closes on my hair, tilting my face up. He moves in, hovering for a moment, stealing my breath away before his mouth even makes contact.

Our lips touch tentatively, like we're testing the strength of an iced-over pond. We pull back at the same time, and I see unabashed wonder reflected back at me. Connor nears me cautiously, and my eyes drop closed as I blindly seek out his lips. He brushes his mouth across mine, a wet, delicious tease. He's more confident with the next pass, growing more insistent…greedy.

My breath is ragged and my heart flutters dangerously as I start to lose all semblance of self-control. Connor's hand rakes further into my curls as we battle our way through a deep and needful kiss years in the making.

He growls into me, incredibly erotic and possessive. Every inch of my body is on fire, and I need him to take me now, the proper send-off we never got to have. It's so fitting here, amidst the scattered memories of our misspent youth.

We're startled apart by the unmistakable sound of someone clearing their throat. Boone gives an apologetic shrug, grabbing blankets from the shelf where Mom always kept them, apparently the one thing in the house the intruder didn't mess with.

After a decadent silent exchange, Connor brushes his thumb across my lips and helps me to my feet, all cool and businesslike.

"Let's get you to bed, Lie."

CHAPTER THIRTEEN

CONNOR

UNDONE

I SHOULD BE sleeping, but this day has me tied in mental knots.

Those pictures had me reeling…and that kiss. Jesus.

Indulgently, I replay the moment for the fifty-third time. Lilah's tongue flicking into my mouth, an unmistakable "come hither" gesture.

I roll over onto my back, since the pressure of the mattress taunts my swelling erection. Knowing Delilah's just a few yards away is miserably tempting. If I dwell on it, I'll be in hellish agony all night, so I purposely focus on the other events of the day.

When Andi had followed Lilah into her bedroom, I turned to Boone, hoping for guidance.

"Fuck." Boone's deep voice nearly made me jump out of my skin. He's a regular chatterbox these days, but I agreed with his sentiment.

We trailed them, ready to referee. I'd stepped into Lilah's old bedroom, like stepping out of a time machine. The place was identical to the last time I'd climbed in her window. No stuffed animals, no lace or frills, no posters of boy bands. Her simple brass bed frame, stacks of books and travel magazines, and framed prints of exotic locals still charm me. She's always been truly unique. A grumpy old man trapped in a body like J Lo's.

Watching Lie and Andi go head to head was awkward, especially since I was the root cause. Lie's hostile contempt took me right back to the night they were fighting about. The night I should have been mourning my mother.

After I hurt Lilah and my brother hurried her out the back door, Dick swung on me, missed, and nearly fell on his ass. Quinn wrestled me back inside, past a houseful of gawking well-wishers. I hid out upstairs while everyone cleared out, but when Quinn knocked on the door, I was too humiliated to answer. He left minutes later, and convinced I wasn't quite drunk enough, I ventured downstairs.

Andi was at the sink doing dishes. Without a word, I pitched in, drying and putting away Mom's favorite china. Tears started a couple of times, recalling the countless holidays around those dishes. I'm sure Andi noticed, but she was kind enough to spare me cliché words of comfort. Though we'd never been close, Andi and I were still stitched together, our lives soldered by years of shared history.

Once we were finished, we relocated to the living room for a drink or three.

"Andi, listen. About Lilah—" I said as she tossed another log on the fire.

"Let's not talk about her." She raised her wineglass to her lips and took a healthy swig.

"I think I really hurt her," I slurred, pressing my palms to my face. I couldn't get Lilah's dazed eyes out of my mind. I wondered if she was concussed, and if she should have been driving. I felt Andi's hand come to rest on my shoulder.

"Kinda makes you even, doesn't it?" She inched closer to me, resting her head on my shoulder. Her hair smelled just like Lilah's used to. My pulse revved, even though I knew she just used the same lotion. In the firelight, she looked enough like Delilah that it made me ache. Her sympathetic eyes hypnotized me.

"I miss her too, ya know." Andi sat her wineglass on the table. "You're not the only one she turned her back on."

When Andi kissed me, I wasn't surprised. Her caresses ate through my weakened armor like acid. She climbed onto my lap and my hands went to her ass on instinct. She felt great, she smelled great, and she could kiss like a fucking pro.

But she didn't taste like Lilah, and though it took me longer to come to my senses than I'm proud of, I eventually did. I broke off the kiss, and that's when I saw movement out of the corner of my eye. Lilah stood in the doorway to the kitchen, her hand on the wall as if the sight of us hit her like a physical blow. She backed away, her resplendent features twisted with incredulity.

"Lie!" Lifting Andi off of my lap, I set her aside, rushing to stand. Andi's stunning eyes grew impossibly wide at the sight of Lilah, and she blew out a long, decisive breath.

I heard Lilah's retreating footsteps and the back door slammed before I could even make it to the kitchen. She peeled out for the second time that evening, gunning Andi's engine as she went. I tugged at my hair, reeling from her brief and mortifying reappearance. Andi put a hand on my shoulder. I jumped up and away from her, distancing myself from another layer of regret.

Andi's expression shifted, a cocktail of sadness and pity in her eyes. "There's nothing to be ashamed of, Connor."

After hurrying into the kitchen, I brewed myself coffee for medicinal purposes. I'd made enough poor choices for one night.

The front door closed a minute later, and I felt a surge of relief knowing I was alone. It was short-lived, though; two troopers banged on that same door an hour later. Andi had been attacked while cutting through the woods between my place and LuAnn's. A neighbor had heard screaming and took his shotgun to investigate. Andi was found cowered at the base of a giant spruce tree, blood all over her face, her skirt missing. Boone was trying to wrap his coat around her. He'd been tossed in a cell, and the cops were holding him until they could rule out his involvement.

LuAnn told the troopers she'd left Andi at my place. I was wearing Andi's lipstick when they showed up, and I ended up in an interrogation room down the hall from Boone. Of course, he wasn't talking, and neither was I, since I knew nothing and had nothing to tell.

It hurt that Lu thought I was involved, but after what went down with Lilah just hours before, I shouldn't have been surprised. Besides, I felt partially responsible. I hadn't hurt Andi, but if I hadn't been so drunk, I would've insisted on driving her home.

After some serious tranquilizers, Andi told the authorities that three strangers jumped out of an SUV and chased her into *the trees. As they hunted her, they kept calling her Lilah and demanding to know about Aurora 10. After they'd cornered her, they figured out they had the wrong sister, but they didn't let that stop their fun. Luckily, Boone showed up before they raped her, and he chased them off, but not before they left Andi with a scar on her cheek to send "her cunt sister a message."*

REPLAYING THAT DEBACLE isn't exactly chamomile tea, and the following morning, I have to drag myself from bed. Considering everything that happened the night before, I'm nervous about venturing out of the confines of Lu's guest room. I scald myself awake in the shower, and as I'm leaving the restroom, I bump into Lie. She's got a mug of coffee in her hands, and I can tell by her damp hair she's fresh out of the shower too. She's all bronze curves and sex personified in her tank top and boxers, and just glimpsing her I feel like I won the lottery while getting laid on Christmas morning. A smile tugs at my lips as I take a step toward her. That's when she holds up Lu's phone.

"I texted Dixon from Mom's phone. Told him we'll meet him and that he's buying." Her haughty expression is painfully sexy. "I want him off-balance."

I can't suppress a smirk. "I'd love to see his face when he gets that text."

"Me too," she murmurs. I'm about to reach out for her, but she's already hurrying toward the living room. I follow, snared in her trap.

She stops short as she enters the living room, and I nearly plow into her since my eyes are on her fine ass. I notice Andi's out on the deck petting Runt and Boone's pouring coffee in the kitchen. Lilah's frozen, staring at the highly stylized decorative map of Alaska that hangs on the far wall. Her head tilts, and I practically hear tumblers click into place.

"She sits and stares at that map," Lie murmurs dreamily, and she hurries over and pulls the large frame down from the wall, scrutinizing the map closely. As I lean over her shoulder for a peek, I see the tiny Xs at each fork where the previous Aurora finds were discovered. Including ours.

"Holy shit, she figured it out. Look." I point to three additional Xs. "She must have been searching for 10."

"She's here or here." Lilah looks a little green as she points to the two Xs that are practically on top of each other.

My eyes catch hers, and I feel my brow wrinkle. "What makes you so sure?"

"They're the closest to Willow. She mentioned Willow when she called me…or at least I think she did. And look." She hands me the heavy frame and hurries out of the room. I study the Xs carefully, noting the third X that Lilah ruled out. It's way up north of Talkeetna, not far from Denali. A stamp of a compass rose, identical to Delilah's arty tattoo, is directly over where my property sits on the Kenai, the place I inherited from my mom.

Lie returns with my laptop. In a matter of seconds, she

has the search grids pulled up.

"Notice anything noteworthy?"

My mouth falls open when I see what's on the screen.

"I'll be damned," I mutter. The two spots Lilah flagged as holes in the air search are directly over the Xs Lu marked near Willow. Where no one had bothered to look.

CHAPTER FOURTEEN

Lilah

Truth and Consequences

I'M ZIPPING UP my boots when Andi enters my room. Bracing myself, I'm nervous and a little curious to see what she's got in store for round number two.

"Boone and I will be back to finish tonight. I don't want Mom coming home to all of this."

I nod confidently, but inside, I'm hoping we live up to her expectations.

She turns to leave but stops, as if thinking. I sit up and wait. Andi faces me, her sheepish expression unexpected. "I really thought you'd moved on. You and Josh...you just seemed...really happy."

"We were." I smile, thinking about how Josh woke me with kisses every morning, smelling like aftershave and toothpaste. How we'd met hiding out on the balcony at a company Christmas party, and bonded over our whiskey sours and our mutual hatred for tamales. How he'd dared me to go to Tahoe with him on Christmas Eve, even though we barely knew each other. How it all started to come apart at the seams before we even said "I do."

"Until I saw Connor again."

A tear escapes her and she brushes it away just before it reaches her scar. "I just felt so bad for Connor. He was so close to his mom. I was mad at the world, and I guess a part of me was mad at you too. I'm a total screw-up, Lilah, and I'm so sorry."

"I'm sorry, too." She's making my eyes sting. I never could stand to see my little sister unhappy.

"I shouldn't have thrown that shit about Dad up in your face."

"I'm glad I know." I swallow hard, then ask the question that kept me awake most of the night. "Do you know who my real dad is?"

Andi shakes her head. "Mom went ballistic when I asked. Made me promise never to breathe a word about it. Guess I fucked that up too."

I climb to my feet and cross to hug her. She's surprised, but doesn't fight me. "I was hurt...and a coward. I should have been here for you, especially after the attack. We've gotta look out for each other, no matter what."

"You're gonna make me cry again." I can hear the fatigue in her voice.

I shake my head and square my shoulders. "No. I'm gonna find Mom and bring her home."

Unlike Andi and me, Connor ignores the events of the previous night as we drive to meet Dixon. Since Connor's not bringing up the kiss, I'm not broaching it. I'd had a few and I'm not a drinker. I'd blame my alcoholic genes, but after last night, I can't even do that. Truth is, I've never once told him no. I'd plead temporary insanity, and no jury would convict me if exhibit A was Connor Garrett.

Being this close to him, his clean scent permeating the air around me, takes me back to the last time we had sex. It was in close quarters, just like this, when he drove me home from the prom.

Our attempt to make each other jealous nearly erupted in a brawl, when Connor shoved Reece on the dance floor. I stumbled, since we'd been dancing, and Reece got right back in Connor's face. Thankfully, Connor's friends broke things up before they came to blows.

We were all kicked out, and as we left, I saw another side of Reece I'd never seen. Hopped up on testosterone, and clearly oblivious to how close to death he'd just come, he told me he had a hotel room nearby. Furious at Connor and ready to prove to myself that sex with someone else was no big deal, I told him to take me there. We didn't get far, since he asked me every five seconds "is this okay…is that okay?" Nothing about any of it was remotely okay, and pushing him off of me, I bolted up and told him I needed some air.

The next thing I knew I was wandering down the side of the highway in the direction of True. Some random older guys pulled over and offered me a cigarette, and I ignored them, which must have pissed them off, because one of them flicked a lit cig at me, and it burnt my arm.

Then Connor was there, chasing them off…yelling at me for being out alone, raving about how dangerous it was. He demanded to know where my date was, and when he finally noticed I was crying, he insisted on taking me home. Turned out Connor was the only imminent danger that night, and we weren't even halfway home before he pulled over.

He kept looking over at my hair and my make-up, which I'm sure was a total mess.

"Did you sleep with him?"

"That's none of your business."

His hazel gaze swept over me, slow, hot, and unapologetic.

"Lie…" He said my name like he was saying something else. The stubborn set to his jaw wasn't as concerning as the agenda behind his gaze. The urge to run was more powerful than it had been with the men who'd come for me at the school. Connor was a far bigger threat, since he held my heart in his ferocious teeth.

"Tell me you don't love me." His steady tone should have put me at ease. It didn't.

"I'm not doing this." I reached for the door handle, though we were miles from civilization. Connor locked it from the driver's side, and I looked away, staring out at the barely visible mountains, trying to muster the energy to fight.

"Tell me."

"I…" I turned to him, ready to hurl the lie at him full force, but I choked on the words. All my good intentions evaporated with his blazing eyes on mine. Connor saw my doubt all over me. He pushed his jacket off my shoulders and I trembled with indecision. My need to have him was at odds with my responsibility to let him go.

"You love flying more than you love me?" His stubble

grazed my temple, while his big fingers stroked my collarbone.

"Please...don't." I didn't sound like myself.

"Say the words, Lilah." His breath fogged my neck, and his lips tickled the curve of my ear. His fingers glided up my spine, then tugged the ties of my dress. "I need the truth for once. No bullshit."

His hand closed around my jaw, wordlessly urging my face to his. I submitted, knowing there was no net to catch me, but unable to stop myself from leaping.

His lips found mine, maddening and...delicious. My traitorous hands gripped his hair, pulling him in for more. The top of my dress fell, and I moaned against his mouth as he eased me back onto the seat, pinning me like he always did. I loved it like I always did, and my legs fell willingly apart.

He fumbled with his zipper and I was right there, helping. Fuck our dreams, fuck the army. I needed to be close to him, as close as we could get.

His eyes shone in the dim glow from the dashboard. "You're mine, Delilah. Say it."

A BLARING HORN rips me from my musings, and an oversized overcompensation vehicle passes me. I realize I'm going the speed limit, which, in Alaska, is considered impeding traffic.

I busy myself with the radio, trying to find a weather report. Connor's got his laptop out, clicking around. He strokes his beard thoughtfully.

I reach over and give it a tiny yank. He looks at me like

I'm mental, and I ask, "Why?"

He flashes that knowing smile that got me into a world of trouble back in the day. "Getting a jump on No-Shave November. I take it you're not a fan."

I turn my attention back to the road. "I liked it better when I could see your face."

"You liked it better when you could read me," he fires back playfully, but there's a mountain of subtext there.

"Got something to hide?" The mysterious four-minute phone call is in the forefront of my mind.

"Nope," Connor replies, far too quickly for my taste. "You?"

A frown overtakes me as I consider all the monumental things that Connor doesn't know about. I take my mirrored sunglasses off my head and place them over my eyes. "I'm gonna wear these until you shave that off."

Cue his seductive grin. "Indoors?"

"Yep," I say. "At night, too."

We arrive at the restaurant, and the hostess drools and fawns all over Connor the entire time she's seating us. When she hurries off he smirks at me.

"Looks like I have an admirer."

I try to appear aloof, which I do well, since I'm wearing shades. "I guess she likes 'em hairy."

His cocky grin reappears. "Seems that way."

When the waitress arrives with coffee, I dump half-and-half and sweetener into mine.

"Want a little coffee with that cream?" Connor arches a brow.

"Just drink your black sludge and be sad," I deadpan.

Wearing a rakish grin, he snatches my glasses off my face. I try to take them back, but he tucks them into his shirt pocket.

We're still looking over the menus when he brings up Aurora again.

"It really doesn't even matter whether we think the gold's there or not." Connor waves the waitress down for a refill. "It only matters if Lu thought it was there."

"And if someone thought Mom had inside information because of us…"

Smiley and his friends immediately come to mind. They'd attacked Andi when they thought she was me. They ran Dad off the road because I wouldn't cough up the coordinates to 9.

Connor's eyes take on a grim cast. "They'd try to get it out of her."

"Covering up her abduction with a bogus crash." I cast my menu aside. I've got no appetite now.

Connor's eyes dart back and forth before locking on to mine. "And look who put himself in charge of the search."

I envision the sneering, rotund man and his white frizzy beard. "Merle Jones."

Merle tried to fence his gold in the lower forty-eight back in the day. It had been quite the scandal, especially since he'd been a trooper at the time. He got away with a slap on the wrist, just fired and a little community service. True's rumor mill seemed to think this was because the judge was his fishing buddy.

"Let's assume for a second that Merle's behind this. Do you think Floyd's in on it with him?" Connor asks. "It seems weird that so many troopers showed up at the crash site."

"And how quickly they got there..." I agree. I'm wondering just how involved Merle's friends on the force might be in orchestrating a missing person's case.

Connor's eyes sparkle with the chase. "Floyd *really* didn't want me looking inside that cockpit."

"Okay..." My heart is beating uncomfortably fast, and though I know we're speculating, what he says smacks of the truth. "Mom said not to trust anyone. Maybe she knew the cops were involved somehow."

"Or maybe just Floyd. He's in charge...so he decides where the others go and when. Maybe Aurora's his retirement plan. I mean, if what Hank Brown said is true, 10 is twice the size of the other finds...but the finder's fee isn't a lot of money when you split it that many ways." Connor's attention wanders off to the right.

"It is if they melt it down for the right buyer instead of turning it in," I counter, but he shoots me a cautionary glance and, standing, slips out of the booth and slides in next to me. He slips his arm behind me to make room for us both. Gooseflesh erupts everywhere he connects with me, and I can smell his aftershave, though I have no idea why he'd use any with his Unabomber manscaping. Still, he smells like a man's man, which reduces my insides to mush. My agitated gaze cuts to his, but before he can speak, Investigator Dixon takes the seat Connor just vacated.

"Morning," Dixon grumbles.

I take in his weary eyes and the dark half-moons underneath. "Sleep well?"

"Not especially." He seems to take thorough inventory of me. I endure his inquisitive once-over with little concern. Dixon's always made Connor nervous, but not me. His fleeing form scrambling down our walk as Mom brandished her shotgun forever solidified my impression of him. All bark and no bite.

How they later ended up lovers is something I can't imagine, even if I was so inclined.

"Coffee?" Connor offers, always the diplomat. Dixon nods, and Connor calls over our eager-to-please waitress. All of the staff apparently has a fetish for porcupine-faced men. Connor's all-white smiles and eye crinkles and the waitress is all lash batting and cleavage baring. Connor uses his cosmic powers for good though; Dixon gets a cup and menu and we all get our coffee topped off. She even leaves us the carafe. I wish like hell I was still wearing my mirrored sunglasses, 'cause I know I rolled my eyes at least twice during her embarrassing display.

Dixon watches Connor in action, and I can tell he's amused. I'm sure he's filing it all away for a rainy day. I know from experience that Dixon's talent is using the right pressure points to get the answers he wants. It's a brilliant strategy, I'll give him that, and I decide to turn it back on him.

"How long have you been sleeping with my mother,

Inspector Dixon?"

It's obvious that I've just confirmed his worst fears about just how much we know.

"How long do you think it'll be before you're named a person of interest once this crash is labeled foul play?" Connor tag teams me on autopilot, speaking in hushed tones.

Dixon's eyes shift from Connor to me. "What do you want?"

Connor steals my line. "Information."

"That's why I invited you here. To talk about LuLu—" Dixon cuts himself off, taking a calculated breath. "To explain about LuAnn and what she confided in me."

"So Lu just called you up…out of the blue…looking to hook up? That's a long time to hang on to a business card." Connor turns to me with a dubious glance.

"No." Dixon's unflinching. "I contacted her."

Connor's eyes narrow to slits. "Why?"

"I'm retiring this spring after thirty years of closing cases."

"Is that supposed to explain how you became my mother's backdoor man?" I sip my coffee, gauging his response over the chipped rim of my cup.

He glowers at me, and I glower right back. I feel Connor watching us, but I don't turn his way. Connor's hand slides down behind me and strokes the exposed skin right above my waistband. I guess it's meant to be soothing, but it's also distracting as hell.

"All these years there was one case I wasn't able to let

go of," Dixon continues. "My very first case. The hijacking."

"Wait...you worked the Aurora case from the beginning?" Connor's rugged features aren't tarnished by his uncertainty.

"Yes." Dixon's eyes flicker, as if transported back to another time. "I was the original agent. I was there the day they found the bodies."

"So you actually interviewed the pilot." I can't squash my enthusiasm. He's the Holy Grail of Aurora mythos, the missing link between the written accounts and real events in 1984.

"What does any of this have to do with LuAnn?" Connor herds us back on topic, and I'm grateful. Gold fever is a disease. You feel healthy for years, but it's still there, dormant and waiting.

I'd been a hairsbreadth away from paying a heavy toll for my obsession with solving the Aurora mystery. Was Mom the first true casualty?

"LuLu was working at the airport back then. When we met, she was a brand-new rookie pilot. She was one of my first interviews. She flew the search plane I was riding in the day we found the bodies. The airport provided a list of all the employees who'd been working the day of the hijacking. LuAnn was on it. And she'd been mentored by Hank Brown, the Aurora pilot who was flying the hijacked plane."

I don't even realize my knee's bouncing until Connor's hand slips out from behind me and stills it. I don't like where any of this is headed.

Dixon's intense eyes are on me. I've seen this look many times, right before someone tells me how much I remind them of my mother. He refrains from saying it, and considering the nature of their relationship, I'm relieved.

"She got her commercial license two days after the hijacking, even though according to Ronald Warren, she'd had her hours in for a month or more. LuAnn passed her test with flying colors, as soon as she could afford the testing fee."

"So you thought Lu was the inside man." Connor isn't asking, just summarizing. My cheeks heat. I open my mouth to speak, and the waitress arrives with our plates. We all pick up our utensils, and though I'm no longer hungry, I drown my pancakes in butter and syrup and force myself to take a taste.

"I was wrong, of course. LuAnn had switched shifts that day. Warren confirmed it later, after I'd already accused her." He shakes his head with a fond smile. "We were in the air at the time. I must have been out of my mind."

"No wonder she pulled a shotgun on you," Connor muses. He digs into the sprawl of a meal he ordered, as I reassess Marcus Dixon. Dixon's smile vanishes.

"Lu and I discovered the first hijacker's body that day. I spotted his chute tangled up in the brush. The second jumper was close by. Both parachutes had been tampered with; it was obvious, even from a distance."

Connor nods, dumping ketchup on his eggs like it's

going out of style. "My dad always thought they sabotaged each other's packs."

I sniff. "No honor amongst thieves."

Dixon is nodding as he continues. "It was another two days before the troopers announced their identities. Later that night, Lu left a note at the front desk of my hotel. Said she had information and wanted to talk."

Connor's stopped eating. I have too.

"LuAnn felt like she may have accidentally assisted with the heist. She'd dated one of the hijackers a few times, the second guy we found. This was months before the hijacking. She said it was nothing serious, but when she heard about his involvement, she suspected he'd pursued her for the purpose of gathering intel about airport operations."

I drop my silverware onto my plate and wipe my mouth with a napkin. "This just gets better and better."

"Of course, the case seemed to be closed after Hank Brown killed himself. Everyone assumed it was an admission of guilt. The only loose end was tracking down all those gold bars. Even though Brown's suicide seemed to implicate him as an accomplice, I wanted to verify that Aurora Corp. hadn't over-reported. The discrepancy between their claim and the amount of gold Hank Brown insisted was on the plane was…significant."

"So you kept coming back." My coffee's cold. I've lost interest in anything except his story.

"Yes," he said. "My gut told me Aurora fudged their losses, but I couldn't prove it. By the time 8 was found, most of the board members were dead or long retired, and my company had moved on to bigger, more lucrative cases. It seemed like I was the only one still looking for the gold, besides a few diehards with metal detectors. And then you two found 9."

Connor and I turn to each other. Much is said without exchanging a single word.

"That bullshit line you both kept repeating…how'd it go again? 'We were so excited we didn't pay attention to the coordinates.'" A wicked smile appeared on Dixon's face and dread washed over me.

"Everyone knew you were lying. I just assumed Lu was using you to turn in what she already had."

"That's a bit of a leap, isn't it?" I demand. I can feel Connor's discomfort, and when I look at him, he's fixated on his toast.

Dixon casually shrugs. "It was obvious by the state of her house and her husband that she was in a bad way…"

I'm instantly irate, and if Connor hadn't been blocking my escape, I would have dumped my orange juice over Dixon's head and left the table. That was my childhood home he was dogging on. It may not be flashy…okay, it's a bit of a shack, but it always kept us warm and dry.

"…I doubted everything I thought I knew about Lu-Ann. She knew it, too. Hence the armed reception when I came to interview you."

"So what changed your mind?" Connor asks.

"You did, Mr. Garrett. The way you were flashing your cash all over town, it was obvious that Lu wasn't pulling the strings. The fact that the only thing Lilah bought was a plane before she paid off Dick's medical bills left giant exit wounds in my theory about LuLu's involvement."

Now Connor's blushing.

"When Andi was attacked, I came back to True. Your mother was hysterical. She swore that neither of you had ever told her where you found 9. I believed her, because she wanted all of it to end, and would have taken it upon herself to end it, if she could have. She was convinced the same men who caused your father's accident and tried to abduct you were the ones who hurt Andi and that they wouldn't stop until someone found 10. That's when we became…involved."

"Those assholes caused Dick's accident?" Connor's eyes blaze, and he seems to have forgotten all about his omelet.

Dixon fixes me with his twinkling gaze. He's flipped this conversation on its side, and now I'm the one with explaining to do. "You want to tell him or should I?"

I lick my lips nervously and turn to Connor. The suspicion in his eyes is cumbersome.

"They threatened my family. Just a few days before Dad's accident."

"What?" Connor's incensed.

"The phone calls never stopped coming," I murmur, and Connor's eyes cloud over. I know he's pissed, but I turn back to Dixon. "How did you—"

"Your mom suspected. Your dog was keeping her up and she'd heard you arguing with someone on the phone before they ran Dick off the road. Besides, what teenager unplugs their phone and leaves it that way on purpose?"

I can feel Connor's anger radiating off of him, so I grab the reins of the conversation and steer us back on course. "None of this explains our current situation. You told Connor Mom was onto something."

"Your mother started looking for 10 while Andi was recovering from her injury. After my visit to True last month, Lu sent me some strange emails. She said someone was following her. She felt like she was being watched."

"Who?" Connor asks.

"She wasn't sure, but the day she went missing she left me a voice mail. Said she'd been digging around at the Willow airport and found something. Something she thought explained everything. It was the last time I heard from her."

"She had it narrowed down to three possible locations. We have her map," Connor volunteers, and I gape at him for revealing this. Dixon seems like he's on the up and up, but I'm still not ready to trust him.

"She was bothered by the fact that the men who attacked Andi kept asking about 10, not 9. She believed they were convinced that Lilah knew where 10 was, and they thought Lilah was the one leaving your house that night. It was common knowledge she was in town."

My palms are sweaty and my stomach feels like a wrung-out washrag. I force myself to take a bite of luke-warm pancake.

"So where does that leave us?" Connor leans back in his seat and rubs his temple.

"I think Lu found a smoking gun implicating someone

as an inside man. Someone who helped cover up Aurora Corporation's paper trail about how much gold was on that plane." Dixon theorizes, "Or she finally found 10 and the thugs who tried to take you were tailing." His deep skin turns a bit ashen at the prospect, and I see for the first time how much he really cares for Mom.

"No." I shake my head, reaching for a drink of water.

Connor's solemn eyes swing to me, and I feel his hand stroke my thigh as if comforting me. "It's the most logical conclusion, Lie."

I sigh and glance around the room. The restaurant's clearing out, and the only person nearby is a young waitress collecting her tip a few tables over.

I lean in conspiratorially; my tone is hushed. "We need to stick to the smoking gun theory, because we're running out of time." My eyes slide from Connor to Dixon, then back again. "You can drop the treasure angle. I already have Aurora 10."

CHAPTER FIFTEEN

CONNOR

OLD GLORY

W E'VE GOT A game plan when we part ways with
Dixon. He's headed to the airport to meet with
Ronald Warren, who's still in charge out there. Dixon will
approach things as if he's there to close the Aurora case.
He's hoping Reece's dad can shed light on what LuAnn
might have been looking into.

Meanwhile, Lilah and I head to the offices of the *True
Gazette*. We're hoping to find connections between Aurora
Corp. and the local Alaskan State Troopers. Researching
will take a lot less time with Sura's help. Lie thinks if we
can connect all the dots, we might be able to figure out
where they're holding Lu. I don't have the heart to say that
it doesn't make much sense to keep Lu if she doesn't have
information on Aurora 10's location, but for all I know, she
does. Maybe Delilah told her she has 10. I have no idea.
Lie's kept me in the dark this long. Who knows what else
she hasn't told me.

I call ahead and Sura's secretary asks me to hold. I use
the opportunity to peek at Lilah. She demanded to drive

again, and she's gunning it like she stole it. I know that she knows I'm watching, and the more nonchalant she seems, the angrier I become.

I'm infuriated, but not about Aurora 10. I'm not surprised that she found the gold. I'd be an idiot to think she'd just quit hunting after our breakup. I want to ask a million questions, but every time I open my mouth, I'm struck muter than Boone.

I'm seething because she never told me those men were still harassing her.

I can't stop myself from replaying that afternoon, when my friends and I got detention for going off campus for lunch without permission. I was supposed to spend the night at Lilah's and was pissed at myself for nearly screwing things up because I was craving a Hula Burger.

"Aren't Lilah's parents out of town?" Brett asked as we rush for the exit. "Andi said something about it in geography, but I can't hear her with all that cleavage."

"Maybe." I worked to keep the smirk off my face, but Matt and Paul exchanged loaded glances.

"Is there something going on with you two?" Paul eyed me closely, and I looked away.

"No comment."

"I knew it! The way you took off after Rucker when he grabbed Delilah's ass...dude!" Paul grinned as we burst through the doors into air so cold it stole my breath. He elbowed Matt. "I fucking told you."

Matt turned wide eyes on me. "You lucky bastard."

We descended into the snow, Brett grilling me about

whether Lilah has tan lines but his idiocy was garbled as I took in the scene transpiring in the parking lot. Lilah's car was parked by the far gate near the street entrance. An SUV idled between it and us, exhaust emanating from the tailpipe. Unease swept over me, and I moved forward on instinct.

My mind stripped gears when Lilah zipped out from behind the SUV, sprinting toward the street. The man chasing her grabbed her hood. The snaps let go, and it came off in his hand.

"Hey," I snarled, hauling ass after them. Lilah slipped on the paved snow, but recovered, attempting a shortcut to the street just beyond school grounds. Lilah was fast, but she wasn't tall, and the deepening drifts were slowing her down.

As I darted in their direction, I heard the SUV rev its engine. Then my friends were shouting after me, their words overlapping.

"Connor! Watch—"

"Look out, dude!"

"Look where you're driving, you stupid prick!"

I dodged just in time to avoid being hit as the SUV barreled backward, trying to plow me down. The driver lost control and counter-steered to compensate, correcting enough that he only knocked the side mirror off of Mr. Smith's Trailblazer. Brett laughed about that later, since Smith was the dick who gave us detention in the first place.

I whipped back around. Lilah had made it to the fence line. The creep behind her nearly grabbed her again, and she faked him out. I silently cheered as she broke away and exited the fence, but my celebration was short-lived. Lie lost her footing and wiped out. The guy grabbed her by her ponytail, and she scrambled to get her legs under her so he didn't rip her hair out by the roots. My blood boiled.

"Gotcha now, bitch." He hurled her into the fence and I lost what was left of my shit. Clenching my fists, I charged him.

"Get your fucking hands off of her!" My throat burned from the cold air I'd been huffing. I heard shouting and honking going on behind me, but the guys could have set off a bomb and it wouldn't have changed my focus.

The stranger noticed me for the first time.

"Back off, hero," he snapped, using Lilah as a human shield. Her frightened eyes produced ice water in my veins, and my heart slammed against my chest wall every time I took a breath. He had one hand on Lilah's jaw and the other gripped her hair. "I'll snap her neck. Don't think I won't."

I had doubts based on the trouble he'd gone to in order to catch her, but I wasn't willing to test the theory. I gestured in surrender. "Don't hurt her, man. Just walk away."

He smiled then. "You first."

A gunshot rang out behind us and we all jumped. The guy flung Lie in my direction and tore off toward the parking lot. I rushed to intercept her fall, missing her by a good two feet.

Lie stood, but nearly toppled over again. I was there to catch her that time.

"Connor." Lilah's voice was breathy and higher pitched than usual.

"I've got you." I clutched her against me. The gravity of the situation hit me full force. If we'd made a pit stop at the men's room, Lilah would have been long gone.

My eyes shifted to the SUV barreling in the direction of the *highway. Matt ran up to us, holding a gun in his right hand.*

"Dude, what the hell happened? Did you shoot somebody?"
I looked in the direction of the parking lot.

He shook his head. "I just shot into the air."

"Where the hell did you get that gun?"

Matt shrugged, as if packing on school grounds was a typical occurrence in True. "Dad keeps it in the glove compartment."

Sighing, I turned my attention back to Delilah. "Did he hurt you, Lie?"

"I'm cold." Her timid reply scared me. Her eyes were dilated black. She looked ashen, but the apples of her cheeks were the color of roses. "My car won't start."

"I think she's going into shock, bro." Matt took off his scarf and handed it to me as if it was a cure-all.

"What happened?" I wrapped the scarf around Lilah's ears and neck, since that asshole had taken her hood like some kind of trophy.

"He knew my name. The smiley guy." A siren approached, and I wrapped my arms around her. Her eyes swiveled to Matt. "Can you jump me, Matt?"

"Ummm…" Matt's lip twitched, but he saw my homicidal expression and forwent whatever wisecrack he'd been considering. "Yeah. Let me start my car."

"You'd better stash that piece, bro." I pressed my lips to the hollow of Lilah's temple. She was ice cold.

"We should get you inside," I whispered to her.

"No." She shivered violently as she shook her head. "I just want to go home."

"SHE'S HERE," SURA'S secretary announces, blasting me out of the past and into the present. "And she said to come on down."

I nod, though she can't see me. "I'll be there in twenty minutes."

Lilah floors it, and I take advantage of the moment to take a hard look at the woman she's become. I flash on that guy who threatened to snap her neck. He still turns up in my nightmares sometimes. I probably have more PTSD from dating Lie than I acquired after I joined up. I make a conscious effort to slow my breathing, but it's a chore. The second we're parked, I take off across True town square.

My strides are long, and Lilah has to jog to keep up.

"Connor, slow down!"

I plaster on a look of mock surprise. "Oh, are we still working together?"

Lilah doesn't break her stride. "What's your problem now?"

"You made me look like an asshole, Lilah."

She smiles broadly. "Trust me. You don't need my help with that."

I stop walking altogether. She does too.

"You can't keep me on a need-to-know basis."

Her expression softens considerably. "Aurora 10 didn't seem relevant."

I shake my head and continue on toward the old brick building where I know Sura's waiting. "Jesus Christ, Lilah,

I'm not talking about the gold! You should have told me those guys were still calling you. I wouldn't have let you out of my sight."

She magnifies her gaze. "That's *exactly* why I *didn't* tell you."

"No. You knew I'd call a goddam press conference and give the world the coordinates to 9. Or had you and Reece already stashed Aurora 10?"

She tugs on my sleeve, forcing me to halt. "Reece has nothing to do with this, Connor. Calm dow—"

I yank my arm away. There is nothing more frustrating to me than Lie telling me to calm down. Especially since she lives to get a rise out of me.

"Don't."

She steps into my space anyway, and the gentle way she strokes my cheek soothes my inner beast. With that one tiny gesture, she douses most of my fire.

"Baby, please, just take a breath." Her bold eyes focus on me, and she seems oblivious to the fact that she just called me what she used to call me, back when our focus on treasure hunting had eroded, and all we were hunting was what was beneath each other's clothes. "Get your head back in the game. Mom needs you. I need you."

I do exactly that, huffing oxygen like I'd been underwater for days. It helps, but I'm still shaking. "It's a sad fucking day when Dixon knows more about you than I do."

Her rich honey-brown eyes go from empathetic to downright disquieting. "Whose fault is that?"

I HUNT DOWN the *Gazette*'s restroom, splashing cool water onto my face. I'm sick as hell, and I can't decide if Lilah's the disease or the cure. This much I know: there couldn't be a worse time to be out of my medications.

When I finally pull myself together, I wander toward the sound of voices, and hear Sura and Lilah talking from behind the partition before I can see them.

"I'm impressed," Lie says. "I honestly thought you'd end up in the big house for dealing. Way to turn it around."

Sura scoffs. "Girl...how do you think I paid my tuition? You're looking good. Divorce suits you."

"Thanks. Some of us are just built to be alone, I guess." It's hard to tell if Delilah's joking, but her dark words depress me. They're too relatable for comfort.

"Preach," Sura concurs. "What's it like living in Vegas?"

"The desert's beautiful." I can hear the smile in Lie's voice. "The party atmosphere gets old, but I enjoy being able to get a steak at two a.m. if I'm in the mood."

"I'll have to come visit at Christmas when this shithole is as cold as a witch's tit," Sura says, and I round the corner just in time to see her plop down unceremoniously into a computer chair.

"Good call." Lie looks over her shoulder and, spotting me, pats the seat next to her.

Sura hasn't changed much. The petite Native American

has added a few blue streaks to her short-cropped hair, and a couple facial piercings. She's still an imposing figure, even though she can't be more than five feet tall and ninety pounds. She swivels her screen so we can see it. "Here's a picture of Aurora's board of directors in 1984."

"Are any of these guys still active board members?" Lilah ties her hair up in a knot on top of her head.

"Any connections to the trooper post here in True?" I lean forward, studying the faces on the screen.

A shrewd smile appears on Sura's youthful face. "Before we dig in, let's talk quid pro quo. If I drop everything to help you blow this wide open, I get the exclusive."

"Drop everything?" I look around at the empty office and the phone that is conspicuously not ringing.

"Deal." Lilah's expression is tenacious, and I know better than to argue.

"And if this helps find Lu, I get to interview you both for a book I'm working on about the hijacking."

"Just what the world needs," I say. Lilah spins her chair to meet my eye. She's waiting for my answer. It's surprising. The Lilah I grew up with would have volunteered me without consultation.

"I will if you will," I tell her. Lilah has a hell of a lot more to spill about Aurora than I do. If she talks, I have nothing left to hide.

Lilah turns back to Sura and nods.

"All right. Here's the list of everyone at the corporate office in 1984. I'll search ties to True, relatives, business ventures, stuff like that. Here's the fax from my source at the trooper post. You two cross-reference the troopers."

I log on to my laptop as Sura hacks away at her computer. Lilah moves to the desktop next to me, and the secretary helps her get past their security and logged on before taking lunch orders. Lie declines. The search for Lu has probably killed her appetite. She barely touched breakfast, and pancakes are her favorite.

As we work, Lilah's phone buzzes on the table between us. Reece's name flashes across the display. She picks up the phone, and as she reads the screen, a hint of a smile appears. Her fingers fly as she responds. This happens twice more, and it's starting to feel like prom night all over again. My stomach clenches when I think about our private after-prom party. I try never to think about that night, because in that moment, I was so certain we were in sync again...that we'd turned the page and she'd change her mind about coming away with me. But the moment passed, and only then did the notion of a condom cross my mind.

I stand up and stretch, and neither Sura nor Lilah look up from their keyboards. Grabbing a bottled water, I gather my wits and talk myself off the ledge. It's ancient history, all of it. We have work to do.

About twenty minutes later, Sura stops typing and snaps her fingers to beckon us. Delilah's on her feet in a flash, peering over Sura's shoulder. I've just taken a giant bite of my meatball sub the secretary brought me, and I scramble for napkins.

"This guy's older than Moses, but he's still alive. This

one is too, but he retired years ago. He still holds plenty of stock though. Of course, Junior Franz is still kicking, but he left Aurora Corp. a decade ago. Talk about a cushy entry-level job. He even looks like he was born with a silver spoon up his ass."

"I remember that guy from my days in the library. Ivy League frat boy. Daddy bought his spot on the board. He was one Jägerbomb away from a date rape scandal at Stanford. His father was a politician or something…"

Sura and I look at one another, eyebrows raised. Lilah doesn't miss the exchange. Defensive, her hands are on her hips.

"What?"

"Lie, Junior Franz is an Alaskan senator now," I say.

Her brow furrows.

Sura spins away, typing furiously on her keyboard. "Oh, it's way better than that. Word on the street is, he's on the short list to be the next vice president."

My mouth falls open as Sura gestures to a recent article showing an Armani-clad Franz posing with a contender for President of the United States.

"That has motive written all over it." Lie's loaded words give me a chill.

"Motive for what?" My mind is already spinning grim tales.

"Tying up loose ends." Lilah's chewing her lip.

"Let's see what Dixon has to say about Franz." I text him, asking about Junior's level of involvement with the claim over the hijacked shipment.

"What does any of this have to do with LuAnn?" Sura takes off her glasses and cleans them with her blouse.

"Worst-case scenario? Franz committed fraud after the Aurora hijacking and Lu found a way to prove it." I'm looking at the ceiling like it's a fuzzy crystal ball.

"The missing manifest," Lie suggests, and I feel goose-flesh spread across my arms. "Maybe Mom found it. And Franz knows somehow?"

"That would explain the break-in at her house." I'm nodding.

"Break-in?" Sura looks exasperated, and deeply troubled. She grew up with Andi and Lilah, same as me. Story or no story, Lu's been a fixture in her life too.

"What'd Dixon say?" Lilah asks, and I glance at my phone. There's no response.

"Nothing yet." I jump back on the computer, image searching Junior Franz.

Lie's phone buzzes again. She picks it up, and her brows meet.

"I'll be back."

I stop what I'm doing. "Where the hell are you going?"

"To meet Reece. He made a pass over those holes in the search grid for me."

"You told him about Lu's map?" I can feel the tightness in my jaw.

"No." She looks up from her phone, a defensive glint in her eyes. "I mentioned that the air search wasn't complete at the hospital, remember?"

I'd been too busy trying to ignore her flirting to hear

anything she said to Reece.

"He's at Wanda's ordering lunch. I figured I should go alone." She's being polite for Sura's sake. I'm not feeling as charitable.

"Whatever." I glance at Sura, who's trying hard to look busy. "We've got this shit handled."

"It'll be thirty minutes tops." Lie's wearing an innocent face and I'm not buying it. "I just need to hear what he saw."

"You don't need to explain yourself to me, Lilah." I turn back to the keyboard. "I mean, why start now?"

I can feel her watching me, but I ignore it. Then I hear her boots on the hardwood and the front door open and close.

"Wow." The word shoots out of Sura like the bullet out of a gun.

"What?" I ask, seething on the inside.

"You're a colossal dick. I can't believe I used to be jealous of her."

I stop typing and cock an eyebrow at her. "She dumps me for Reece, gets knocked up, blows town, and *I'm* the dick."

"She didn't knock *herself* up." Sura stops what she's doing and glares at me. "You won that blue ribbon, stud."

"So she says." I'm outraged, but I picture the stain on the back of her prom gown as she fled my truck without a word.

"Connor..." Sura's eyeing me like I'm some tragic figure in a Jane Austen novel. "I was there when she found out she was pregnant. Trust me, that baby was yours."

I stare at the keyboard, but I'm so discombobulated that I can't even pretend to type anymore. My eyes sting, and I'm working too hard to breathe. If I live to be a hundred years old, I'll never understand why the head-strong girl who fought so hard for everything she ever wanted never bothered to fight for us.

CHAPTER SIXTEEN

LILAH

CHOICE

CONNOR'S GOT ME so keyed up that I'm muttering to myself all the way down Main Street. He acts like I'm some bully he's turned the tables on. We're both responsible for the consequences of our carelessness, but I had to pay the toll alone.

I take a breath and remind myself about all his empty pill bottles. Antidepressants, anti-anxiety…the number of different drugs was staggering.

I'm heartbroken that Connor's struggling. No matter what he says or does, I still worry about him. He's a scar on me…one that refuses to fade even though we've been apart nearly as long as we were together. That time apart has been just as defining.

I can recall the cloudless skies and crisp mountain air as I lay amidst the last few gleaming bars of gold. I was waiting to feel victorious. That feeling never came.

Desecrating Aurora 10's resting place without Connor felt like sacrilege. It wasn't right, and I wasn't right, and I was pretty sure I'd never be right again. I broke down sobbing.

Like a tree falling out in these woods, no one bore witness. The only evidence dried before I climbed back in my plane.

By the end of June, I could no longer deny I was in trouble. Though my periods had been sporadic thanks to cross-country and training with Connor, I was overdue even for me. Andi and Sura were dispatched to the drug store and returned with a two-pack of pregnancy tests and three pints of Cherry Garcia. Watching my dreams die was evidently a spectator sport.

The bright pink line appeared immediately. Sura and Andi didn't need to see the results once they'd seen my stricken face.

"I can't do this!" I hurried out of the bathroom and into my bedroom.

"Of course you can." Andi was empathic.

"You're Lilah Fucking Campbell," Sura agreed.

I crushed my pillow to my belly, as if I could snuff out the reality of my situation. "How am I going to fly? I can't just toss a car seat into the cargo hold. What am I going to do with a kid?"

"You practically raised me all by yourself." Andi's dismissive remark didn't comfort me, considering our absent mom was a pilot.

No one said a word for what seemed like forever. I had time to use a third of a box of tissues.

Andi finally ended the silence. "A miniature Connor."

"It's gonna be a ten-pounder for sure." Sura shook her head, and her expression said "better you than me."

I pictured a chubby baby with my unruly curls and Connor's devilish eyes.

"You need to tell him." Andi made herself at home on my bed. "As soon as possible."

"He's in basic. He's got enough going on." I wiped my wet cheeks and tried to mask my anguish with my game face. Connor and I hadn't spoken since the night of prom, not at graduation...I didn't even go to say goodbye when he shipped out. I was afraid I'd fracture at the sight of him, so I stayed away.

"This is life-altering shit right here, Lilah," Sura insisted. "If you don't write to him, I will."

Her threat prompted a short letter to Connor, asking him to call me. Recruits had sporadic access to mail and phone privileges, so I was on pins and needles 24/7. Ten days later, Andi handed me the phone. She mouthed his name.

I took a deep breath and raised the phone to my ear. "Connor?"

His response was level, like he was in mixed company or being monitored. "I got your letter."

"How're you holding up?" I was breathless. He sounded terrible, and what I had to say was going to make things so much worse.

I heard a heavy intake of breath. "I don't have time for small talk, Lie."

"Okay." I crossed to the bay window. "I have to tell you something."

"I figured." He sounded hardened, which made sense, given where he was. Somehow that helped me spit out my news.

"I'm pregnant."

The silence went on for so long that I turned to Andi and Sura, who were pretending to read the Victoria's Secret *catalog. Their expectant eyes questioned me and I shrugged.*

"I think it happened on prom night," I added, just to fill the distressing void.

"You…think?" Scorn and accusation traveled the long distance between us.

More silence descended, this time from me. Shame overwhelmed me, and then righteous indignation since it takes two to tango.

"That's all you have to say to me?" I vowed I wouldn't hang up, no matter how much he pissed me off.

"What do you want me to say? Congratulations?" he spewed like venom.

I gathered myself, unwilling to let him hear a tremor in my voice. "I thought you should know." My words were reed thin, since I could barely breathe.

"Are you saying it's mine?"

I had the sensation of falling…like I was rushing through a loop on a roller coaster. All this time I'd been torturing myself with doubt and this fucking piece of work was who it had all been for.

I stubbornly pushed on. "I guess that tells me what I needed to know."

"Lie—" He started in with his signature frustrated sigh. I was over being treated like a situation he had to put up with.

"Screw you, Connor."

"Delilah, listen—"

"No, you listen, asshole. Never call me again." I slammed the phone down so hard I broke a piece of it off. Andi and Sura, who'd been watching me like I was a one-woman telenovela, jumped.

Hate reinvigorated me, helping me through what came next. I scoured the internet for any place that might hire me. Even before the pregnancy tests, I'd considered leaving. Everything here reminded me of Connor. I couldn't escape him, whether grabbing coffee at Wanda's or circling Mt. Redoubt at 4,000 feet. He'd invaded the smallest parts of me, and I hated myself for allowing it. I'd just have to go somewhere and wring myself out until I'd rid myself of every last drop.

A small airline in Las Vegas called me for an interview several days later, and I threw some clothes into a bag and made Andi drive me to the airport.

She seemed upset as she pulled into short-term parking. "What are you doing, Delilah?"

"Making it rain, Sistah," I joked, but Andi was a tough crowd.

"I mean about the baby." She watched me carefully, as if worried that she'd set me off.

My smile vanished. "I'm taking care of that too."

THE LINES ON the sidewalk blur a little, thanks to my gut-wrenching memory and my stinging eyes. Connor chose to leave and I chose to stay. Now he's home and I'm gone and neither of us really ended up with what we'd hoped for. The irony leaves a terrible taste in my mouth.

The bell rings as I enter Wanda's Diner, and Reece waves from a table in the far corner. A room full of state troopers sits between me and Reece. Eight sets of eyes turn my way, and I'm a little paranoid, so I hurry past their table.

Reece stands and pulls out a chair for me.

"Hey, gorgeous." He flashes his model-like dimples, and his large hand cups my shoulder. "How ya holding up?"

"I'm all right," I say, comforted by his touch, and delighted by his pleasant scent. I realize that I'm not only hungry and tired, I'm also a little hard up.

We both take a seat.

"How's your side?"

"Bruised…but better. It only hurts when I poke at it."

"So don't do that," Reece jokes, and the waitress appears with a carafe. Reece takes it and pours into the empty mug in front of me. "I ordered coffee. I hope that's okay."

"Coffee's more than okay." I immediately dress mine with all the trappings that make it impossible to drop the extra weight I'm lugging around, and take a long drink. "Tell me about your flyover."

"Okay. Ummm…well…since I'm not looking for the fuselage anymore, I wasn't really sure what you wanted to know."

"Topography would help." I'm honestly not sure what I'm looking for at this point, and acknowledging that— even just in my own head—exhausts me.

He nods. "The more easterly section is heavily wooded. There's nowhere to land without floats that wouldn't be dicey, even for you, Ace. The western section is very floatplane friendly, though there are some shallows you have to look out for. There are more manmade structures in that section. If you want, I'll take you out there right now and show you."

"I can just take Cherry out."

"I'm not crazy about the idea of you wandering around out there all by yourself." His concern is wearing as thin as Connor's mood swings.

I take another long swig of my coffee. "Connor will be there."

Reece goes silent. I look up from my cup with apprehension. The mention of Connor rankles him. He sits back and folds his arms, flipping his hair out of his narrowed eyes. "Lilah...I wasn't going to say anything—"

The waitress reappears with two waters and asks if we're ready to order. We both order the special, and she hurries away.

"Where were we?" He turns furtive eyes my way.

"You were lecturing me about Connor." I drink long and deep from the water glass to cool my building temper. It works, and I realize my comment sounded catty, considering how much Reece has done for me. "Sorry. That was rude."

He looks belligerent. "After the way he treated y—"

"I remember." I shut him down with a sharp gaze. Reece thinks he knows me, but he doesn't have an inkling of how severely Connor wounded me. I haven't shared that with anyone, not even my ex-husband. I rarely allow myself to even think about it.

"I don't have to understand it, but I get that Connor

meant a lot to you. I hate that you sought him out for help instead of me. I want to help you, Delilah. I'm here. And I can't imagine ever abandoning you."

I rub my eyes tiredly. "That's not fair, Reece. Connor had obligations."

"The army. I know. Which brings me to my next point," Reece presses on, undeterred by historical facts. "Rumor is he's…unstable. That's why Stephen let him take point during the search. He didn't think you needed a scene on top of what you're already dealing with. Did you know Connor's been arrested for assault twice?"

I look up from my coffee, the oppressive weight of the conversation zapping my energy. I rest my head on my hand. "What the hell are you talking about?"

"He hit someone with a chair, Lilah."

"I can't believe…" But I trail off, because I can believe it. When I'd gone to Claire's house after the funeral, trying to clear the air before we didn't see each other for another decade, Connor had shown me his dark side…

I barely got his name out before he had my wrist and the pressure was excruciating.

"Don't fucking touch me. Who the hell do you think you are coming here?" he'd slurred and I could see he was already drunk.

"I just came to say how sorry——"

"Not half as fucking sorry as I am, Lilah."

"I know how much your mom meant to you. I always liked her." It was the speech I rehearsed, but he looked like he might spit in my face. I slipped my wrist carefully out of his grasp.

He turned back to his drink. "You never gave a shit about anyone but yourself."

I moved a bit closer and lowered my voice, hoping he'd follow my lead, since a houseful of people were on the other side of the door. "Connor."

"Why are you here? To rub that goddam ring in my face? Just go. Take that fine ass of yours back to Vegas, sweetheart. You fit right in with the rest of the whores."

"You take that shit back." I was shocked, not angry.

"Or what?" he taunted me. "I'm not your bitch anymore, Lie. I did my time."

Just like that, I finally felt the oppressive weight of him easing off of me, and I was glad I came, even if the result was the polar opposite of what I'd hoped for when I arrived.

"You know what? I'm done. You're a piss-poor excuse for a man, Connor. Have a nice life."

I turned to go but he yanked me back by my hair. My instincts kicked in.

"I'm not d—"

I slapped him with everything I had.

"The fuck you're not." I raked at his injured eye, but his hands gripped my arms so tightly that I had bruises for a week after. Then he shook me so hard it felt like I had whiplash, and my head cracked against something solid. Pain rocked me, stealing my breath. He stopped as suddenly as he started.

"Oh, Jesus, Lie…" His voice trembled, and when I was finally able to focus on him, he looked like the little boy I used to know. A mordant chuckle escaped me.

"Look at the big bad soldier. The army did a real number on you."

Rage contorted his features and his hand was on my throat. I didn't even struggle. I'd wasted a decade crying over this monster, what we'd made, what we'd lost. I was ready for his eyes to be the last thing I saw.

"The army didn't fuck me up, Lilah." His eyes swept me, less hostile and more lustful. "You did."

He'd pinned me against the wall when he'd grabbed me, and his heavy breaths smelled like whiskey. Our gazes entwined, and for a second I was sure he'd kiss me. Then Quinn yanked Connor away from me and Boone jumped in, pinning Connor to the fridge.

"Let's go, Lilah." Quinn rushed me toward the back door. I understood why. Connor was a trained killer, and we were all screwed if he really decided to throw down. Before the door slammed behind us, I heard Connor yelling my name.

"DID CONNOR TELL you that he has Lu's old plane?" Reece rips me from my recollection, and my eyes pop wide when I process what he's said.

"The De Havilland?"

He nods. I sip more coffee, my head spinning.

"He bought skis for it from one of our pilots."

I look out the window at nothing in particular. Connor...a pilot. The knowledge somehow makes me feel...less relevant...unimportant. Why didn't he tell me? My mouth feels dry and I take another drink of water. The waitress arrives with our sandwiches, and I use chewing as an excuse not to speak.

"Did Connor tell you that LuAnn owes his dad money?"

I know he's seen the horror and shock on my face because he nods, pursing his lips.

"The authorities pulled your mom's bank records. Her phone records too. Connor was the last person she spoke to."

I drop my sandwich, unable to stomach it. His suspicion is valid, but how does Reece know about the phone records? I'm about to ask when he presses on.

"The investigation's just getting started now that they found the plane. There's obvious foul play. They've brought in the FAA and they've called the FBI. They'll get to the bottom of this, Lilah. Nothing stays buried."

I'm nauseated, and I'm sweating. I wonder if I caught something in that germ factory of a hospital. I'm tempted to put my head down, like a child who's in trouble at school. I try to pour more coffee and almost knock over the carafe. Reece reaches out and pushes the carafe away, taking my hand in his.

"Lilah. You don't need him. We can do this together."

"I…I'm…"

"You know you can count on me. Can you say the same thing about Connor?"

"I knew my ears were itching for a reason."

I turn toward the sound of Connor's voice in slow motion. He takes the chair next to me, flipping it around backward and straddling it. His gaze sweeps over me, his mysterious eyes settling on my hand as I pull it free from

Reece's.

"You look worn out," he tells me softly as he reaches out to stroke my hair. I move away, and his eyebrows shoot skyward. "Do I need to take you home?"

I'm tempted to acquiesce, because I haven't slept well in days. I can barely keep my eyes open. I shake my head, going for the coffee again. Connor takes my mug and fills it to the rim.

"So, Reece. How's married life treating ya?" Connor sounds so genuine, I almost believe he's looking for an answer.

Reece's discourteous expression tells me he'd love to disembowel Connor. "I'm divorced."

Connor turns to me, a roguish smile transforming his shrouded face. "You know who he *was* married to, right?"

"I didn't know you got married," I slur. Reece is blushing, and his eyes have trouble staying with mine. I see his jaw pulsating.

"Your old pal, Cyndi." Connor's eyes are alight with pleasure at the damage this does to Reece.

I regard Connor with critical eyes as his deplorable announcement collapses on me. Reece can't even look at me.

Don't trust anyone.

I'm starting to understand what Mom meant.

"I hear *you're* sleeping with her now," Reece pops back at Connor. That blow dampens Connor's megawatt smile, and his shifty eyes flick to mine. I lift my coffee cup to my lips and drink deeply, though the urge to vomit is strong.

"Ready to head out?" Reece's ignoring Connor now, as

if he isn't even present.

I push my chair back, planning to leave them both with their smug smiles and shared STDs. I'm done with their tug-of-war and I'm in a "trust no one" kind of mood.

I stand, my knees shaky. Attempting to maintain my dignity, I focus on getting to the door without falling into the laps of my fellow diners. The troopers have cleared out, which is good since I stumble into their table. My head swims, and I lurch in the direction of the exit. I smell fresh air, but nearly fall face-first down the stairs. Someone grabs me by the arm, wrenching it painfully. I cry out.

"Lie, w—"

"Dammit, Connor. Just go away!" I try to shrug him off, and make for the sidewalk, slewing side to side. I lose my footing, and put my hands out to block my face from the sidewalk.

I never make impact. Big hands pull me backward and flip me over. Both Connor and Reece hover over me as I fade to black.

CHAPTER SEVENTEEN

CONNOR

WAR WOUNDS

"**W**HAT DID YOU give her?" Terrified and furious, I grab Reece by the collar, ready to mop the sidewalk with him. Delilah's only been out of my sight for thirty minutes, and she's been roofied. I've apprehended targets using similar tactics and recognize her symptoms for what they are, and just how little can be done about it now that the drug is in her system.

"What?" Reece seems horrified and confused, and though I'd like to believe he was behind this, he's not stupid, and there are too many witnesses around. "We need to call an ambulance!"

I sweep Lilah up off of the sidewalk and hurry for the SUV. I'd seen troopers leave the restaurant as I was coming in, and I wonder if one of them slipped something to her somehow. I can't take her to the local hospital if law enforcement is involved. There's nothing they can do but monitor her anyway.

I hear Reece shouting for someone to call 911 as I reach the SUV. I speed off, and as soon as I'm far enough away, I double back in the direction of the airport. Dialing Boone's number, I'm unsurprised when I get his voice mail, and I sound surprisingly normal in my message, asking him to feed and water Runt until I make it back to Lu's.

Carrying Lilah to her floatplane, I get a couple of curious glances, but no interference. Good Samaritans really are a thing of the past.

As I'm running through a quick preflight check, I chew on my quandary. GHB takes effect in about fifteen minutes, and based on the amount of time she'd been gone from the *Gazette*, it's the most likely culprit. I know from black ops that the life of this drug class is three or four hours. Lie's respirations are normal and her pulse is strong. I need to make sure she doesn't have breathing issues or seizures. If either happens, I'll have to chance a trip to the ER, but I'd rather be in Sterling or Soldotna, outside the reach of the local troopers. Plus, I have an arsenal at my place to protect her, should the need arise.

I'm buckling her into the passenger seat when her eyelids flutter. Her hair clings to her sweaty brow, and I brush it aside as I check her pulse again. Still regular. She looks like she's trying to talk, but no words come.

"Don't worry, baby. You're all right," I say, more as a pep talk to myself than to her. It's unlikely she'll remember any of this anyway. When I get out on the water, the tower radios me, and I ignore them. No one is landing or taking off, so I take advantage of the hole in air traffic.

Once we're in the air, my focus is back on how and why Lilah was drugged. GHB is potent shit; a very small amount can have a big effect. I gave some to a terrorist cell leader once and within fifteen minutes he was seizing and choking on his tongue. It comes in many forms, so it could have been in her food, the coffee, even something she drank at the *Gazette*.

I shake my head. She hadn't been dosed at the paper. She'd refused lunch and I never saw her drink anything. It definitely happened at the café. I consider what might have gone down if I hadn't gone after her as soon as I had. Thankfully Sura is as nosy as ever, and pressed me about the baby. Our baby. I had no reason to doubt Sura when she told me Lie's baby was mine, because Sura knows a true story when she hears one, or she wouldn't do what she does. This gets me thinking about my reaction to the news, and the state of mind I was in when Lilah told me she was pregnant.

Dad warned me not to give my drill instructor any lip. He didn't warn me that his former coworkers at Ft. Benning were waiting for me, ready to pounce. I was called out in front of my entire platoon on day one.

"Listen up, recruits! We have a celebrity in our midst. This here is the *Connor Garrett, a world-famous treasure hunter." The drill sergeant was so close that the brim of his hat nearly poked my right eye out, and I could smell his two-pack-a-day cigarette habit as his spittle landed on my cheek. I wasn't prepared to be singled out in such a spectacular fashion, but I had plenty of experience with being yelled at. I focused my gaze on the terrified kid across from me. "This pretty mug right here was on the cover of* People *magazine. Try not to swoon when*

you encounter his radiance."

Before I could acclimate to this development, they were pairing us with battle buddies. I was matched with the wide-eyed kid bunking across from me, who looked as if he may have shit his pants.

We were on our way to lunch when he introduced himself. "I'm Max Moore."

"Connor. Garrett." I saw him nod out of the corner of my eye.

"I heard the drill sergeants talking about you in reception last week. Your dad used to be an Airborne instructor here, right?" His near-set blue eyes searched me for verification.

"Yeah." Things made all sorts of dreadful sense now.

"They sure don't like him." Max huffed out a humorless laugh.

For the first time in my life, I wished I'd chosen the Air Force.

The heat and humidity took some getting used to, and the first two weeks we did an obnoxious amount of marching around, and tons of PT. I always finished first when we ran. The drill sergeants had balloons and a poster-sized version of my People *magazine cover waiting for me at the finish line. They started calling me Hollywood, and made me autograph the poster, then announced that I was so special they'd decided to make me squad leader. It was another way to isolate me. If my squad fucked up, I'd get in trouble. If I tried to correct the men, they'd hate me. It was a lose-lose situation.*

As if things weren't shitty enough, they hung the poster in our barracks, just to remind everyone what a giant douchebag I am.

"Hey, Hollywood!" We were in the midst of personal time, and the Hispanic kid and his battle buddy were loitering near the poster. "Is this your girlfriend?"

I looked up from the envelope I was sealing to see his fingers trailing over Lilah's image.

"She used to be," I admitted. Delilah still dominated my thoughts when I wasn't too tired to think.

"Mind if I borrow her?" his buddy asked. "I just need some scissors to cut you out of the picture. And a little hand lotion."

"Shut the hell up, limp dick," Max called to him.

"Fuck you, shitbag," the Hispanic kid stuck up for his pal. "Hollywood can't keep your ass out of jail if you don't step up."

The two loudmouths wandered away and I eyed Max curiously.

"What the shit was that about?" I asked.

Max turned red. "We were all talking about how we got recruited. I was too honest."

Max's cheeks appeared as if they were stained with cheap wine. "I took the ASVAB last year just to get out of class. Fast-forward a few months to when I get charged with possession with intent to sell. The judge gave me a choice. Jail or the military. Here I am with you dildos."

I nodded. This explained why Max was so unprepared. I'd been worried about him. A couple of days before, he had gone completely ape-shit at the obstacle course because once again, he'd been in last place. The guy in front of him had tripped and fallen, and Max had run right over him, hollering like he was charging the battlefield carrying a battle-axe and wearing a kilt. He had stepped on the guy's head, forcing him to eat a mouthful of mud. It had been so ridiculous that even the drill *sergeants had laughed. After that, everyone had started referring to him as Mad Max.*

With the first couple of weeks of basic behind us, I was finally adjusting to the three to five hours of sleep we got every night, which had been the second hardest thing for me to adapt to. The hardest thing was being so disliked. I wasn't some insecure little bitch who needed everyone to be my best friend, but I'd never had a problem fitting in or getting people to listen to me. These Smokey-Bear-hat-wearing dicks in charge did their worst to make sure everyone hated me. Half the guys on the squad resented my enthusiasm, calling me a "kiss ass." The other half hid behind me, like Mad Max, who I suspected had only survived this long because I was his battle buddy.

I liked him, but there was no denying that Max Moore was our weakest link. We'd been smoked twice in the past two days because of his inability to lock shit down. I knew if I didn't do something soon, someone would beat him down. It was my responsibility to be that someone, and the idea was about as appealing as kicking a blind, starving puppy with mange.

He and I were on fire guard one night and he was shooting his mouth off, like always.

"...Drill Sergeant was so close that I could smell the tuna he had for dinner." He frowned, as if a truly tasteless idea had just popped into his head. "At least I hope that was his dinner I was smelling..."

"Moore..."

"Yeah?"

"This can go one of two ways. I kick your ass and tell you not to fuck up again, or I help you learn and you just don't

fuck up again. Your choice."

"I'll take door number two."

"Wise choice."

He looked relieved.

"Don't think I won't beat your ass, Max. You look bad, we look bad. Don't make me be that guy."

"Just tell me what to do."

He worked his ass off after that, listening carefully to every tip I dreamed up. Soon the other guys were giving him pointers too. We were moving into the second half of basic, and learning tactics and how to use all the gear. Clever and mechanically inclined, Max outshone most of us. Everyone was grateful that we weren't getting smoked with extra push-ups every day, and squad morale improved exponentially.

Two days later, I received a letter from Lilah. My heart raced and my hands shook so badly I was afraid I'd rip the letter clean in half. When I smelled her lotion on the stationery, it was hard to catch my breath.

Connor,

I hope you're giving them hell. I need you to call me as soon as possible.

Lilah

"Shit," Max said after I showed it to him.

"Maybe she's ready to get back together," I said.

"Maybe." Max's weighty gaze was a direct contradiction to his optimistic tone.

I read Lie's words over and over again, like I was going to divine something new about her intentions. I thought about her and Reece, feeling less and less confident by the minute. When I finally got her on the phone, my squad was milling around, waiting to witness their leader get his nuts handed to him.

Andi answered, and I knew something was up by her overly polite behavior. She put Lilah on, and I could tell Lie was super nervous. I had about four minutes to talk before they cut off the call, and I told her I didn't have a lot of time. Speedy, our totally un-PC nickname for the Hispanic kid, was making obscene gestures and, irritated, I turned away from him. Then Lilah told me she was pregnant.

I should have known. Lilah wouldn't have written to me unless the sky was falling. When she added that she thought it happened on prom night, I felt pins and needles all over my body.

"You…think?" Prom was the one and only time we hadn't been safe. She had doubts, so she must have been with Reece after all.

"That's all you have to say?" The incredulity in her tone was unmistakable.

"Congratulations," I spat, images of Reece's hands all over her on the dance floor feeding my building anger.

"I thought you should know," she declared.

"Are you saying it's mine?" Even as the words left my mouth, I saw her ruined prom dress and the pins all falling out of her wild hair.

Delilah lashed out, an uncharacteristic tremor in her voice. I started to interrupt her rampage, but she told me never to call her again and before I could say anything, the line was already dead.

I started firing off letters knowing she might not receive any of them for weeks. I tried to call her, but Andi hung up on me every time. Finally, I called my mom. Confessing that I'd knocked up her best friend's daughter was awkward, but Mom didn't even seem upset.

"Oh, honey, I wish I could go talk to her for you." She sounded hoarse, but I was so spun up I was barely aware of it. "I just can't."

"I don't think you grasp the gravity of the situation, Mom." With so many battling emotions I gripped the receiver until my knuckles turned white.

"Connor, I'm in the hospital."

I felt my heart start to pick up speed. "What? Why?"

"Time, Garrett!" the drill sergeant hollered.

"I found a lump, honey. Turns out it's malignant."

"Garrett!"

I went numb. My stomach was on the floor at my feet. I had a sinking feeling that my troubles were just getting started.

The second I could get back home to Alaska, I went. Lu-Ann seemed shocked to see me.

"Connor!" she blurted. "When did you get back?"

I couldn't speak. The silence was deafening.

"She's not here, Connor," Lu insisted. "Come inside. Have a beer and we'll go see your mom."

"I've seen Mom. I want Lilah. She needs to hear what I have to say." I held up the flowers I'd brought, as if they were evidence that I wasn't a giant dickhead.

"She's been gone a month. I have no idea where she is." Lu looked sad and afraid.

Andi hurried around the corner, and when she spotted me,

she froze. She knew where Lie was; it was written all over her face.

"She doesn't want to hear from you," she seethed.

"Please, Andi. I don't have much time before I have to fly b——"

"I don't give a shit, Connor. And neither does my sister. Just take your sorry ass back to Georgia. Your services are no longer required."

"She's carrying my baby, Andi," I hissed.

She folded her arms. "Not anymore, she's not."

I GLANCE OVER at Lilah, counting her breathing for fifteen seconds. Still normal respirations. Still terminally beautiful. I owe Sura a debt of gratitude, because, because during my tirade at the *Gazette*, I'd tossed out Lilah's abortion as evidence that she was the villain of our story.

"She just got rid of it without giving me a real chance to process the news, Sura. That wasn't fair—and then she was just gone."

The gobsmacked look on Sura's face made my blood run cold.

"Connor." She leaned forward in her seat, and seemed to contemplate for a long moment before continuing. "There was no abortion. Go find Delilah. Right now. I got all this, but you two really need to talk."

I was on my feet and out the door, hurrying down Main Street in the direction of Wanda's. Why would Andi say that if it wasn't true? Do I have a kid out there somewhere? Lilah loves her secrets, but has she really kept something like that from me all these years?

I take several deep breaths, pissed at myself for letting her go to the café alone, even though I know there's no "letting Lilah" do anything.

By air, it's not a long trip to my house on the Kenai. Cherry is easy to fly, and the landing is the smoothest I've ever managed since Lu first gave me lessons. The current jostles the wet floats I'm balancing on as I lift Lilah out of the plane. I don't breathe easy until we're safely on the dock, and I race to get her inside.

She's still sweating when I lay her on my bed, so I peel off her jacket and her boots and socks. After a half-second debate, I pop the button of her jeans and slide them off. It's not how I'd hoped to get her out of her pants, and realizing someone might have had this very thing in mind, I'm so angry I can barely see straight. I cover her with the cool sheets and a light blanket and leave the room, but not before snagging Lu's cell phone from her back pocket.

Back in the kitchen, I examine Lu's call log. She called my number, all right, around the time the storm was blowing in, and the hipsters and I were passing around a bottle of Jack. At four minutes, I couldn't dispute a connection. I rub an exasperated hand over my face. Had I even had my phone out of my pack?

I dial Andi from my own phone. She picks up after three rings.

"What?" How she makes a living interacting with the public I will never know.

"Sura said Lilah never had an abortion."

"Hello to you too, Connor."

"Andi…"

She sighs. "Why don't you ask Lilah?"

"You're the one who said she did. So I'm asking you."

There's a pause. "I thought that was her plan."

"So…"

"So that is all I have to say about it. Talk to Lilah. You're thirty fucking years old. Start acting like it." She hangs up.

Exasperated, I lock up and kick off my boots. Next thing I know, I'm leaning in the doorway watching Lilah sleep. She's so little in my California king, her long chestnut and mahogany hair splayed out around her like a radiant crown. Climbing in beside her, I admit to myself that I need to hold her like a scared kid needs his teddy bear. I put my hand gently on her belly, feeling her steady inhalations and exhalations. Trying to match her breathing, I hope it'll calm my jangled nerves.

I study her face, from the tiny freckle I remember so well to the barely visible smile lines around her eyes. Restless, I wonder if she's dreaming about all of her secrets. I stroke her cheek, noticing that she's no longer sweaty.

Being this close to Delilah feels right, but the circumstances nauseate me. I pull the blanket more snugly around her and breathe her in. I would never have guessed it possible, but she lulls me to sleep.

"That was some straight-up Rambo shit." Max took off his shemagh and poured water over his head. I know I'm dream-

ing, and it's a terrible feeling, because I have this dream all too often, and it isn't just a dream. It happened, and no matter how many times I'm here, I can never change the outcome.

I gulp down my water instead, since I have a healthy respect for desert life. Max shouldn't be impressed. What I'd just done was fucking idiotic…an act of desperation.

In the last twenty-four hours, we've lost three friendlies. Their truck was engulfed in flames, and with so many motherfuckers bearing down on us, we couldn't retrieve their bodies. At this point, I don't give a shit about anything but getting everyone else home with a pulse.

If I hadn't retrieved Max's pack after the strap broke, he'd have gone back for it and gotten his head blown off. I'm faster than he is, especially since his damn Chucks are worn out after months on assignment. Speed is measurable. Simple math. There's nothing courageous about math.

Another bullet whizzes by me. I duck as it hits the stone wall behind me, taking out a chunk the size of a softball.

"Get down!" I bark, wishing like hell we were wearing helmets and not kafiyas. At least we have concealable body armor, so that was something.

We have very little cover between us and the extraction point, and I have no idea how the hell we'd get out of this one. I return fire in the general direction of the sniper and then I drop flat on my back behind the half wall.

Nothing happens for over a minute.

"Get to the truck," the team sergeant orders into the walkie-talkie. He and Max race in the direction of the truck, and the rest of our team barrels after us from the next building over where they'd been taking cover. I hang back, my M4 deafening

as I provide cover fire. Blood splatters my face as Mike takes a head shot. Without hesitating, I drag him with me, hurrying after the accelerating truck. I toss Mike over my shoulder, jumping onto the tailgate. Max and our fellow squad member Frank pull us the rest of the way in.

I'm shaking, and I can't even look at Mike. He'd planned a trip to Euro Disney for his kid's fifth birthday. We gave him so much shit about how much that place sucked, and I want to take it all back. At least I won't have to face Mike's widow without bringing home something for her to bury.

"Bad news, boys." Max has his 117 to his ear. "Air support's in black. We have to go another ten miles."

"Motherfucker," Frank spits. Whenever weather conditions at this altitude got bad, we were on our own.

"There are two trucks waiting at the extraction point to take us there."

I can't wait to get the hell out of hostile territory. Get the intel home and hand off to those who knew how to use it ASAFP.

We ride in unmolested silence. The ominous sky is oddly beautiful, and the monochromatic terrain resembles the southwest United States. I think of Lilah, since the last time I was home my mom mentioned Lie was living in Nevada. I pull her picture out of my pouch. It's worn and faded from years of carrying it with me, but one glance at her immortalized under the aurora borealis, and I'm calm. Her potent gaze still reaches right down into my chest a decade later, and I'm not sure what to do about that or if anything could be done.

"Still carrying that picture around?" Max's tired eyes shift from the old snapshot to my face.

I nod.

"You gonna go see her when we get out of here? Talk your shit out like grown-ass adults?"

I shake my head, and the corner of my mouth turns up. "I'm going to party with a couple of pros for a week."

Max looks at me like I'm speaking Chinese and he's waiting for an interpreter. Then he frowns and turns away. "Fucking pussy."

I squint as if trying to read his lips. "What did you just call me?"

"You heard me."

I glare at him in surprised disbelief. "Fuck you, Moore."

"No fuck you, dude. Parker wants you to be our kid's godfather. I told her you need to grow up first."

I raise my eyebrows, surprised that Max's wife had suggested it, since she told me off every time she saw me. I'm more hurt by Max's objection to the idea than I'd ever admit. "You locked yourself out of a four-star hotel naked not even a year ago, and I need to grow up."

Max looks genuinely pissed. "Remember dam? 'Cause I sure as shit do. You fell apart and nearly landed us on the no-fly list. Man the hell up, Connor. Jesus. This Delilah bullshit has gone on for about ten years too long."

I can't believe he brought up Amsterdam. A few months before he met his wife, we had a four-day leave and decided to party. The flight attendant leaned in to ask what I wanted to drink, and I'd smelled Lilah's lotion on her. I spent the rest of the flight getting drunk on those tiny bottles of booze and I can't remember what I said to Max, but he'd been tiptoeing around me like I was a minefield ever since.

I ignore him the rest of the way to the rendezvous. It isn't easy, since we're packed like sardines. The QRF that is waiting are also Green Berets, and they've brought their guerrilla force of friendly locals. We all breathe a small sigh of relief.

"Come on!" Max yells, moving toward the closest truck. I'm not ready for more advice on my lack of a love life. I wave him on.

"I'll get the next one."

Max's close-set eyes narrow, offended and resigned. "Sir, yes sir."

He hurries after the team sergeant and hops into truck number one. I climb into the second truck with the rest of the team, and we convoy in the direction of extraction site B.

"I'm going to drink my weight in Cuervo when we get back." Frank always says this when we're close enough to taste the finish line.

"I'm gonna eat so much barbecue they gonna kick my fat ass out." Brooks, the biggest black dude I'd ever encountered, chuckles and his deep laugh echoes off the walls of the cab. "What about you, Chief?"

I half-smile and wink. "I'm gonna eat so much pus—"

An explosion rocks the truck with such force, I'm sure someone set a bomb off under my seat. I duck and cover, and though my ears are ringing from the blast, I'm aware of the screech of metal and I'm showered with broken glass. My left eye stings, and my face is wet. The truck stops hard with a tremendous crunch, and I turn to Brooks, whose chest heaves like he's just shoved an elephant off of it.

"Brooks! You okay?"

"I think so." His dark eyes find my face and grow to the

size of beach balls. "Shit, Connor. Are you okay?"

Figuring he's in shock, I lean into the front seat. The windshield is mostly gone, and both guys in the front seat are slumped over. There's glass everywhere, but it's the shooting flames from the road in front of us that grab my attention. We weren't hit. The truck in front of us was.

The truck Max is in.

My door is jammed, so I brace against Brooks, kicking it repeatedly with both feet until it flies open with a thwack. *Jumping down, I sweep the surrounding area, my Glock at the ready. I see no one, but I hear gagging, wailing, and coughing up ahead.*

Men in the act of dying.

I approach Max's truck, desperate to see what's left. The heat from the flames is intolerable, and the smoke is so thick I'm coughing before I get within ten feet. I can hardly see, but I make out that the truck is lying on its side. I can't get close enough to do anything but listen to the screaming coming from inside.

"Sir!" I hear Frank call, and I look to see where my superior officer is. Then I realize I'm the "sir" he's addressing. "Here."

I hurry to where he's crouched. I can only assume someone crawled or was thrown from the truck. As I near him, I see a Converse Chuck Taylor, and my throat closes.

"Max!" My trashed vocal cords make me sound like a stranger. I shove Frank aside. One of Max's legs is missing from the thigh down. He has a large sliver of metal sticking out of his side about the size of a tent stake, and his eyes dart wildly, until they settle on my face.

"Con—" It's barely a whisper.

"You're all right, Max. Don't talk. Save your breath."

"Park…" he murmurs, his pale eyes fluttering, then focusing on me again, fierce and alarming.

My heart is in my already grated throat as I yank my belt off, using it as a tourniquet on what's left of Max's appendage. "Don't you die on me, Max. Don't you fucking dare."

"Tell Parker—"

"Shut the fuck up, Moore," I choke out, my eyes stinging with tears and my face dripping with sweat and God knows what else. "Tell her your fucking self."

I FEEL LILAH wrench herself away from me, but surfacing to consciousness is like swimming through quicksand. I usually medicate myself to suppress these nightmares, but today's drifts away, replaced by the enticing scent of Lilah's hair.

"Shhh…" I pull her back against me, my lips brushing the hollow of her temple. "It's all right, Lie."

"Connor." She's not posing a question, just confirming her lot with agonized resignation.

The sudden movement of the bed makes my eyes spring open. By the time I sit up, Lilah's gone, the door wide open behind her.

I scramble out of the bed and hear her rifling through the kitchen. By the time I round the corner, she's standing in the center of the room, brandishing a carving knife.

"Lie—"

"Stay where you are." Her wild eyes and jerky movements have me playing through scenarios to disarm her. "I
don't want to hurt you, Connor, but don't think I won't."

"Put the knife down, baby."

"Make me." The hard set of her jaw dares me to try.

"Lilah, this isn't what—I would never hur—" Her
tempestuous glare hits me like a sledgehammer. We both
know I'm perfectly capable of hurting her. I try in vain to
fight the fire roasting my entire face. "I'll never hurt you
again. Not intentionally."

"How did we get here?" she demands, and I take a
breath and say a silent prayer that I can talk my way out of
my questionable choices.

"Your plane," I say. "What do you remember?"

"I remember I was wearing pants." Her words are accusatory. My eyes slip to her bare legs before I can stop them.

"I wanted you to be comfortable." I realize how awful it
sounds right after I say it.

She huffs out an incredulous laugh and flips the knife
over in her hand. It's the move of someone alarmingly
familiar with how to handle a blade. I can take it away from
her, but now I'm not so sure I can do it without injuring
one or both of us.

"Nothing happened, Delilah," I say gravely, taking a
step toward her.

"I guess I'll have to take your word for it." She backs
out of the kitchen and into the living room. I follow her
cautiously, my hands up like she's holding a gun on me.

"When I got to the café, you were out of it. You tried

to leave. Do you remember?"

"Reece told me you were the last person to speak to Mom. He said you have her plane."

I stop moving, genuinely caught off guard that Reece knew about the call, and disturbed that he's mentioned it to Lie.

"She sold me her plane when she bought her new one. And I already told you, I don't remember talking to her."

I can see she wants to believe me. History tells her she should. I've tossed a pebble into Reece's version of events, and the ripples of doubt are forming.

"I was drunk," I admit.

Her startling eyes bore into me. I can't decide if she's judging me for day drinking, or if she truly believes I was involved in Lu's disappearance. "I don't know any more about where Lu is than you do. It was storming that day and I was on a hunt. There were seven of us in the camp. Someone else might have picked up my phone. No one mentioned it."

"Reece said Mom owes your dad money."

My mind's reeling at the seeds this asshole managed to plant in such a short window of time. "Since when is Reece such an expert on me?"

"Is it true?" She spits out the words, but she's practically to the sofa now, and the only way out of the room is through me.

"Dad and I aren't exactly on speaking terms." I put my hand out, palm up. "Just give me the knife, Lie. Let's figure this out together like we always do."

She shakes her head and takes another step back, bumping into the sofa. It's all the opening I need. My hand strikes out and with a simple twist of her wrist, I disarm her, tossing the knife aside. "Now it's my turn to ask you questions, so let's start with the big one. What did you do with our baby?"

CHAPTER EIGHTEEN

LILAH

EVERY LAST DROP

C ONNOR HAS ME literally backed into a corner. You'd think he'd know better, considering the teeth-shaped scar I gave him in junior high after he pushed me into the creek. He's being careless, and it's almost disappointing. He ought to know I'll do whatever's necessary to get away from him.

I recognized the house on the Kenai the second I opened my eyes. Connor's family spent most weekends here at the river house when we were kids, and Mom and I often flew down to deliver supplies. Connor and I played while our moms visited, so we'd grown up exploring the surrounding woods, claiming the old homestead cabin as our fort. The older we got, the crazier our playtime got.

It was in these same woods that Connor first kissed me. He didn't ask permission—his lips were just on mine, so suddenly and unexpectedly that I'd inched backward in surprise. He refused to accept that, holding me in his powerful grasp as his mouth claimed me, exploring me without hesitation. I bolted the second he released me, but not because of what he'd just done to me. I fled because I'd felt wild and out of control in his arms and I knew I'd let him do whatever he wanted if I ended up back there again. I should have trusted my instincts.

This place is a vault of memories I'd rather not unlock, but that's the least of my concerns. I'm inexplicably over one hundred and fifty miles south of True, and I've somehow lost six hours.

Kneeing Connor in the groin seems appropriate, so I go for it. He dodges with wide-eyed surprise and twists my arm hard. I gasp at the sudden pain, and I bring my head up, solidly connecting with his jaw. I hear a satisfying crack and surprised grunt from my hulking opponent. He loosens his grip on me, and I spring away, up onto the nearby coffee table and into the center of the room, scanning the floor for the knife he'd tossed aside. It's smoldering in the crackling fire that Connor found the time to build while I was conspicuously unconscious.

Connor's laughter is so inappropriate that my attention shoots straight back to him. He rakes his long hair out of his playful eyes.

"Not bad, Lie." He opens and closes his mouth a few times, testing its functionality. Satisfied, he prowls in my direction as if this is all some sort of game.

"Don't touch me," I caution him. There is nothing playful about how I say it.

"I'm not touching you." He's wearing his innocent face, one he's used on me since we were four. I'd like to smack it right off of him. "But you're not going anywhere until you tell me what I want to know."

"That's why you brought me here? To dredge up shit you didn't have the balls to talk about when I *needed* you to?" Connor's expression darkens.

"I brought you here because we can't trust anybody. You said so yourself." His harsh tone makes me take a step back. "Quit trying to make me the villain. Someone drugged you *before* I came looking for you."

My hands are still up, ready to go nine more rounds if I have to. He's making sense though, and I'm disturbed at the obvious deduction. "Reece?"

"I don't know." Connor seems doubtful, and that surprises me. I figured Connor would be as ready to discredit Reece as Reece had been to defame Connor. I lower my defenses just a hair to ask him more, and Connor moves in, lightning fast. He snags both of my wrists. I tense, kneeing at his thigh and bringing my arms down full force. Without releasing me, he reverses his grip on both of my arms, easily sidestepping my knee.

"Hey, now. Settle down," he says mildly, and I head-butt him as hard as I can in the mouth. I mean to use the top of my head, but I catch him with my hairline. It hurts like hell and tears spring to my eyes, but it wipes the cocky sneer off of his face. I have time to mentally gloat at the sight of his blood before he lets go of my right arm and grabs my left. He spins me, grappling me to his chest from behind.

He scissors my legs with his, pulling us down backward onto the bearskin rug and holding me immobile. Thankfully he absorbed the impact, and other than a twinge in my side, I'm fine. I throw my head back, trying to screw up his handsome face for his trouble. Our height difference thwarts my assault, and I smash my head ineffectually against his sternum.

"That's enough." His deep voice reverberates against the back of my skull. "I'm not going to let you hurt me and I don't want to hurt you."

Whatever drug took me down at the diner has left me pretty drained. My energy wanes and, resigned, I abandon my struggle. When I go limp, Connor rolls us onto our sides, one vise-like arm around my chest, the other firm around my waist. I'm trying to steady my breathing when I feel his beard tickle my ear.

"Lie…" He nudges my hair aside, his lips remarkably soft as he murmurs against the back of my neck. "We're on the same side."

A sentimental heat rises between my legs. I'm ashamed, and I tense, readying myself for round three. I'm more comfortable fighting with him than I am with this. This is too dangerous and has longer-lasting effects.

When I feel his hard shaft press against my ass, I'm completely derailed. I release a desperate moan, arching into his impressive length. I'm trembling, afraid, and aroused. My flesh remembers every inch of Connor fondly, but unfortunately my scarred heart does too.

Connor rolls me onto my back and comes down on top of me, trapping my legs with his hard, muscular thighs. I immediately bow off of the rug, aching to feel more of him.

He frames my face with his elbows, pinning my long hair under his forearms so I can't look away or move my head more than a fraction of an inch.

He studies me, as if comparing me to long-abandoned memories. His hazel eyes are alight with promise and dripping with unmasked lust. I see everything underneath the surface of his gaze, the helplessness, the doubt, the desperation. I can relate to it all. What Connor and I have, what we've always had, is bigger than us. My craving for him is uncontainable, making me question my sanity.

His brows meet as if he's pondering, his features bare and exposed. "Lie…"

"We shouldn't…" I agree, since he's working up the fortitude to say it. Even as the statement leaves my mouth, I'm straining underneath him, undulating against his powerful body. I want him inside me, not off of me. Biology is a powerful thing, and I've exhausted my willpower along with everything else. He seems to be on the same page, and when he ghosts his lips over mine, I'm quivering with anticipation.

"I know," he acknowledges, but he reaches back one-handed and pulls his shirt off over his head in a single fluid motion. His clean, masculine scent makes me crazy. I run my hands over his shoulders and down his arms, enjoying the sinewy peaks and valleys.

"We should—" I try to tell him we should already be in the air, but he swallows my words. His resolute kiss tastes as good as he looks. A soft moan is all the response I can manage. Our tongues sync like our combat did, matching each other move for move. I can taste his blood, metallic, vibrant, and poetic in the midst of this unholy union. Thrashing beneath him, I pull at his overgrown beard to bring him firmer against my lips.

Connor rolls onto his back, bringing me with him. Now I'm on top, with his hands sliding up my bare thighs till they grip my ass, locking us pelvis to pelvis. His glittering eyes submit control, telling me to make my choice.

There's no alternative as far as I'm concerned. Sex with Connor has been on the agenda since he first turned up in Mom's kitchen. We may as well get it over with so we can both think straight. I sit back on my heels so that I can unbutton and unzip his jeans. His mossy eyes flash, deadly serious as I swing off of him to remove his pants, sending them skittering across the hardwood and into the kitchen without a second glance.

Nude Connor was always impressive, but his evolution borders on intimidating. He's ripped muscles from head to toe, and before I realize what I'm doing, I'm running my fingers along his cut midsection, following the trail of dark hair down to my favorite part of him. He's standing at attention, and I can't resist a taste.

I flip my hair aside and take him greedily into my mouth.

"Jesus, Lie," he exhales, his tone all gravel and heat. He throws his head back, a bronze god on the thick cushion of fur. I take pride in my work, watching his every reaction. He's bigger and stronger than me, but I own his body now, at least until the sweat dries. I intend to teach him what he's been missing all these years.

"Come here," he growls, tugging on my hair. I shake him off, and he smooths a hand over my ass and yanks unsuccessfully at my panties. It's not long before he's gripping my hair, bucking and moaning, so big and unchained that I nearly choke before I finally have to pull away to breathe.

Connor moves so quickly, it's startling, and before I know what's happening he's on his knees, sweeping me to my feet. The animal look in his eyes drenches me in an instant.

"You won't be needing these." He hooks his finger on the waist of my boy shorts and rips them down to my ankles. I kick them off, already struggling with my shirt. His wet kisses on my stomach have me weak-kneed, and as his mouth travels south, I yank at my top feverishly. He reaches up one-handed and unfastens my bra, which vanishes with one quick flick of his wrist.

Connor sweeps his eyes over the entirety of me, leisurely taking his time. His forehead crimps and he reaches out, placing his warm hand on my bruised side.

"Did I hurt you?" I can tell he's recalling every move he made during our short-lived skirmish. It's a sweet sentiment, but I'm impatient and hungry and don't have any time for sweet.

"Shut up and do me like you mean it." I advance on him, and with an approving flicker of the eyebrow, he intercepts me, lifting me to straddle his lap. He reaches between us, poised to enter me.

"Is it safe?" He kisses my collarbone and the sensitive skin between my breasts. I understand that he means protection, and considering what happened last time, it nearly wrecks the moment.

"Safe as it ever was," I mutter, and he forcefully pulls me down onto his shaft. He fills me, and the searing heat of him steals my breath. His body's tailor-made for mine, and we fall into the rhythm of two people who've not only done this many times, but who've thought about doing it a million more. His hands clutch my hair, forcing me to look up into his beautiful eyes.

"Look at me, Lie," he insists, rocking into me, steadying me with one large hand on my sacrum. I cinch my legs tighter around his waist, struggling to do as he asks. "I want to watch you come."

He strokes his fingertips up my spine, tingles and gooseflesh trailing in their wake. Sounds escape me that I can't claim responsibility for, and Connor murmurs some encouragement I'm too dumbstruck to translate. Heat blazes in his eyes, eyes that haunt my dirtiest dreams. Mumbling curses against my lips, his hand closes around my throat. My eyes drop shut as I surrender to the sensation of him owning me. He forces my chin to extend just a tiny bit farther, and I arch my back, groaning wantonly. Connor strokes his beard against my cheek and his primal growl in my ear takes me right to the edge.

"All fucking mine."

He's made similar claims every time we've been together, but he's never sounded so desperate, so demanding. I cling tightly to his hair, afraid one or both of us might not make it through this bedlamized coupling unscathed. I'm so close to coming that if anything or anyone gets in my way, I won't be responsible for my actions.

"You feel so fucking good," I whisper against his lips.

"You make me crazy, Delilah." He snarls my name between gritted teeth and I come completely unraveled. My orgasm rips through me in unstoppable waves. My quaking sets Connor off, and he shudders, swallowing my cries with a hungry groan as we ride out our dueling climaxes, still locked tightly together as we spiral all the way back down. When our grinding ceases, Connor collapses onto his back, pulling me down with him to rest against his chest.

Neither of us speak or move, just lie there, breathing in unison. I'm trying hard not to think past this moment, afraid anything I do or say will taint what just happened.

"That was even better than I remembered," he says, after a time. He's stroking my hair, and I'm enjoying it far too much. I remove myself from him and climb to my feet.

"We were always good at that." I feel what's left of him dripping down my inner thighs, and I suddenly need a shower and some space.

I hurry to the restroom and start the water. When I turn to lock the door, Connor's there watching me from the doorway. "We were good at everything when we did it together."

I step into the shower, unable to look at him anymore. "Nothing lasts."

"Especially when you refuse to try," I hear him say, and

I dunk my head under the water. When I feel his hands soaping me, I'm not surprised. Connor has no concept of boundaries.

"I would have stayed if you'd asked me to." He spoons my body, running his hands over my breasts. I turn to face him, too distracted by his fragile eyes to succumb to his sensual touch.

"I wanted you to *want* to stay, Connor. But I *never* would have asked you to."

Frown lines appear, hurt and confusion wrestling for control of his features. When he finally speaks again, his tone is measured. "Why haven't you answered me about the baby?"

A tidal wave of memories crash into me, and I'm tempted to let the undertow take me out into hostile waters. I could confess everything. Lying awake the first time she moved, wishing Connor was there beside me so he could feel it. Seeing her suck her thumb on the ultrasound just like Connor used to when he was little and deciding there was no way in hell I could give her up for adoption. Writing a letter to Connor about her and never sending it. Finally packing up her nursery after months and months of ignoring it.

I manage to grasp control of myself before I'm too close to the ledge. "This thing between us would have played itself out in a year or two tops, baby or no baby."

His arms encircle me, pulling me against his broad chest. His eyes hold mine, unrelenting. "This doesn't feel played out to me."

I pull away, breathless, and turn, reaching for the shampoo.

"Look how unhappy you are right now, stuck here like this when you could be out saving the world. At least you have your injury to blame and not some kid you never wanted." I fumble with the bottle and dump shampoo into my hair and lather, glad I don't have to see his reaction.

When I open my eyes, Connor's out of the shower, directionless and dripping onto the rug. His eyes accost me, throwing all sorts of accusations my way. He snatches a towel and vanishes from the room, leaving me alone in the steam with my agonizing memories. I take advantage of the time alone to mask my tears with what's left of the hot water.

When I finally exit into the hallway, Connor's got his phone to his ear.

"Hold on, Sura. I'm going to put you on speaker so Delilah can hear this."

"All right! So, your pal Dixon blew town. He checked out of his hotel and no one has seen him since." I gape at Connor, and he just shakes his head. I can tell he's as bewildered as I am.

"How do you know that?" I'm loud, so Sura can hear me.

"I have sources at the hotel, but my contact at dispatch confirmed it. I guess Lieutenant Colonel Floyd went to question Dixon about Lu's cell phone records, and he'd just checked out. Anyway, that's not all I called about. Everyone's looking for you two. Apparently Reece told the police

Connor drugged you and carried you off like a caveman. Andi says they've been to your dad's and the B&B trying to find you. People are already saying that Connor's trying for a matching set of Campbells."

"Goddam it." Connor tugs at his hair.

I sigh. "We don't have time for this shit."

"I found some things you're going to want to see. I'll email them to you, Connor. You should get out of there, though. And fast. The Kenai's probably the next place they'll look."

"Thanks, Sura."

"Don't thank me. Just go get Lu." The phone goes dead.

"We're probably gonna be camping until we figure this out or find your mom, whichever comes first." Connor's all business, handing me his phone with the email pulled up. "Get dressed. I'll load the plane." He's already raiding his cupboards while I scan the contents of his inbox. I see several unread emails, including one from the *Gazette*.

Connor hurries outside, and I open the email from Sura. It's a link with an attachment. I open the link to see a website about some fraternal organization for Alaskan businessmen called The Brotherhood. The "About Us" section is a bunch of self-indulgent ego-stroking nonsense, and as I click through the asinine menu, I spot a dropdown that says "Our Lodge." I click on it and find a gallery of photos.

Senator Junior Franz is in several of the photos, but there's nothing else remarkable as far as I can tell. I tap on the hyperlink that says "directions" and suddenly can't breathe as all the air leaves my lungs. The Lodge is located smack dab in the middle of one of the neglected search areas, near Willow Lake.

I take screenshots, then I open the attachment Sura included.

It's an editorial article about the Anchorage Winter Gala, some ritzy ball put on by a law enforcement association. I know I don't have time to read it. I quickly tap through the photographs, and the third stops me dead in my tracks.

Reece's dad, Ronald Warren, along with Merle Jones and Senator Junior Franz are all posed together like chums. The last person in the photograph, smiling wide with his hand on the senator's shoulder, chills my blood.

It's Connor's dad, Archer Garrett.

CHAPTER NINETEEN

CONNOR

ASCENSION

I PULL CHERRY up onto the riverbank where the trees will camouflage her from the river. I unfurl a tarp and toss it over her, hoping it will mask her from the air. Doing so costs me precious minutes we may not be able to afford, but hiding the fire engine-red plane may buy us some time. I hurry back to my own plane, all the while worrying that Lilah's been inside for fifteen minutes. I've got a sinking feeling with every passing second that she's out of my sight, and I'm starting to wonder if she's bolted.

I'm about to go back in for her when she races down the porch steps. She slows a little when she sees me firing up her mother's old plane, but seconds later she's climbing into the copilot's seat. I hand her a headset and she puts it on, her arresting eyes full of questions.

"They'll be looking for Cherry," I explain, but her thousand-mile stare never wavers. She leaves me light-headed, especially after what just went down between us on my living room floor. I indulge in an instant replay, how unbelievable I felt encased in her again, Delilah, naked and glistening, her eyes closed and her features transformed by obvious ecstasy. Her skin sizzled under my lips, and I hoped it was enough to melt her icy heart. If that was our farewell fuck, I intended for it to haunt her forever. I wanted her to still be able to feel me on her deathbed.

Drunk on her salty taste and her sweet smell, that cabin could have burned down around us and I wouldn't have noticed. I fisted her hair, seeing a flicker behind those golden-brown eyes that had long been my hearth and home.

After, as she made a break for the shower, that flicker was gone again, shuttered away somewhere deep and hidden.

I fumble my way back to the here and now, and I realize I haven't explained what she wants me to, though I have no idea what that might be. Lilah turns to the controls, but I can't take my eyes off her. "I was starting to worry—"

"I couldn't find my bra." The apples of her cheeks are glowing, and her hard expression dares me to laugh. "It was behind the couch."

"Sorry 'bout that." I'm unconvincing, and the corner of her generous mouth curls just a hair.

"I'll fly. You need to see this shit." Lilah thrusts my phone at me. She takes the controls, and after an impeccable liftoff, she circles back in a northerly direction.

"What the hell…" I blink at the photo of my dad, all smiles and glad-handing the senator and Merle Jones.

"Yeah…I know."

"Who's this guy on the left?"

"Reece's father." Lilah sounds troubled, even distorted by the headset.

"He's the one Dixon went to see at the airport?"

She nods as she veers northeast, sailing over the old homestead cabin near the edge of our property. I catch sight of the fading white wall Mom built sometime after I left for basic. Ivy spills out of the planters, trailing halfway to the ground. I glance over at Lie, whose amber eyes sparkle as she takes in the strange addition to our old hangout.

"It's not a picket fence…" I jest, but Delilah averts her eyes. I take another long look at the structure. The dilapidated fruits of Mom's labor depress me, so I flip to the link Sura sent us, perusing The Lodge.

"Well isn't this just the ultimate man-cave for entitled rich pricks. Did you see that wine cellar? And this trophy room? There's a stuffed elephant head complete with ivory tusks, for fuck's sake. Someone's overcompensating for something…"

Lie nods, adjusting dials on the console. "It's the perfect hideout."

I study the photographs closely, trying to get a feel for the layout in case we end up kicking the doors in.

"Do you believe Dixon took off?" Lilah's wearing her mirrored shades now, so it's harder to read her. "Or do you think he's wearing a pair of cement shoes?"

"I think we should ask my father," I reply, worried that she's losing faith. "Seems he's part of the in crowd."

"Won't the cops be looking for you at your dad's?" Her

brow wrinkles as her eyes roam me.

"Worried about me?" I refuse to look away.

Reticent, she turns back to the view of the mountains ahead. "We have unfinished business."

Her cryptic response dampens my spirits. "Nobody who knows me would ever look for me at my dad's."

She nods, afflicted by some thought she chooses not to share. "I guess some things really don't change."

"Lie?"

"Yeah?"

I blunder forward, fueling my courage with a sudden intake of breath. "When did you find Aurora 10?"

She sits up a little straighter in her seat, as if fortifying herself for an interrogation. "Not long after prom."

My mouth falls open. "So you had the gold before I shipped out."

"Most of it. With just one person to carry it—"

It's out before I can stop myself. "Why didn't Reece help you?"

There's a weighty pause. "I didn't need help. And I was never with Reece, *never*. So can you just stop with that shit?"

I sit back in my seat and ponder this revelation.

She glances at me, hyper focused for the split second she spares me. "Don't you want to know where I found it?"

"North of Talkeetna?"

She's openly astonished, and it's an unfamiliar expression on her. "How'd you know?"

"Your tattoo. And the matching rose on Lu's map."

She turns back to face forward, and chews her bottom lip.

I point straight ahead. "Dad's place is just over that ridge."

Fortunately, Dad's overpriced house is nestled on a small lake with several other cookie-cutter McMansions. Landing the floatplane is a snap for me, and Lilah could do it blindfolded.

"Nice place," she remarks as we tie her down, suspicion woven into every syllable.

"Yeah…he needs everyone to know he's still a big deal." My dry acknowledgment is met with a nod of understanding.

Cyndi answers the door, all neat and fresh in her fitted light pink scrubs.

"Connor. It's been a while." She's all sexy smiles until Lie emerges from behind me. Cyndi's face contorts as if she's seeing an abomination in a horror flick. Lilah just nods at her old nemesis, brushing past her like she's inanimate.

"He's dialyzing right now." Her previous pleasantness vanishes, as she glares over her shoulder at Delilah.

"This can't wait." I sidestep her and follow after Lie as she proceeds into Dad's foyer, navigating through his military collectables. Since diabetes and a bad ticker forced him into early retirement, Dad's ignored his doctor's orders like a man who'd never heard the phrase "chain of command."

Last fall, he went fly-fishing and a hook went through

his boot. His neuropathy was so bad he hadn't even felt it. Now his wound won't heal, and between that and his dialysis, he's pretty much housebound. I told him so the last time I visited, when he started bitching about the fact that his superiors had asked him to retire.

He'd started in on me, of course…how he wouldn't roll over like a defeated little bitch like I had. Then he went off on a tangent about Quinn, calling him a worthless fag, who my mom always indulged, and I lost it, raving at him about what an epic failure of a father he was. By the time I came to my senses and stormed out, we hadn't just burned our bridges; we'd napalmed them.

Dad's kicked back in his recliner watching ESPN. His dialysis machine makes a swishing sound as the pump whirls. He looks over at me and mutes the TV right away.

"Well, well, well. If it isn't my prodigal son. How's my washed-up baby gir—" The moment he sees Delilah, he bites down on what he was ramping up for. Unlike Cyndi, though, he seems delighted to see her.

"Delilah. What an unexpected surprise." Dad looks Lilah over with something akin to glee.

"Archer."

He turns to me. "I bet this made your goddam year."

Anger smolders within me, and I give him a look of warning to watch his mouth in her presence.

"The troopers were here looking for you. I told them neither one of my daughters visit me anymore. Guess I spoke too soon."

I hand my phone to him, immune to his brand of bullshit. "Recognize these smiling faces?"

He takes it and looks at the screen. He pales a little, or maybe it's just a side effect of his treatment. Regardless, Dad gestures as if to imply he couldn't care less. "Obviously."

"I didn't know you dabbled in politics." I take a seat across from him, as if we're having afternoon tea.

"Everything is politics, Son. But I haven't seen Junior in a couple of years."

"Bullshit. Does this asshole have my mother or not?" Lilah demands. She's still standing, hand on her hip.

"LuAnn isn't exactly his type." Dad's snarky tone ruffles my feathers. "He's always been more interested in the barely legals than cougars, if you catch my drift."

"This isn't about sex, it's about the goddam gold," I interject.

Dad takes a sip of whatever he's got in his tumbler. "Sounds like your department, kids. Not mine."

"Why'd my mom borrow money from you?" Lilah makes herself at home in the seat nearest to him. Dad's definitely unprepared for this question, and he turns his sharp green eyes on Lilah.

"You asked her to sell your precious plane. Christ, Delilah, you know LuAnn. She'd rather light her own hair on fire. She needed the money for you so you could ride off into the sunset with that lawyer of yours, or whatever the hell you did with all that cash. Your dad trashed her credit years ago, so she couldn't borrow from a bank. I guess I'm the only person she knew with that kind of money."

Lie's skin takes on a green cast, and I wonder if she'll be sick.

"She'd probably have paid it all off already if your dad hadn't lost his boat."

"I don't see how." Lilah's clearly unconvinced. "That was so much money…"

"Rumor has it she found Aurora 10. She's been paying things off for months. The house, her car… I heard she finally saw a lawyer about drawing up divorce papers. She's been meeting with that insurance investigator, you know, the black one. Probably trying to negotiate a better finder's fee for 10."

"Who'd you hear that from?" I glance briefly at Cyndi, who's trying to act like she's charting on her computer. It's obvious that she's listening to every word we say, and is probably the source of most of his gossip. Too bad I can't make her leave while Dad's on treatment.

"Word gets around." I don't trust the expression he's wearing. "I also heard she faked that plane crash. Ran off with the treasure while half the damn state was out looking for her."

Lilah stands. She's fed up and ready to leave.

"Dad. Have you ever been to this place?" I pull up the link to The Lodge, and turn my phone to face him.

"Oh, sure." He smiles fondly and hands my phone back to me. "Tons of fun. Not exactly the good clean kind, though."

"Okay…" I slant my gaze toward Lilah, who looks like she's in the middle of a high-stakes poker game.

"I'm told it was crazier back when Junior's dad was in charge. That man loved a good orgy. Half the country club came down with the clap after a New Year's party there once. Made the divorce attorneys in the area a small fortune. Those boys were animals back then."

"Disgusting," Lilah mumbles.

Dad gives her a measured look. "Your father's been there several times. As my guest, naturally."

"Who, Dick?" Her aggressive gaze makes my pulse race. "Or my real father?"

Cyndi looks up from her computer and Dad bursts into unfriendly laughter.

"You finally figured that out? Nice work, Nancy Drew." His smug satisfaction makes me want to unplug his machine.

A storm is brewing behind Lilah's eyes. "Do you know who my real father is, Archer?"

"Don't you?" He's glib, but Lie isn't fazed. She's known him as long as she's known me, and she's fully aware of what a sadist he is. When she doesn't bother to respond, my father shakes his head.

"I'm not even sure LuAnn knows which one of her many conquests was your sperm donor. She sure as hell knows it wasn't Dick. Claire said she was already knocked up when she got her hooks into him. Wanted to get a ring on it before she popped you out."

Lilah is on her feet, her face flushed a deep shade of pink. She heads for the door. "I think we're done here."

I follow her without a backward glance.

"Good luck!" Dad calls after us. "Don't forget your bug spray!"

We're in the air and nearly to Dick's boathouse to pick up Runt when Lilah finally speaks.

"I'm sorry you had to grow up with that man, but you should know how much he loves you." She smiles ruefully. "I wanted to throat punch him the day he showed up at my house but he was looking out for your future."

"What the hell did he say to you?" The very idea that my dad approached Lie makes me homicidal.

She gives a tiny headshake. "He said we needed to have a chat. That you were talking about not joining up and your mother was beside herself."

"Motherfuc—" I start, but she interrupts me.

"He said you'd take some shit job that squandered your talent and preparation so you could play house with me. Then he asked who I thought you'd blame when the shine wore off. I could picture this future perfectly. In fact, it was the only future I was able to see if you didn't go. And this conversation was after Dad's accident. Before prom and—"

She trails off, but I know where she was going with it. Before prom, and our careless fumbling in the cab of my truck.

"He was right, Connor. You'd have blamed me for ruining your dreams and we'd have killed each other."

I don't have time to argue with her. Lie descends onto the choppy water and maneuvers up to the dock at her father's boathouse. I climb out, and Runt is there, tail wagging. I pick his lard ass up and hoist him into the back seat. When I climb in, Runt's already up where he shouldn't be, licking Lilah's face. She's laughing from deep in her gut, and my heart twists at the sound.

Once we're in the air again and I've calmed down a little, I reach out and touch Lilah's knee. She glances at me apprehensively. "Sura says you didn't have an abortion."

Delilah breathes deeply.

"I need to hear it from you," I demand. She makes a heading adjustment and then meets my eyes. Turning away, she sets her sights on the horizon.

"I couldn't do it." She doesn't say anything more at first, so I assume she's done talking. But you know what they say about assumptions.

"I named her Sky." She's visibly trembling, and I can feel my pulse in my neck at the sight of her. "Please don't make fun of it. I was young and clueless."

Stunned, I can't speak, and I don't know what I would have said if I could. Fortunately, Delilah continues, so I don't need to.

"She was born on Black Friday. Mom and Andi flew down to Vegas to be with me. Labor wasn't bad. I'm really not sure what all the fuss is about."

The set of her shoulders and the tremor in her voice tell me this story doesn't have a happy ending.

"I knew that she was dead before the wand touched my belly. She hadn't moved since I went to sleep on Thanksgiving. Nuchal cord asphyxia. That's what the death certificate says." Lilah shakes her head, her lip quivering, her chest rising and falling at an alarming rate. "The medical examiner said she was absolutely perfect otherwise. She was just really, really unlucky."

I blink back hot tears, trying to picture her, the baby, and Delilah facing something like that alone. Pushing through it because she didn't know any other way to be. I'm devastated for her, with her, and I want to take her hand in mine, but she's flying and she's fragile, and it's a perilous combination.

"The holidays are still a bitch. All the lights and music...it's a lot to take."

I see a tear slip out from under her sunglasses and trail down her bronze cheek. I reach out for her, but she inches away. She pulls off her glasses and tosses them aside, swiping at her eyes one at a time so that she can keep the controls. Seeing how badly she'd wanted our baby shatters what's left of my walls, and I realize I'm crying too. "Lie...I wish I could take back those things I said when you told me."

"It wouldn't change anything," she says, her coal-black lashes weighed down with tears. Her calm, philosophical tone fractures what's left of my heart.

Even though we're just inches apart, I've never felt her absence so strongly. I'm glued to her beautiful face, trying to figure out how I'll be able to say goodbye again when all of this is over. A look of horror transform her features, and I whip my head toward the windshield just in time to see a shower of blood and feathers spray the windshield. There's a crack in the glass on my side of the plane, and I realize we've struck a bird with the propeller.

"I have to put her down," Lie blurts, and she leans to get a better view around the carnage. I know she's right. What's left of the bird could clog the engine and contaminate the air in the cabin. Bird strikes have taken down planes and killed everyone on board.

"Over here." I point out a fairly straight waterway with no visible obstructions. Lilah banks hard to the right and lands quickly, though it's a rough touchdown. Runt whines like a baby, and I can relate to his apprehension.

Lie kills the engine, and I release my seat belt, yanking off my headset. I reach for her and though she's still clutching the steering column, she collapses against me, allowing me to hold her against me like it's the most natural thing in the world.

"Hey." I take her face in my hands. I can tell she's more freaked out than she wants me to know. I also know if I'd been flying, we would have crashed. "You did good, baby."

She nods, though she doesn't look remotely convinced. When I finally release her, she steers the rudders to the right and we drift onto the rocky beach. We try to tie the plane down, but the smell of the blood and guts is overwhelming. Runt keeps trying to leap up and lick at the carnage, and Lilah knees him, grimacing.

"Gross! Runt, get down!" She sounds like she's trying not to breathe through her nose. "We need to rinse her down. Now."

We use a couple of camping thermoses and a percolator from my pack as makeshift buckets to douse the propeller and windshield with river water. It's a half-assed job at best, but once the gore has a chance to age, the smell will be rank as hell. We can't be sure we've gotten everything out of the intake, but at least there's no structural damage to the plane. It looks like the loon disintegrated when it hit the propeller, which is fortunate since it could have come straight through the windshield.

"What do we do now?" I ask, once we've finished our sad attempt to decontaminate my plane.

"We have no way of knowing if there's mechanical damage." Lie wipes her hands off on a towel, and tosses it aside.

"But she landed fine." We can't be more than a few miles away as the crow flies, and I'm hyped up on adrenaline.

"It's too risky to take her up without a proper inspection." Delilah's a risk taker, so if she's apprehensive, there's cause to be. Her disappointment is obvious.

"So now what?" I sigh.

She peers in the direction we need to travel, as if the shrouded wilderness is a crystal ball, showing her what's to come. "We could run it."

I shake my head. "Lilah...you were drugged just a few hours ago. And you have bruised ribs."

She shrugs a single shoulder.

"I come from hearty stock." There's a slight pause, and she pulls a face. "At least...I think I do."

I snort at the obvious dig at her parentage. She cracks a smile.

"We're losing daylight. I don't know these woods. It

sucks, but we probably need to make camp and leave at first light."

"So we bed down here for the night?" Awash in the pinks and oranges of sunset, the surprising sharpness of Lilah's gaze takes my breath away.

Time stands still as I admire her. Lie's resilience never fails to amaze me. She's a permanent stain on my soul and a complete and utter pain in my ass, but I'd walk through fire if she asked me to.

I nod, shivering at the idea of another night with her.

CHAPTER TWENTY

LILAH

COLLIDE

ONNOR AND I work in tandem, erecting the tent as
the first streaks of the aurora borealis appear. My
hands drop to my sides and, head back, I bask in them,
baffled as they creep across the eastern sky, competing with
the sunset for my attention. It's very early in the season to
glimpse the northern lights, and for the first time since I
left for Vegas, I feel at home.

The temperature drops rapidly along with the vanishing
sun, and I zip my jacket all the way up over my chin.
Connor looks up from unrolling a sleeping bag, and he
pulls his gun out of its holster. I freeze mid-step, and his
eyebrow arches high.

"Still don't trust me?"

I roll my eyes. I'd made up my mind on his bearskin
rug that if I couldn't believe in Connor, I couldn't believe
in anything. Him on all fours was what I'd reacted to, not
the stupid gun. I'd be damned if I'd tell him this, though.
Connor's colossal ego doesn't need any stroking. I'd be
interested in stroking other parts of him, and my cheeks

feel hot enough to blister. He still leaves me breathless, and I despise him for it.

Connor flips the gun in his hand and presents the handle to me. "You remember how to use one, right?"

I nod, unwilling to admit how long it's been since I've even held a gun.

"Go find some firewood. Take Runt with you. I'll finish this up and catch us some dinner."

I check the safety, and then tuck it into the waist of my jeans.

He hands me a flashlight. "Don't stay out long. If anything moves, shoot it."

"Ten-four." I try to keep the sarcasm out of my voice and fail.

His hand comes down on my shoulder. In the deepening twilight, his expression is a bit more mysterious. "Maybe I should go."

"Connor, it's gonna be slow going if you worry about me 24/7."

I start to turn away, and he pulls me unceremoniously back around. His large hand cups my face, and tips my chin up so I can't ignore the anxious dedication in his hazel eyes. "Then I guess it's gonna be slow going."

I swallow through a throat so acrid I can barely stand it. The shadow of our lost love looms large enough that I could rest comfortably in its shade. But I won't.

He reads something in my expression, because his darkens, and he removes his hand and backs away. "Be careful."

Runt and I sojourn away from the riverbank, and I

have to whistle for him several times when he wanders, sniffing at every damn bush he encounters. Andi told me years ago that Connor had left Runt with his friend Matt while he was deployed. Matt and his father raise sledding dogs, so Runt's behavioral training was world class. Unfortunately, the mutt doesn't listen to me at all. Guess he was better off with them.

When I return with my arms full of kindling, Connor's already gutting his second trout. Since I need to prove I'm not useless, I build and start the fire as quickly as I can.

"Do you think your dad knows more than he's saying?" I look up at Connor and see him blink rapidly as he considers his answer.

"Probably." He places the clean deboned fish onto his over-the-fire grill. Washing and sanitizing his hands, he kicks back on the ground beside me.

I shiver, uncertain whether it's due to the chilly night air or his answer. I reach out to pet Runt to keep from fidgeting.

"I don't usually put much stock in anything that comes out of my dad's mouth anymore, but I guess someone has to ask the question. You don't think Dick is involved, do you?" Connor's hand grazes mine as he joins me, his large calloused hands stoking the malamute. "He seems pretty hung up on your mom."

"He's more hung up on Samuel Adams." My mind wanders away from Dick to my real father, whoever he may be. I wonder if he even knows I exist…if Mom ever told him. Maybe Archer's right. Maybe she isn't sure who it is.

Considering the way I'd coped with my unplanned pregnancy, I'm not in any position to judge her. The laundry list of parallels between my mother and I aren't lost on me, and I realize Connor's overdue for an apology.

"I'm sorry I didn't tell you."

He turns my way, brow furrowed. "Hmmm?"

"About Sky."

His eyes are shrouded as he stares into the dancing flames. I have no idea what he's thinking, but I've come far enough that I have to spit the rest out.

"I wrote you about her. I planned to send an ultrasound picture along with an explanation." I recall how Sky pressed on my bladder the whole time I was composing Connor's letter. It's hard to string the words together, but I press on anyhow. "She was strong, Connor. Every night she'd kick the shit out of me. She was a thumb sucker, too, just like you used to be. I have pictures. Maybe, when this is all over…"

I trail off, unsure what will happen after our search is done. Connor's fidgeting with the grill, and he can't seem to look at me. I decide I'm okay with that. It makes it easier to tell him the rest. "I planned to give her up for adoption, but I just couldn't go through with it. By the time I decided to keep her, I wasn't sure how to tell you. And then I lost her…and you already thought she was gone, so—"

"I understand." His hushed acknowledgment silences me. He's clearly upset, angry, maybe. As much as I want to share, I'm only willing to press him so hard. It's not like there's any escaping him out here if he loses it on me.

We eat in relative silence, and I'm glad. Talking about Sky took a lot out of me, and though I'd never admit it to him, my side is a bit sore after the action earlier, both the naked and not-so-naked kind. After so many restless nights, I'm hoping I can nod off. I've never been able to relax enough to sleep well in the woods, and I'm already jumpy at every little sound.

"Runt will bark if anything approaches camp," Connor assures me. My face grows warm. I don't want him to notice, so I poke at the fire with a stick. He clears his throat. "Lie."

I force my eyes to his and see they're glistening with desire. He leans in for emphasis. "I'm not going to let anything happen to you."

He sits back and takes his hair out of its halfhearted topknot. I watch it tumble around his incredible face, marveling that I ever imagined I'd get over him. He takes a sip of water and offers me one. I shake my head.

"Can I ask you something?" I'm nervous, and I catch myself biting my lip.

"Of course." He thrusts the water bottle at me again, and I take it this time without thinking.

"Reece said you were arrested twice for assault."

Hazel eyes pin mine. "That's not really a question."

I tense, but I'm too curious to drop the subject. "Will you tell me what happened?"

He exhales. "The first time was a bar fight with some loudmouthed assholes in Sterling. Boone was visiting me on the Kenai. I take him out with me sometimes when I want to hunt off the clock.

"Anyway, we ended up at a bar on the way back to the house. Some rednecks recognized us from the papers, after we were questioned about Andi's attack. They waited until I was pretty sloshed and then started shooting their mouths off about Andi, saying she probably dropped the charges because she liked us double teaming her, shit like that. Boone was about to get himself into trouble, so I head-butted the guy and broke his nose. His buddies scurried off and left his sorry ass bleeding all over the bar. Paul, you know, from school? He got the charges dropped. He's a damn good lawyer.

"The second time was at The Corner Tap. Some tourist with a black belt thought he'd show his friends that Green Berets ain't shit. Came at me with a pool cue. It didn't end well for him. That time, I had to pay some damages, and a fine and go to group therapy at the V.A., since the court-appointed shrink said I have self-destructive tendencies because I have survivor's guilt."

I pass the water back to him. "Do you?"

He shrugs, but he's avoiding my eyes. He riffles through his coat pockets and pulls out a chocolate bar, ripping it open and breaking it, shoving the bigger half at me. "Sorry. I didn't have time to pack the marshmallows."

It's impossible to suppress my enthusiasm. "Thanks."

Connor takes a giant bite and I follow his lead. I'm savoring the creamy candy when he surprises me by continuing his story.

"Max and I had been together since basic. He was like a brother, Lie. His truck was hit by a roadside bomb, and he was thrown from the wreckage. I carried him on my back for most of a day before we finally got evacuated, but he was probably dead hours before we were picked up."

Stunned, I search his eyes, seeing the anguish there that he'd been trying to drown with drink and prescription drugs. His father had always tried to beat the empathy out of him, but Connor is his mother's son, and his heart is just as big as the rest of him.

He shakes his head and points to his scar.

"One hundred and forty stitches. Every time I look in the mirror, I think about Max, and his kid who will never get to meet him." He tosses another stick on the fire, a slight scowl twisting his features. "They gave me the Silver Star and a Distinguished Service Cross. I wanted to refuse them both, but that's a slap in the face to everyone who didn't make it out with us. No one wants a goddam medal for surviving when their best friend didn't."

His eyes are misty and I almost reach out for him before I remember it's not my place anymore. "I'm sure it sounds stupid, but the bond…"

"It doesn't sound stupid at all," I say gently. His hazel eyes search me with cool mistrust, but when I refuse to shy away, his expression thaws.

"Max had a new wife…a baby on the way…people counting on him. I should have been on that truck with him or put him on the other truck. Nobody would have missed me."

I stare fixedly at the fire, afraid to look his way.

"We were arguing just before he got killed. He thought I should find you." I scan him quizzically, and he hangs his head. He steals a guarded glance at me, and exhales apprehensively. "He said that we needed closure. He was right and I didn't want to hear it."

I take another tiny bite, though my stomach is in knots and it's really hard to chew.

"Right after Max's funeral, Mom called me saying she had bad news. I thought 'how much worse can things get?'"

"Her cancer came back…" I fill in the blanks of his story for myself, realizing how our violent reunion fit into this jumbled puzzle of his past.

Connor nods, grief consuming his ruggedly handsome face. "She told me she was done fighting and wanted both of her sons home."

I can see the sequence of events he'd faced as if I'd been there myself, and I shiver. He motions for me to come closer, and unzipping his jacket, he pulls me back against him, wrapping me up in his arms.

"Can I ask you a question?" I hear him say.

I nod, the warm skin of his neck against my face, his scent intoxicating. "Fair is fair."

"What's the story with you and that Andrews guy?"

I run a hand over my face. "You really want to hear this?"

"Yes." He sounds committed, but not thrilled at the prospect. The fact that I can't see his face makes discussing my love life with him seem less insurmountable.

"After Sky, my job kept me going. My work family had my back, but I partied a lot, and made some really stupid choices."

"Like…" Connor urges me to continue.

"Like throwing myself at the worst men I could find. I guess I had a touch of survivor's guilt too."

I feel him nod, his soft beard brushing against my temple. My heart aches, wishing he'd been this close to me all those years ago when I was alone and mourning in a strange city.

"After having my car stolen and covering up a couple of black eyes, I decided I was celibate."

I feel Connor's body stiffen against me, then his arms tighten around me. "That's when I met Josh, at a work thing."

"He's a pilot?" Connor looks doubtful.

I snicker. "No, he's my boss's tax attorney."

"Ah." Connor nods, and I rock my shoulder into his.

"It wasn't meant to be anything serious. He was an excuse to ditch out on an awkward Christmas party. I didn't like that I liked anything about him, so I gave him a fake number. But he's persistent, I'll give him that. And he really is a good man. Laid-back, easygoing. I guess he kind of snuck up on me and tricked me into falling for him."

"But…" Connor says, providing me the transition I need for the second half of our story. I turn to face him.

"But…we rushed things. The week before your mother died, he surprised me with a ring. I was still kind of reeling from that, and with what went down after the funeral…I knew you and I were done…*really* done. So I talked him into eloping with me in Hawaii instead of flying home."

Connor winces, and I can relate. We never had a shortage of shit to talk at each other, but we could never seem to say what we really needed to.

"Josh wanted to have a family, and we hadn't even talked about kids. I couldn't…I just…" I cringe, working my jaw and grasping for the right turn of phrase. "Sky isn't a puppy you can replace with a trip to the pound." My voice cracks, and when I look up at Connor, his piercing eyes won't let up. My chocolate is melting, and I no longer have the stomach for it. I take in a breath, deciding I can't hold it in. "And if I'm being honest, I wasn't over you. And Josh knew that. And he married me anyway."

Connor's pensive gaze is enchanting, and I have to reel it back before I'm taken in by him. I look away, overwhelmed by visions of what might have been.

He leans in and I think he's going to kiss me. Instead, he swipes at the corner of my lips, then shows me his thumb, covered in milk chocolate. He pops it into his mouth. "Sorry. You had a little somethin—"

I yank him by the collar, pulling his lips to mine so suddenly that he almost falls on top of me. He tastes like salty candy, raw sex, and unimaginable danger. He deepens the kiss, and when I realize I'm falling off the wagon and into his arms, I break away and hurry to my feet.

Connor looks up at me expectantly, though what he's expecting, I'd rather not think about. I take a step backward, fidgeting with my hair and the wrist of my coat.

"I'm gonna turn in." I hand him what's left of my chocolate bar. I'm far more emotionally drained than physically. "We have a long hike ahead of us tomorrow."

I hurry into the tent and kick off my boots. I notice that Connor has our sleeping bags zipped together into one giant bag. After the day we've had, it'll be an awkward arrangement, but preferable to dying of exposure. I doubt I'll be able to turn my brain off, but I'm asleep the minute my head hits the pillow.

Sometime later, Connor climbs into the bedroll with me. He's blessedly warm from the campfire and, barely lucid, I burrow into his ambient heat. His arm comes around me, and I'm rousted when his rough fingers delicately graze the curve of my ass. I drowsily slip my hand up under his T-shirt and rest it over his heart, stroking the thick tufts of curly hair on his chest.

"I missed this," I whisper on the tail end of a lengthy and serene sigh. His bearded cheek strokes against my forehead, and he brushes tendrils of my hair out of my face, kissing my temple.

"I missed you." His husky murmur rouses me fully, and I inch back, searching his face by the light of the electric lantern.

He casts a curious glance down at me, and I swallow hard. "I'm scared, Connor."

His brows shoot high, and he shifts so he can look me directly in the eye. "What are you scared of, baby?"

I hold him tighter, releasing a shaky breath as he strokes my hair. "Us."

"You aren't the only one." He moves his arm out from under me and he rolls over onto his elbows so he's looking down into my eyes.

I raise a hand to his cheek and stroke his beard. His eyes drop closed and he kisses my hand gently.

"I won't be able to sleep tonight unless I've said this and know you've heard it," he whispers. "Are you listening?"

His eyes are so insistent that I'm nervous. "Yes."

"I still love you, Lie. In spite of all the bullshit we put each other through… It's twisted and fucking crazy, but I never stopped loving you even though I *really* wanted to."

"Connor…" I'm stunned by his candor.

"I know I hurt you. It makes me sick to think about it, and I'm not sure I'll ever forgive myself. But…I really hope you can forgive me, because *this*…it's everything I've ever wanted."

He's expectant, waiting for me to say something. I've never been good with words like he is, so I rise up to kiss him, desperate to show him everything I don't know how to say. He meets me with eager lips, and I surf the wave of euphoria as his taste floods me in a welcome rush. Connor's caresses and kisses overwhelm my senses, and it's not long before my inner animal rattles the cage door. I'm tearing at his clothes, trying to get closer. He's doing the same and moments later he enters me roughly. I gasp and Runt whines from outside the tent.

"Shhh…" Connor covers my soft whimpers with his mouth. He rolls his hips, burying himself farther inside me, hurting so good that I dig my nails into his muscular ass, urging him on. He puts his everything into fucking me, his anger, his passion, the unresolved remnants of hurt and betrayal. I don't mind one bit. I revel in it, reflecting everything right back at him, clawing him, nipping his flesh and pulling his hair.

Ravishing me with his eyes, he flips me over. Feathery kisses on my back drive me crazy, as does his ragged breath on my neck. He tugs on my hair, and I arch back with a desperate groan, needing him inside me again where he belongs. "Tell me you're mine, Delilah."

"You know I am," I moan harshly, because it's always been true. I rock back against him, and Connor's calloused fingers slip around front and stroke me deliciously while he enters me again, driving deeper into me than before. The world around me slips away, and there's nothing left but us.

So familiar,

so intense,

so achingly right.

Home sweet home.

I WAKE TO the sound of Runt rustling around outside the tent. The sun is just peeking over the horizon, and my neck aches from using Connor as a pillow. His steady breathing tells me he's still asleep, so I gingerly inch out of his grasp, taking a long moment to admire him, all wild disarray and peaceful beauty.

The steamy events of the previous night are firmly rooted in the forefront of my thoughts. It's crazy how easily he can get me going...and almost unfair how quickly he can get me off.

I frown, realizing Josh never stood a chance. Connor spoiled me so early in life. And it's impossible to put your heart into anything when someone borrowed it and never gave it back. First loves aren't supposed to be the forever kind. They're meant to burn bright and burn out, like a comet streaking across the inky night sky.

I brush a strand of hair out of his face, greeted by the constellation of freckles on his cheek not far below his scarred eye. My heart hurts when I see the scar, and it's more than I can handle. What Mom said about Connor was right. He's constant, like the moon...even when he was absent from my life, he was there every night, controlling the tides. There's no telling which side of him I'll see today, but I want to believe he meant all the things he said last night. The notion that we're together again terrifies me. There's too much whiskey under this particular bridge for us to make it over without drowning...but I don't think either of us really have a choice in the matter. We'll just need to swim like hell and try to make it to the other side.

Well-rested and sufficiently screwed, I need to get up and move around. Grubby and disheveled, I put my hair up to keep it out of my face, and I scoff at myself. One night in the woods and I'm already fantasizing about a hot shower and a venti caramel macchiato. Thank God Connor can't read my thoughts or I'd never hear the end of it.

I slip quietly out of the tent and suppress an uncomfortable groan. Stretching to work out the kinks, I scan the campsite, admiring the looming mountains beyond the lush forest. There's a crisp chill in the morning air, and I slip my jacket on as I enjoy the serene sounds of the river.

Movement in my peripheral vision draws my attention, and I whip in that direction. Runt's sniffing the ground over by the tree line, his pluming tail wagging exuberantly.

"Runt." It's a loud whisper, yet he doesn't turn my way. He's fixated on the woods when he freezes, ears perked up, his attention on something too faint for my human ears to register. Suddenly, he dashes off into the trees and vanishes into the darkness before I can see which direction he's headed.

With a dramatic eye roll, I reach back into the tent, and grab the revolver before hurrying after him. Runt's likely chasing a rabbit or a caribou, but if he's tracking a wolf, or worse, a bear, I'm unloading the chamber and running like hell.

Wandering into the trees, I scan for Runt as my eyes adjust to the darkness. I hear rustling in the bushes about twenty yards dead ahead. I hurry in that direction, maneuvering around the thick bushes where I find my way to a small clearing.

I turn in a complete circle, hoping for any sign of the rambunctious malamute. Noticing some cracked branches and broken twigs off to my left, I peer into the underbrush, hoping to catch a glimpse of him. I take several steps in that direction when I hear distant barking and then one distinct, blood-chilling yelp. The hair on the back of my neck stands on end, and my heart gallops ferociously. I pull my gun from my waistband and, grudgingly, I move farther into the carnivorous wilderness.

The first thing I notice is the complete absence of noise. Typically, the bush is bustling with random sounds, especially this time of year when so many animals are preparing for the looming winter. Now I hear nothing but deafening silence. This sends a chill down my spine, and I cock the hammer of my revolver, cringing as it echoes all around me.

I come over a small rise and freeze mid-step. Something large and gray lies on the ground directly in my path. I blink, trying to make sense of what I'm seeing. Runt's lying on his side, not moving, not breathing. Blood pools around him coating the bed of pine needles he's resting on, soaking into his gray-and-white coat.

I suck in a painful breath and slap a hand over my mouth, choking back a sob. I'm frantically looking everywhere at once, worried the predator responsible might still be nearby. When I see and hear nothing, I step closer to the puppy I spent so many nights nursing back to health.

I'm fighting back bile and tears as I gather myself before I'm able to investigate my lifeless dog. There's so much blood I assume it had to have been a bear to silence him so quickly. If that's the case, Connor and I need to get the hell out of Dodge.

When I roll him over, something pink dangles from his

feathering, and it takes effort to yank the object out of his tangled hair. Holding the tranquilizer dart up, I now understand how someone took down an Alaskan malamute without much ruckus. And I'm shaking with unbridled outrage.

The copious amounts of blood result from the surgically precise wound near Runt's jugular. Someone tranqed him, then slit his throat.

I swipe at my tears and realize my hands are covered in his blood. Wiping them numbly on my jeans, I reach blindly for my gun. I pick it up, and with one last look at my sweet dog, I'm off and running, back in the direction of camp.

Connor.

I have to warn Connor.

CHAPTER TWENTY-ONE

CONNOR

DIVERSION

I ROLL TO my side, and reaching out for Lilah, I come up empty-handed. Prying my eyes open, I notice that her gun is missing. That gets my blood pumping.

My reaction to her unexpected absence only strengthens my resolve. I'm going to ask her to stay. Now. Before she convinces herself getting tangled up with me is a mistake, or that last night was just for "old times' sake."

I'm not the same guy I was before the army. That's not necessarily a bad thing. Yes, I have baggage, but I also have hard-earned perspective. I've learned that I'm not invincible, and that I don't know everything. I also know that tomorrows aren't guaranteed, and that no matter how shitty things get, they can always get worse.

Lilah kept me centered, which is why I carried her picture with me so long after we'd cut off ties. When I struggled with a decision, I'd imagine her take on things and give myself her counsel. She's always been my unwitting north star. My mistake was never telling her so, and it's time to remedy that.

Lilah's changed too. She's been to hell and back, fighting her own private war, but she's grown as only someone with her innate strength and fighting spirit can. I know she has a life somewhere else, but I'll follow her to Vegas if that's what she wants. No matter how shit shakes out with her mother, Lie and I belong together.

My chest hurts as I consider everything I've missed. The times she needed me and I was oceans away. Those wasted years apart, both of us trying to forget each other. Convincing ourselves that we weren't as amazing as we remembered. Lying to ourselves and everyone around us.

It took our separate journeys to appreciate just how good we had it. You can't live the same moment twice, I get that, but I know opportunity when I see it. This is not a second chance for us, it's a new beginning.

I listen for her movements outside the tent, but I don't hear any. I listen for Runt, and I don't hear him either. All I hear is a whole lot of nothing.

Nothing isn't what you want to hear in the bush.

Scrambling out of the tent, I'm standing when the gleam of metal catches my eye. I tuck and roll just as the distinct sound of an air rifle bids me good morning. I hit the dirt and glimpse the fanned tail of a tranquilizer dart sticking out of the ground where I'd been just seconds before. Long strides in heavy boots approach, and I rise and spin in time to see a large figure rushing at me like a linebacker.

I'm startled when I recognize Reynolds, the apprentice I've been hunting with all season. He was kind of a slacker, always off smoking, or joking with me like we were old pals when we weren't. Reynolds's shirt and face are splattered with blood, but before I can get caught up in that detail, my muscle memory kicks in and I block his fist as it jabs at my face.

"You should have just stayed home, Garrett." Reynolds's eager grin tells me he's enjoying himself. Those blood-splattered clothes have my attention now. Almost as much as the blood-tinged knife he's trying to drive into my chest.

"Where is she?" I snarl, restraining his knife. He's one big son-of-a-bitch, but he's all brute strength and no skill.

"Who? The dime who carries your dick around in her purse?" Reynolds forces a laugh. "Don't worry. We'll find her for ya."

"Reynolds," someone shouts, and I glance up to see a smaller guy who looks like he should be surfing in Southern California. He's rushing toward camp, waving his hands in a defensive manner. "Don't kill him, dude. Bossman wants him alive."

"Big bossman or little bossman?" Reynolds grunts, his eyes never leaving me as we square off. The blond guy laughs uproariously as if we're all out for beers at a comedy club.

"Good one."

Reynolds sweeps at my bad knee, narrowly missing it and catching me in the shin. Pain shoots through me and, dropping low, I catch his wrist, twisting hard enough to nearly dislocate it as I send the knife flying. His smile is gone, replaced by a pallor indicative of the onset of shock. Pulling him around by his bad arm, I use his considerable weight to throw him. The clang of his girth landing on top of my grill is highly satisfying.

I turn on the little guy, who's suddenly lost his sense of humor. He's scrambling for his holstered gun.

I stalk toward him. "You better pray she's not hurt."

I see Reynolds in my periphery stumbling to his feet. Before he can get to me, I spin in place, catching Cali in the side of the head with my foot. I turn on Reynolds, who launches himself at me.

Reynolds knows how to take a punch, but he's several years older than me and not half as fit. I can wear him down if it's just him and me, but someone's out there shooting tranqs, and as my friend Brett pointed out so many years ago when I was joining up, I make a really big target. I'm hoping Lie doesn't resurface until all this is over. With calculated footwork, I retreat behind the tent for cover from the shooter.

"Don't be a bitch, Garrett. I've been waiting months to kick your ass," Reynolds sneers, his hands moving in a showy manner that telegraphs exactly what fighting style he'll be using. I wait for him to throw his first punch. Ducking his fist, I smash three quick jabs into his floating ribs. The pain takes him out of his stance and I use his lack of focus against him. Grabbing his weakened arm, I twist, using all my rage, until I hear the bone snap. His scream is like music to my ears. I release his arm and drop-kick him, sending him ass over elbows into the brush.

Cali takes one look at Reynolds's motionless boot sticking out of the bushes and turns tail. Since he's armed and I'm not, I slip into the brush to see if Reynolds is carrying.

Flipping my sweaty hair out of my eyes, I search him for a second weapon, since his knife rests near the remnants of last night's fire. The distinct sound of a cocked hammer reaches me. It sounds like my revolver.

"Step away from the tent." Lilah's inner bitch is center stage, based on her deadly tone. I can't see her from my vantage point, and my anxiety level skyrockets. Lie's hardcore, but these guys are dangerous and they aren't fucking around. This isn't target practice, which is exactly why I hoped she wouldn't return to camp. I wonder if she'll pull the trigger when the chips are down.

"Here she is," Cali calls in a smarmy used car salesman voice. "Connor's been worried about you, Delilah."

"I should have known it'd be you." Her voice has true grit. I roll Reynolds and remove his gun from his back holster.

"You *do* remember me! I have to admit, I was hurt when you didn't recognize me at the airport. You were too busy rubbing your tits all over flyboy to pay me any attention."

"Shut up and move," Lie commands.

"Aww, don't be like—" he starts, and I hear the blast of her firing a shot. "Whoa! Take it easy!"

"That's the only time I'll miss. Now shut the fuck up and do what you're told." She's goddam savage and I'm bursting with pride.

I hear him slowly shuffling away from my current location. I peek out and see Lilah, covered in blood. She waves the revolver, directing him away from the tent. "Connor, you can come o—"

"Lie! Come to m—"

But I'm too late. The shooter comes out from behind the plane and aims his air rifle at Lilah. I dive at her, knocking her out of the way. Lilah cries out in surprise as she hits the ground and loses her gun. I feel the sting of the dart as it enters my tricep. Cali's laughing again as my vision begins to blur.

"Connor!" Lilah's scrambling to her feet, and I turn in slow motion. I search her body for injuries, but all I see is her blood-smeared face and wide worried eyes. Cali's behind her, and I try to warn her, but my tongue's too big for my mouth. Lie doesn't notice him until he presses the gun barrel to her temple.

I pull the dart out of my arm, but it's too late to matter. I stumble toward Lilah as the tranq shooter saunters into camp. I recognize him immediately as the thug who threatened to snap her neck years ago. The one Lilah told the cops looked like a hawk.

"Damn." Cali smiles at me like he's about to hand me a participation trophy. He's calm, like we're all hanging out having a smoke. "I can't believe you're still conscious. You're a beast."

"Should I shoot him again?" Hawkman's still got both hands on the air rifle. He's a little gray at the temples, but otherwise he looks the same.

"Leave him alo—" Lilah blurts and Cali grabs her by the ponytail, giving it a good yank.

"No, dude. You'll kill him." Cali sounds like they're arguing over what office supplies to order from Staples. "Go check on Reynolds, for shit's sake."

My legs give out and I lose my balance. I stumble sideways, crashing into the tent pole before I collapse, coming to rest on my stomach. Lilah's calling my name, and as an extra dose of torture, I helplessly watch Cali frisk her, his fucking hands all over her. He murmurs softly and I can't hear what he's saying, but Lie yanks away and elbows him in the mouth.

"Get your goddam han—"

He pistol-whips her, and she goes down hard. Hawkman reappears with Reynolds, whose arm hangs at an awkward angle. Reynolds gives me a swift kick in the face, and I can't even move my fingers, let alone raise my arms to block. All three of the men stand in a circle around Lilah, and thankfully my vision fades to black.

I COME TO, sucking in breath like I've been underwater for a minute too long. My head throbs with a vengeance, making every hangover I've ever had seem like child's play. My shin aches where Reynolds kicked me, and my jaw feels like I've had a tooth pulled. I'm shivering on frigid cement, which does nothing for my aching head. Zip ties on my wrists cut off my blood flow, and I struggle to sit up in order to spare myself the searing contact with the basement floor.

"Morning, kiddo." I recognize LuAnn's hoarse croak. "I thought you were dead. I've never been so happy to hear snoring in my life."

I'm awash with relief. Lu's alive. I blink to focus my dry eyes. She's sitting a few feet away on a pile of ratty sleeping bags. "You okay, Lu?"

"I could use a bacon cheeseburger and a shot of Jim Beam, but I'll pull through. That muscle-head who dragged you in here didn't look so good. You must have done something very right to get that kind of VIP treatment."

My eyes finally adjust enough to get a look at her injuries. Lu's pale and gaunt, and she's sporting two black eyes that are on the road to recovery. Her split lip looks fresh, and her long hair is matted and greasy. The scent of sweat and fear permeates the basement.

"What the hell happened, Lu?" I'm fuming that these assholes laid hands on her, but not surprised. I push back against the wall behind me, inching my way up to standing.

"Ronnie Warren saw me coming out of the Great Northerner with Marcus Dixon last month and thought I called him to cash in Aurora 10. He tried to bring it up the next day at the airport, all nonchalant. You should have seen his face when I told him we were just old friends with benefits." She chuckles. "He didn't believe me."

I shake my head at her ability to find humor in any situation, not to mention her frankness about her extramarital relations. "Ronald Warren. Reece's dad?"

"Yep. After running into him, Marcus got to reminiscing about Ronald's 'scheduling oversight' implicating me in the Aurora debacle and that got me thinking. I paid a visit to Willow, where they store the old records. In the eighties, we used carbon-copied manifests. In triplicate. I found the third copy of the Aurora manifest, and Hank was right. Aurora Corp. over-reported their losses to Anderson and Hart by forty-two bars, and Ronald signed off on it."

"Senator Franz is a buddy of his," I explain, and she laughs condescendingly.

"Kiddo, Reece's mother is Junior Franz's first cousin."

"Holy shit." I twist at the zip ties hoping these goons applied them with the same attention to detail they'd used to fake Lu's plane crash. "So Reece is involved?"

She shrugs and leans her head back against the wall. "If he is, he hasn't shown his face around here."

I come across a nail sticking out of a wall board, and I start working frantically on the zip ties.

"This Warren guy? Is he capable of murder?"

Lu frowns.

"He's a walking Napoleon complex who'd whore his own mother if he thought the market would bear it. He tracked me down at my customer's private airstrip near Willow. Claimed the weather forced him to land there and offered me a cup of coffee from his thermos. I don't know what was in it, but it sure as hell wasn't Bailey's. I knew something was wrong, so I went to my plane to call Lilah. She said I was cutting out, so I called you. You were acting weird, answering in grunts. I saw Patrick and another one of Ronald's lackeys coming for me, so I stashed my phone."

"I never talked to you, Lu. But one of Ronald's guys, the really big one? He works for my company and he was out with me that day."

"That explains that." She's nodding.

I frown. "Who's Patrick?"

"He works at the airport. I'm not sure what he does, besides stand around like a shaggy Ken doll with pubes where his beard should be."

"He's one of the guys who jumped us this morning. These are the same guys who tried to abduct Lie at the high school."

Lu's gaze settles on me, her swollen eyes making my skin crawl. "Wait. You just said 'jumped us.'"

I brace for the tirade headed my way. "Delilah's with me."

"Goddam her! I told her not to come here!" LuAnn erupts.

"Have you met Delilah?" My reply elicits a sardonic grin that doesn't make the trip up to Lu's worried eyes. I scour every inch of the basement while filling Lu in on all that's happened and what we've learned. I feel one of the zip ties give way, and I scratch myself in the process. "Ouch."

"Hope you had your tetanus shot," Lu quips, moving toward me. She's limping, and I see her hands are mangled and discolored.

I manage to do enough damage to the second zip tie

that it cracks, and I shake my hands, desperate to regain some circulation.

"Good to see the military puts my tax dollars to good use," Lu jokes as I hurry to inspect the ankle cuff chaining her to the wall. I search for something to pick or break the lock, but it appears I'm going to have to get creative.

"There's something else you should know," I tell her cautiously. "Dixon went to see Ronald. No one's seen him since."

Lu's battered features are genuinely grim. "You think they have him too?"

"I hope not," I say, though I can think of a far worse scenario. Dixon's curiosity might have gotten him killed.

"Listen, kiddo. It's time we face facts. They broke three of my fingers and shattered two of my toes. I would have given up Aurora 10 if I had it."

I keep a neutral expression, knowing this isn't easy for LuAnn Campbell to admit. "Yeah?"

"And, they still haven't disposed of me." She stands tall, and I can tell it's not a simple task for her. "You understand what that means?"

I narrow my gaze at her, feeling the frown lines forming. "They kept you for bait."

Her swollen eyes are forlorn. "They know better than to try to break *you*, Connor. They won't waste their time. I'm surprised they didn't just shoot you and leave you in the woods."

I look up at the unfinished ceiling, saying a silent prayer that I'm wrong about what's coming next. "We're both here for the same reason."

Lu nods, her pale eyes sunken and haunting. "They're gonna use us against Lilah."

CHAPTER TWENTY-TWO

LILAH

CHOICE

"HURRY UP, LITTLE girl. Daddy'll tuck you in." Smiley, who I didn't recognize due to his bushy surfer hair and beard, pushes me down the hall toward Hawkman, who's standing by an open bedroom door wearing a lascivious grin.

"I'll tuck something in, all right." Hawk reaches out for me, and though I backhand him solidly, he hurls me across the threshold. I slam into the heavy four-post bed frame, landing in a heap. My injured side burns, and my wrist throbs. Standing takes work, but I grit my teeth and make it happen.

Hawk shoves me face-first onto the bed. I flop onto my back as he starts to unfasten his belt, but Smiley puts a hand on his shoulder.

"Not yet."

Hawkman's heavy brow furrows and he glares hostilely at Smiley. "Says who?"

Smiley loses his amused expression, and it chills me when I see what hides underneath. "You know who."

Whoever "you know who" is must be pretty important, because Hawkman refastens his belt.

"How's the lip, asshole?" I nod toward the injury I bestowed on Smiley when he touched me between my legs back at camp.

"You can kiss it later." Smiley's retort is automatic, but he seems distracted. He hurls my backpack at me. "Clean yourself up. You smell like a wet dog."

Hawkman chuckles, and I glare at them, truly unable to respond.

"Awww. Too soon?" Smiley's cocky now. My silence bolsters his machismo, and his simpering self-satisfaction returns. "Seriously though, get in there and wash that shit off of your face. The boss will be here soon."

They leave, and I hear two bolt locks engage on the outside of the door. I set to work immediately, searching my makeshift prison cell for flaws. These guys are sociopathic, but they're also idiots, as evidenced by their half-assed job trying to abduct me from the high school back in the day and how they fumble-fucked their way through staging Mom's plane crash.

The room looks like the honeymoon suite at some bed and breakfast in big sky country. The rug is an actual polar bear's hide, and I wonder how many of Archer's orgies went down in this room. I wish for a black light. Then at least I'd know whether it's safe to sit on the tacky comforter.

After verifying that the mirror isn't of the two-way variety, I peer out the small window. Judging from what I see below, I'm locked in the A-frame loft at The Lodge's center. I'm on the west side facing the woods, and though I could squeeze out the window, I'd have a three-story drop to the stone patio below.

I note the darkening sky. A storm is moving in. Even if I survived the fall, I'd be drenched and shambling through mud, miles from what could pass as a main road. I could try to make it to the plane, but the whole point of coming out here is to get Mom, and I'm not leaving here without her.

I can no longer stand the smell and the sticky sensation on my face, so I barricade myself in the bathroom. As I lean into the tiled stall to turn on the water, I'm deeply disturbed that the shampoo and conditioner sitting inside are my brand of choice. Turning toward the sink, I see an unopened box of toothpaste, also the kind I use. I start to feel hot around the collar. Truth starts to fall like dominos. This was all a trap, one tailored just for me.

The poorly staged crash site kept the authorities busy, but sent me the message that Mom was still out there. The holes in the air search weren't something everyone would catch. When Connor got me away from the diner, he only delayed the inevitable. Getting me into this room had always been the end game.

Knowledge is power, and I plan accordingly. I take a long, steamy shower, scrubbing myself raw and rinsing until the water runs clear.

I'm dried off and putting on clean clothes from my backpack when I hear a plane approaching. Whoever's piloting is flying very low. My heart clenches. The big guy—the one who'd been driving the day of my attempted abduction—dragged Connor away from camp. Smiley and Hawkman flew me here in Connor's plane, and the big guy hadn't resurfaced since we arrived at The Lodge. I've been clinging to the notion that he drove Connor here. But Connor's far too lethal to hold hostage, and his knowledge of Aurora is redundant as long as they have me. My chest feels leaden as I start to suspect Connor and Runt now share a shallow grave. This gruesome image brings on a sudden crying jag. My heart tells me I'd feel it if Connor was really gone. Even so, I see the strategy in disposing of him, so I assume that's what they've done.

The heavens empathize, releasing a torrential down-pour. Rain batters the tin roof in a percussive attack, and thunder claps so close that it startles me out of my sorrow. I hear footsteps on the stairs, and I wipe my face on my shirt, preparing for whatever fresh horror is about to unfold.

Both bolts slide open and I ready myself to charge the door. It swings open and Hawkman tosses a bloodied and bewildered Reece at me. I catch him, wincing at the shooting pain in my wrist.

"Hang with your girlfriend 'til Daddy gets here," Smiley calls from over Hawkman's shoulder. "Don't do anything I wouldn't do, Delilah."

The door slams. Reece slumps onto the bed. His nose is bleeding. I rip handfuls of tissues from the box and move to help him.

"Pinch the bridge of your nose," I insist.

"Did they hurt you, Lilah?" He sounds like he has a cold due to his stuffed-up nose.

I shake my head.

"Thank God." Blood trickles down onto his shirt, but he ignores it. He strokes my cheek with his thumb, and the presumptuous contact disturbs me. I move away.

"Why are you here?" I want to know how long he'll keep up the charade that he isn't involved.

"I'm here for you." Rankled, he struggles to maintain his cool. "I keep telling you that."

"Really? So now that your scumbags killed Connor and I'm locked in your bedroom, what do you plan to do with me?"

His brow furrows and something flickers behind his eyes. "This isn't my doing, Lilah. And Connor's not dead."

I exhale a quick breath. I can't tell if he's lying or not, but just that tiny beacon of hope gives me strength. "You expect me to believe that you aren't in on this?"

"Yes." He seems genuinely baffled.

"That man works for you, Reece," I hiss. "The blond one with the slick grin."

"No. Patrick works for my father. I've been trying to keep you away from this." He's dim, like he's exhausted. "Everything I've done, I've done to keep you safe."

"Like abducting my mother and killing my dog?" My voice sounds strained, but I don't care.

He inches toward me, his expression possessive and raw.

"Delilah, I didn't do either of those things. I would

never hurt you…"

I move to the other side of the bed—better with a barrier between us.

"You drugged me." I'm antsy and disagreeable, but I know I need to tone it down. Reece is a honey versus vinegar type of situation.

"I did," he admits, and I'm exalted that he hasn't bothered with some lame denial. "But it's not what you think."

His eyes implore me to listen to his explanation. I press the heels of my palms against my forehead. I wonder where he sees this charade ending. I cross my arms over my chest and meet his gaze. He's still consuming me with his eyes. "I'm listening."

"I didn't know they took your mom until they already had her. My father was twitchy for days before she went missing, making us change our passwords…tightening security. He flew up to our Willow location, claiming he needed to do an audit. After he landed, he called, spouting off about the weather, asking me to radio LuAnn and divert her to a private airstrip near Willow. The weather reports were ugly, so I didn't question him."

Reece is moving closer. His hands caress my upper arms, and his voice is overly calm. I want to gouge out his earnest eyes, but I maintain my cool.

"Dad said she never arrived. I notified the authorities, and then Dad showed up at my place and told me he had Lu. He said the cops would think I was an accessory. I didn't know what to do."

"Is that going to be your defense after you kill me too?

Sorry, Your Honor. My daddy made me do it?"

Reece reacts like I slapped him. He drags a desperate glance over me, and his expression spells trouble in all capital letters.

"You ended up here because you stuck with Connor. They would have taken him and left you alone. I tried to get you away from him. The Special K I gave you just worked too fast. Then he showed up and took off with you. When Cyndi emailed me and told me you were on your way up here, I tried to get to you first, but I was too late. Now that you're here, I don't know if I can stop any of this. Maybe…if you tell me where you found Aurora 9…"

I laugh out loud. "I'm not an idiot, Reece. Those guys you have working for you didn't bother wearing masks. I'm not getting out of this alive no matter what I do, so why the hell should I tell you anything?"

"Because I love you, Lilah." That irrevocable adoration appears on his boyish features. "I'm the only reason you're still alive!"

I contain the urge to slap him, though it's arduous. "The coordinates inside my head are the only reason I'm still alive. But 9's coordinates don't matter. I already have Aurora 10. I've had it for a decade."

His eyes bulge. "Seriously?"

I nod. "So go tell Daddy we're making a deal."

Reece scrutinizes me, and then bursts into hysterical laughter. I startle at the inappropriate outburst, my hair standing on end at the unnatural sound.

"I should have fucking known." His words escape as his

jag winds down. He sweeps in suddenly, his hand gripping the back of my neck.

"Reece—" I want to tell him what a piece of shit he is before he gets me into a lip lock, but kissing isn't what he has in mind. Reece forces me in the direction of the door.

"Let's get this fucking show on the road then." His cold demand echoes in the trashy boudoir.

CHAPTER TWENTY-THREE

CONNOR

ALL IN

JUDGING BY THE cataclysmic creaking, Reynolds is descending the stairs. I'm behind the door, my finger to my lips. LuAnn's battered face is harder to read than usual, but her body language is indisputable. *No shit, kiddo.*

"Reunion time—" Reynolds bursts through the door, and my fist connects with his throat. The cracking sound turns my stomach. I don't enjoy hurting people, but he kicked me in the face while I was paralyzed, so fair is fair. I deliver a second blow to ensure he stays down. He lands in a heap next to Lu, and no longer bound by her ankle chain, she crouches down to feel for a pulse.

She shakes her head. "You kicked him straight through the goal posts of Jesus."

My shoulders sag. Lu crosses to me and jerks my injured jaw mercilessly so I look down at her.

"Stop that shit now, Connor." She hurries back to pull his weapon from its holster much like I had several hours ago. "This son of a bitch broke my fingers and laughed about it. I'm glad he's dead. The world's a prettier place.

Now let's go find my daughter."

"Maybe I should take the gun."

"Hell no." Broken fingers aside, Lu handles the gun like it's an extension of her arm. "I'm not right-handed."

We move out into the hall and up the stairs, each step cautious and deliberate. I can hear voices, and my empty stomach clenches hard when I recognize Merle's. I knew that piece of shit was involved in this somehow.

"How you gonna break it to him?" Merle asks, and I hear someone pouring something into a glass.

"Break what to whom?" says a sanctimonious voice I don't recognize.

"Your son. When are ya planning on tellin' him he can't keep his eye candy?" The smile in Merle's voice tinges my vision red. I shoot LuAnn a look and she mouths the word *Ronald*.

"Reece isn't stupid, Merle." The elder Warren's retort is curt and cold. "There'll be plenty of pussy to take his mind off of Delilah Campbell when he's sitting on a pile of gold in Puerto Vallarta."

"I'll drink to that," I hear Cali dude, the one LuAnn calls Patrick, chime in.

Their glasses clink audibly.

"Damn, that's good whiskey," Merle says.

"Aren't you thirsty, Stephen?" Elder Warren asks, just as Lu and I move into the foyer and flank the door.

"I'll celebrate when we have the gold." Stephen's gruff voice is unmistakable. His involvement agitates me further. He could have doped Lilah's water and dragged her here that first day of the search had I not forced myself into their party.

"Here's hoping she spits out those coordinates before Reynolds breaks out the torture kit. I could do without all the screaming." Merle smacks his lips like a lord at a midsummer's feast.

"Fat chance," Patrick snipes. "We've been after her to cough that shit up for years. She's gonna make us work for it."

"Speaking of which…Reece has had plenty of time to get a piece." The elder Warren sighs impatiently. "Go fetch him, Patrick. The girl, too."

"Aye aye, Captain." I hear Patrick's quick footfalls as he retreats.

"Where the hell is Reynolds?" Warren asks. "I told him to retrieve LuAnn."

"He probably stopped to piss." Merle sounds jolly in the midst of this horror show. "I think that guy has overactive bladder or something."

"I'll go," Stephen says, and Lu and I exchange a sideglance. We know he's coming our way. I hear his boots clomp, but I also hear Lilah viciously cursing as she draws nearer.

"Touch me one more time and you'll lose a testicle, asshole."

Stephen steps through the doorway and a steady calm settles over me. He can blow our position with a single word. I slip behind him as he clears the doorway, clamping one hand over his mouth. Lu points her gun at his face, and I yank his belt knife from its sheath hard enough to snap the leather. I raise it, ready to bury it in his chest. LuAnn shakes her head, and I pause to read her gestures. She wants to use him as a hostage.

I press his blade to his throat and murmur softly, "Just give me a reason."

He's putty in my hands after that, and Lu and I both shove him back into the room, using him as a living meat shield.

I recognize we're entering the sprawling trophy room these douchebags were so proud of on their website. Animal heads cover nearly every surface, and the assembled men lounge on expensive furniture by a stone fireplace, as if they're on vacation. They're all turned away from us, watching Lilah make a spectacle of herself. She's swearing like a sailor at Patrick, who once again, has ahold of her by her hair.

"Take your hands off my daughter." LuAnn puts Dirty Harry to shame as she brandishes Reynolds's weapon, aiming it steadily at Patrick. All heads whip in our direction, and weapons turn our way. I allow myself a moment to look at Lilah, but only one. She seems unharmed, and she overflows with relief as she looks from her mother to me. I turn in Hawkman's direction, since he's obviously had military training and seems to be the biggest threat in the room.

"My, my. What an unexpected surprise." Reece's dad was probably quite the player back when open shirts and gold chains were all the rage. His eyes are cool and reptilian, and though he's an ankle biter compared to me, I see I've misjudged the situation. Killers know their own, and Ronald Warren is the most lethal person I have to contend with. The animal in me bows to the animal in him, and he's evaluating me in a similar manner.

We all stand, listening to the rain beat down on the steel roof of the remote log fortress.

"Reece, let my daughter g—" LuAnn starts, but Ronald nonchalantly raises his gun and shoots Stephen in the face. Spray from the gaping exit wound showers Lu and me, and I release my grip on him as he falls to the floor with a resounding thud.

"I'm sorry, LuAnn...you were saying?" Ronald turns to her with benign interest, like they are making conversation over a hand of bridge. Lu says nothing. She's staring down at our former hostage in disbelief. Merle's gone as lily white as his beard and Patrick's breathing like he's delivering a baby. Hawkman lunges for LuAnn, who puts a bullet into the hardwood inches from Hawkman's foot. He freezes in place and Ronald chuckles merrily, like we're having a grand old time.

"Seems we have a Mexican standoff on our hands." Ronald perches on the edge of his antique desk, his gun resting casually on his thigh with menacing panache. "But there are just so many more of *us*."

"I have a Green Beret." Lu nods at me, her gun trained on him unwaveringly.

"And only five rounds in the chamber. When was the last time we fed you anything? What's it been? Two days?

You must feel pretty weak..." He smiles. It's obvious he finds us as intimidating as a couple of toddlers throwing a tantrum. "Pity. This could have been fun."

Ronald points his gun at Lilah's abdomen. "Belly wounds won't kill you right away...but I hear they hurt like hell. Now, I think I've been pretty damn patient. Who's going to tell me what I want to know?"

"I am." Lilah's laser-focused on Warren Senior. "But you need to let them go first."

Ronald moves in her direction, watching her like a cat stalking a goldfish. My impulse is to bury my pilfered knife into the base of his skull. "Oh, Lilah. You always seemed like such a smart girl. Don't disappoint me now. You don't have the cards to play this hand."

"Dad." Reece moves between his father and Delilah.

Ronald Warren holds up a hand without taking his eyes from Lilah. "Not now, Reece. The grown-ups are talking."

"She has Aurora 10." Reece is abrupt, emotionless. His odd demeanor bothers me nearly as much as the cold-blooded murder we'd just witnessed.

"Bullshit," Ronald says without missing a beat.

Lie lifts her chin. "And you're not getting one bar unless Mom and Connor walk out of here."

Ronald scoffs. "You're out of your mind."

She graces him with a curlicue smile. "That's my offer."

"Or what?" Merle inserts sarcastically.

"Or you can kill all three of us." Lilah chuckles, fatalistically. "And pray that your treasure-hunting skills improve dramatically. I've had that gold for years and none of you had a clue."

Everyone is staring at Lie, and I don't like that at all. The elder Warren gets right up in her face, like he's sniffing out weakness. I grip the knife in my hand tightly, ready to tear through every man in the room to get to her if I need to.

"You mean to tell me that you've wasted *years* of my time and money hoarding *my* gold?" Ronald Warren fumes, and for a minute I believe he'll shoot her on sheer principle.

"You mean *my* gold." She's pushing the envelope, unflinching and aggressive. "It's tucked away safe and sound. Nobody knows where but me. So let me tell you how this is going to go. My mother and Connor go free. Then I'll take you straight to it."

"He's not screwing around, Lilah," Reece insists.

She turns sultry eyes his way. "Neither am I, Reece."

The elder Warren roars and hurls the contents of his desk onto the floor. Lie keeps her game face, but just barely, and Lu looks like she might shoot *him* just for the heck of it. Hawkman keeps his gun trained on Lu, and Patrick, who looks overheated, has his on me. Merle coughs and clears his throat nervously, and he's perspiring so much I can see the circles of sweat around his pits.

Reece scrubs his hand over his face, digging deep, trying to negotiate. "I don't think you understand—"

"I understand perfectly." Lie's remarkably calm.

"They'll kill you," I blurt. Lie's fearless eyes shoot to mine, scorching, liquid amber that forged me into a man, for better or worse.

"I was dead the moment my plane touched down in Anchorage." She holds out her hand for the knife I'm brandishing. I'm lost, and she must see it in my eyes, because something shifts behind her smooth expression.

"Guess there's no white picket fence for us after all."

I squint, perplexed by her uncharacteristic sentimentality. Against every instinct I have, I present the knife to her, handle first. She flips it in her hand and holds it out to Hawkman, who accepts it with blatant surprise.

She crosses to LuAnn and places a hand on her mother's shoulder. "Mom. Give me the gun."

"No." LuAnn's scathing tone doesn't even make Lilah blink. Lie places her hand on top of the revolver, her resigned eyes holding her mother's rebellious ones. Lu's lip is trembling. "No, Delilah Anne."

Lilah takes the gun from Lu, and Lu collapses, as if her final stores of strength were used up all at once. I've never seen anyone look so despondent and it chills the marrow of my bones.

Lie turns to Reece. "She needs to eat something. Right now. Since drugging folks seems to be all the rage with you people, I'll cook for her. Tomorrow, once they're both safely out of your reach, you can have the goddam gold."

"There you go again with those demands." Ronald's sharp eyes bore into her. "You can't take all of us out with five little bullets."

"No." She places the gun to her own temple. My heart climbs into my throat. "But I can take me out with just one."

Ronald Warren tilts his head, his sinister grin trouble-some. He turns to Reece.

"You really know how to pick 'em, don't you? She's a real piece of work, this one. What you've got yourself here is an untamed mare, Reece. She'll let you believe she's broken long enough for you to climb back into the saddle just so she can buck you off again." His smile wavers as he turns back to Lilah, the wheels visibly turning behind his dead eyes. "You messed with the wrong cowboy this time. You took *my* gold. Twice. Tell me again why I shouldn't choke the life out of you right here and now."

He's been gesturing with his gun the entire time, and Lilah swallows hard. She's seeing what I'm seeing. He's a mad dog in desperate need of being put down.

"Because you lost that gold before I was born...and *I* found it, twice." Her eyes sparkle as she lowers her gun and moves in on him, going toe to toe with a psychopath. "And Aurora 10? She's a double pallet, Ron. Eighty-four perfect gleaming bars. You should see them. Smooth, shiny, perfection. They're one hell of a sight."

She's hooked him, and it's obvious to everybody in the room. She's played his pathologic gold fever like a well-tuned fiddle.

"So what's more important to you? Punishing me, or getting rich?"

Ronald's eyes have a faraway look.

"I'm not asking for much." Lie's wearing that innocent expression she wore with Reece in the hospital. "Mom and

Connor can tell everyone Stephen's the one who kidnapped Mom. No one needs to know you were involved. Or drop them in the bush. By the time they find civilization, you'll be drinking something fruity on a tropical beach somewhere."

Ronald's nodding, already living her vision, but Reece's expression is dark and labile.

"Take them to the kitchen," Ronald says, eyes still locked with Lilah's. "Do not give Mr. Garrett utensils, not even a spoon, do I make myself clear? Reece, if anyone tries anything, shoot him between the eyes."

Reece nods, his icy eyes telling me he can't wait for me to give him a reason. He might just shoot me for sport.

Ronald turns to Hawkman and gestures at Stephen's bloody corpse on the floor. "Get that thing out of here before it starts to stink."

CHAPTER TWENTY-FOUR

LILAH

WEST

I'M AWAKE TO see my last sunrise, but I miss it anyway. Reece tucked me away in the same room I'd been placed in upon my arrival, so I stare at the dark westerly woods. The bright and pungent odor of spruce permeates the air after last night's downpour, and I inhale forcefully, savoring the scent.

It's hard to sleep under the same roof as a homicidal maniac. There's no way out of this predicament...I know that. I just hope Connor doesn't try some kamikaze stunt.

I had to warn him off several times while making dinner the night before. Connor kept eyeing the guns, taking stock of the knives, and plotting moves to turn the tide. Sensing every option he was considering, I was so distracted I nearly burnt the meat. As if he could hear my thoughts, Connor stroked my hair.

"Lie—" Before he could say any more, Merle stuck a gun in his back.

"Other side of the counter, Garrett." Merle's bloodshot eyes made him less attractive than ever. "No fraternizing."

Connor glared at Merle like he wanted to rip his throat out, and Merle stepped away. Luckily, Connor followed Merle's instructions. He was only a couple of feet away, on the other side of the island, but it may as well have been miles. It didn't stop our communication. We just talked with our eyes. His pleaded, mine apologized. I caught Reece watching us, and I had to look away.

Merle's compulsive coughing did nothing for my nerves. Patrick looked just about as bad as Merle sounded, and I wondered if I'd live long enough to catch the flu, or whatever plague they were coming down with.

"Delilah, you can't do this." Mom leaned on the breakfast bar, commanding my attention. "I won't allow it."

"I said no frat—" Merle started, then coughed thickly. The phlegmy sound made me want to gag.

"Ask me if I give a shit what you have to say, Merle," Mom snapped, and she turned back to me. "I didn't bring you into this world to watch you trade your life for mine."

"This is *my* fault, Mom." Her battered face strengthened my resolve. "I should have told them where I found 9. We wouldn't be here if it weren't for me. They hurt Dad, Andi, now you...all because of me and my childish secrets. I gotta make it right."

Our last supper was a sober experience. Even though Connor and Mom had just washed Stephen's blood off of themselves, they ate. Connor cleared his plate, but Mom ran from the room mid-meal to vomit.

Afterward, they marched us up the stairs and forced each of us into separate bedrooms. Reece followed me into mine and locked the door behind us.

"We can walk out of here. Right now." Reece was stern and completely serious. "We can go anywhere you want. That much gold—"

"Don't you get it?" I jabbed an accusatory finger at him. "You could have stopped all of this. This all could have been different if you'd just been honest. You disgust me. If anything happens to Mom or Connor, you'd better hope I'm dead."

His injured expression repulsed me and I turned my back on him. Big mistake. Reece swung me around by my sore wrist, forcing a frantic kiss on me. I could feel his erection against my belly and, disgusted, I shoved him hard. I expected that to be the end of it, but he came right back at me, tackling me onto the bed. My ribs throbbed, but with gritted teeth, I reached up to gouge his eyes. Then he backhanded me, hard enough to stun me and scramble my brain, leaving me cloudy.

Oh my God, this was really happening. This son of a bitch thinks he can just help himself...to me.

As he struggled with the button on my pants, one clear thought clawed its way out of my gut and into my swirling mind.

I am nobody's bitch.

I relaxed under him, lifting my hips. The corner of Reece's mouth turned up in a sly grin. He actually thought I was eager for him to undress me. Too bad for him, I was retrieving the gun from the back of my waistband. He sat up on his knees to tug my jeans off of me, and I pulled the hammer back with a satisfying click. He froze, his eyes glued to the iron barrel pressed against his unzipped fly.

"Get the fuck off of me and get the hell out of here."

I trained the trembling gun on him until I couldn't see him anymore. I heard him lock the door behind him and once I heard his retreating footsteps, I collapsed back on the bed, struggling not to hyperventilate and blinking back unwelcome tears.

Now, I wonder if I should have just gone with it. Maybe I should have seduced *him*. I might have been able to turn him against his father, then clubbed his sorry ass over the head. I breathe, therapeutic and decisive. I don't regret my decision. I'd rather die with my self-respect intact, thank you very much.

I spend my last hours focused on Connor, allowing the tears to fall. These aren't sad tears, they're grateful ones. I'm so thankful to Connor, for seeing past his bitterness to help me find Mom. I'm also grateful that I finally had the chance to tell him about our daughter, and I hope one day he'll see all the mementos I kept of her. I double over, physically aching as I recall our night in the tent. Knowing that he missed me like I missed him affords me some measure of peace, but knowing he still loves me is absolute torture, and fate's final cruel joke.

When the door swings open behind me, I hurry to wipe my eyes.

"Rise and shine, beautiful." It's Hawkman. His voice has lost its bitter edge. Curious, I glance over my shoulder. He looks frazzled, and the bags under his eyes imply he's had a sleepless night too. "It's time."

He leads me downstairs, past the bloodstained hard-wood, and out onto the stone-paved drive. Reece glowers at me from the pilot's seat as I cross the lawn. I breeze by Ronald, and as I climb into the plane, I notice Patrick and Merle look as pale as vampires, and Mom and Connor's heads are covered with black hoods.

"What the hell—" I start, but Ronald silences me with a blistering glare. His devious smile is nowhere in sight, and he just seems perilously close to some sort of cataclysmic breakdown.

"If you want them to live, they can't see where we're dropping them."

I feel my pulse spike, but I see his point of view, and I try to sound collected. "How will I know they're safe?"

"We'll leave your boyfriend a knife," Reece snaps in response, and my eyes widen at his blatant hostility. "Now shut up and get in the plane or you'll be wearing a hood, too."

CHAPTER TWENTY-FIVE

CONNOR

THE BUSH

ETWEEN THE ITCHY material on my face and Merle
and Patrick hacking their lungs out in stereo, I'm
thoroughly nauseated. I ate way too much last night, and
not just because Lilah makes a great steak. Warren plans to
dump LuAnn and me in the woods, and if he doesn't circle
back and slaughter us, we'll need every ounce of that
protein to survive.

By the time we land and my hood comes off, I'm so
ruffled it takes me a minute to get my bearings. Merle's
resting his forehead on the back of the seat in front of him,
looking less like St. Nick and more like an extra from *The
Walking Dead*. LuAnn's eyeing him with a combination of
fear and disgust. I find her trepidation is highly relatable.

"Merle?" Patrick also looks like he's on death's doorstep, and Merle's distress is obviously freaking him out. I
assume the lack of oxygen during the flight exacerbated
whatever's ailing them.

Merle gasps and wheezes. "I...I can't...breathe—"

"Don't just sit there; help him out of the plane," Patrick demands, and Hawkman and I exchange an apprehensive glance, both afraid we're about to expose ourselves to the Ebola virus or some such atrocity. We work together to lift Merle's portly ass out of the cramped space.

I glance around at where we've landed, but it seems like the middle of nowhere to me. We set Merle on his feet, but his legs go right out from under him. Hawkman and I catch him under the arms in time to break his fall and lower him to the ground. Merle continues to gasp for air, turning more and more purple with every passing exhalation. He's racked with another coughing fit, and bright blood sprays out of his mouth.

"What the fuc—" Patrick's pallor increases as he looks down at Merle. "Roll him over! He's gonna choke."

"Jesus wept!" LuAnn tries to help Patrick, and Hawkman jumps in too. Lilah ignores Merle, turning her scrutiny on Ronald, who seems to be taking Merle's dire situation in stride.

Merle stops coughing, then he stops gasping, and after about ten seconds, I realize he's stopped breathing. Without thinking, I move to start chest compressions, but six compressions in, Ronald's insistent command snaps me out of my rhythm.

"Don't bother, Garrett. He's gone."

I look up to see Patrick with both of his hands on his head, terror contorting his all-American features.

"I need a doctor. You gotta get me to a doctor!" Patrick cries, pleading eyes shifting to anyone who will look at him.

"I haven't had enough coffee for this," Ronald sighs.

"Dad...I think we—"

"Don't go thinking, Reece. It doesn't suit you," Ronald replies, his clinical tone unnerving me more than Merle's corpse. "Get back in the plane, and get ready for takeoff."

"You said you'd leave Connor a knife." Lilah's all business, ignoring the second gruesome death we'd just witnessed, just like she had Stephen's. Patrick is pacing back and forth, his frantic breaths making me nervous. He gets a little too close to LuAnn and Hawk, and Hawkman reaches over and pulls LuAnn away from Patrick, like he's afraid Patrick will give them both cooties.

"So I did," Ronald says agreeably, and he reaches over to Reece's belt and removes his hunting knife. Then, in one swift motion, he plants the blade firmly in Patrick's chest. Lilah gasps loudly, and Patrick slumps awkwardly to the cold, hard ground.

"There ya go, Connor." Ronald nods. "One knife, as promised. And what do you know? We even left you some meat for the long weeks ahead."

No one speaks. I hear the white noise of a nearby river, and something big moving in the nearby trees. From the slow, plodding steps, it sounds like a moose.

"He was already dead anyway." Reece sounds far too much like his father for my taste. "The poisoned whiskey just worked faster on Merle, because he's a gluttonous pig."

Ronald turns to Hawkman with a wide, welcoming smile. "More gold for us."

I glance at Hawk, the only non-Warren still kicking. He didn't know about the poison, I have no doubt about that. His preference for beer is probably the only reason he's still breathing. Lilah's gripping her revolver, and I have no idea when she drew it.

"The gun, my dear?" Ronald says, his hand out, palm up. "Hand it over, please."

"Not until we're in the air for a good ten minutes."

"Fine," Ronald sighs, but he's glowing. Considering the way he tossed his own men aside like used tissues, I don't find his indulgence of Lilah's terms remotely comforting. "Reece. Get the plane ready for takeoff. Delilah, say your farewells. Make it quick, please. I'm overdue for an appointment."

Lilah and LuAnn hug for what seems like forever, and I keep one eye on Ronald the entire time. Hawkman stands at attention, but I see his gaze drop to Merle and Patrick more than once. He seems to be having a very bad workday.

Lilah pulls out of Lu's grasp and advances on me. Her golden eyes slay me, and I'm unprepared on all levels for any type of goodbye. Her lips meet mine, and regardless of her mother's presence or who else is watching, I give as well as I get. It's Lilah, after all, and she was built to be kissed by me.

She finally breaks away, dragging my bottom lip along with her. Her curls slip through my fingers, and her poker face slips back into place.

"Take care of Mom." She backs away radiating far more confidence than I'm comfortable with. "Get somewhere warm, fast. Maybe there's an old homestead cabin like ours out here."

Watching her willingly climb aboard Reece's plane, I tap into that deep reservoir of wrath set aside just for Delilah. It feels good, like a well-broken-in pair of boots. No one infuriates me half as much as she does, and definitely not with such spectacular flair.

She places her hand on the window in a final goodbye, and I watch her until they're far enough downstream that I can no longer see her features. I turn to LuAnn, and she's got one foot on Patrick's unmoving chest, trying to pry the knife out of him. She notices me beside her and offers me a turn. I pull it out and I wipe it off on his jeans. When I stand up, LuAnn is surveying our surroundings. She snorts and a smile pulls at her swollen lip.

"Idiot," she says. "Reece dropped us by a ranger's station. Due south. Can't be more than a few miles."

"How do you know that?" I'm hurrying after her when she bleats out a bawdy laugh.

"I used to visit Ranger Harding on Sundays for...waffles." She's hobbling in a southerly direction. "Those were good times till he went and got married on me."

I frown. "Do you think Reece left us here intentionally? He had to know—"

Lu scowls. "Maybe. But it's too damn late for that little shit to play hero."

"Level with me, Lu. Do I need to carry you?"

"What's the hurry, Connor?" She avoids my eyes, and I know she's really hurting but she'll never admit it. "It's not like we know where they're headed even if we could go after them."

"Does this Ranger Hard-on *of yours* have a plane?"

She chuckles at my pun, out of habit, not happiness. "Of course he does."

I swing Lu's frail frame up into my arms, hoping Lilah can stall the Warrens long enough for me to catch up to them. "Lilah told us exactly where she hid the gold."

"What?" LuAnn frowns as if I have a screw loose. "When?"

"When she mentioned the picket fence and our homestead cabin," I reply in a rush. "Aurora 10's been on my property all along."

CHAPTER TWENTY-SIX

Lilah

X Marks the Spot

MY HEART'S SO heavy, I don't know how the plane can stay in the air. As I take in the pale blue of the sky, the fighter inside me won't accept my fate. I keep examining and discarding strategies to get away, but deep down I know I'm done for.

Because of our detour to the east, we have to fly around some weather before veering south to the Kenai. I'd finally surrendered the revolver to Hawkman. I feel better about handing him a deadly weapon than Ronald, or even Reece for that matter.

Reece touches down on the scenic stretch of river by Connor's house and he and his father hop out to tie down the plane. Hawkman offers me his canteen.

Though I'm parched, I purse my lips.

"You're joking, right?"

Hawkman rolls his eyes, gulps some down to show it's safe to drink, and offers it again.

"*That's* supposed to ease my mind?"

Understanding dawns, and his serious expression thaws

around the edges. "I filled this. I've had it on me ever since."

I appraise him, then drink deeply. I decide to make my play. "I guess you and I have something in common."

His heavy brow twists with perverse approval. "Oh, yeah?"

"Yeah. We're both on borrowed time. What do you think your life expectancy is after you help them load that gold?"

Hawk and I find ourselves in a stare-off. As our gazes snarl, I can feel his doubt as surely as I could feel Reece's erection the night before. He knows I'm right, but he hasn't decided what to do about it yet.

"There are two of us and two of them," I point out. "I like those odds."

He shrugs, but it's not a no, so I press on.

"You take the gold. I just want to go home." My eyes silently beg him to man up and see things my way.

Hawk's my only way out of this now. I didn't drop my hint about 10's hiding spot so Connor could ride in like the cavalry and save me. There's simply no way. I just wanted him to know where I hid it, even though I'd never be able to tell him why.

The homestead cabin is our white picket fence. He said it himself back before we broke up. It's our happily ever after. Maybe he'll get it…maybe he won't. I'd just like him to find my body before the wolves do.

A fist thumps loudly on the window, and Hawkman turns away as the door swings open.

"I hate to interrupt, but it's time for a hike." Ronald eyes me fiendishly before he turns them on Hawk. "Pretty, isn't she?"

Hawkman nods.

"You can have her." Ronald smiles reassuringly. "After."

Hawk raises a brow. "I don't think your boy would appreciate that."

"She's no good for Reece. He knows that now."

My body prickles at his lunacy. The bastard's toying with my life...and he's smiling about it. I look forward to watching him die.

We work our way into the woods, traveling the badly overgrown paths that Connor and I used to explore as kids. Without us around to trample the flora, Mother Nature took it all back. Twice I have to stop and think about which way to go. Ronald jabs me with the barrel of his gun.

"Quit stalling."

"I'm thinking." I scan our surroundings. "I haven't been back here in years."

"Give her a second." Reece steps between us, and Ronald lowers his gun so he's not pointing it at his son. "You know how much the landscape can change from season to season."

"This way." I can't stand another moment of Reece's backhanded chivalry. Father and son are arguing again, and I glance over my shoulder to see they've stopped in the middle of the trail. They aren't paying attention to me, and I'm about to bolt when Hawk hurries past them as if to tail me. I wonder if he's leaning toward Ronald's offer or mine.

I proceed down the path with Hawk breathing down my neck. Reece is getting loud.

"I've busted my ass to clean up your mess. It's not my fault you surround yourself with incompetence."

"This is all your fault, Reece. We would have had her and the gold years ago if I hadn't been so afraid you'd hurt yourself when she went missing. You were always so fragile."

"Fragile?" Reece sounds like he's about to snap.

I press on, expecting Reece's father to start shooting. This off-kilter feeling is what a master terrorist like Ronald is aiming for. Too bad it's unraveling what's left of his team.

We come to a sharp bend in the path when Hawk pulls me off the trail, pressing me against the cool stone of a neighboring rock wall. His hand clamps over my mouth.

"Take this." He thrusts a tiny throwaway gun into my hand. "I don't want to see it again until I see the gold or I'll have to hurt you. Nod if you understand."

I nod, and he takes his hand away and replaces it with his lips. He tastes like breath mints and desperation, but I've had worse kisses in my time, and I do my best to indulge his ego. My best must be enough, because when he finally pulls away, he looks satisfied. He yanks me back onto the path, summarily answering my question about which offer he likes better. Hawk wants the whole pie with a little something on the side. Treasure a la mode.

At last, I can finally see the finish line. The Garretts'

original homestead cabin looms at the far end of the clearing, well placed by Claire's ancestors. The sight of the whitewashed wall she allowed me to build chokes me up. Neglected by its creator and left without a caretaker, the white paint has started to peel and fade.

I take several deep breaths as we near my monument to a long-dead dream. That Connor would come back for me. That he'd want the life he'd talked about the night we spent here when we were young and madly in love. That two broken kids could find a way to heal each other and make a family of their own.

When Sky died, my battered dream died along with her. I wanted nothing more to do with the gold or Alaska, or anything that reminded me of Connor. I just wanted to forget.

Back when I came to Claire with my bizarre request, she never pressed me on why I wanted to build the fence. She probably assumed I was missing Connor since he'd just shipped out, and messing around at our former clubhouse was some sort of therapy.

The planters Claire added on top are a nice touch, but years of neglect has left them with peeling paint, and housing more weeds than plants. It doesn't matter. Today's the wall's last day too.

"I need tools," I explain. "There should be some inside."

"Are you fucking kidding me?" Reece barks at me, and I flinch.

I can see Ronald working complicated algorithms as he

studies me. "Take Reece with you. Son, if she tries any-thing and you don't shoot her, I'll burn that cabin down with you inside it, I swear to Christ."

Reece follows me to the door, and we find it padlocked. He blows out an exasperated breath and pushes me behind him. Shooting the wood above the lock, he kicks in the door and moves swiftly inside. I'm tempted to pull Hawk's gun from underneath my jacket, but Hawk's still my best chance to get out of this alive.

"You lucked out." Reece sounds bitter as he points to the rusty tools a few feet in front of us. He's trying to detach from me, and borrowing his father's demeanor to do so. It's not a color that flatters him.

"Luck has nothing to do with it." I move to the toolbox that's sat in this spot for as long as I can remember and rummage until I have a large hammer in one hand and a smaller ball-peen hammer in the other. "Let's go get Daddy's treasure. Wouldn't want to keep those margaritas waiting."

"Lilah…" His sigh is longing and tragic. I ignore him, afraid I'll punch him if I make eye contact, and I hurry outside. Ronald opens his smarmy mouth to say some-thing, but stops short when I swing the hammers hard at the planters. I take all my frustrations out on them, and then I chip away at the seam between the cement blocks.

Finally, it gives way, and I'm able to remove the top block. I turn it on its side, and two pieces of red velvet fall out onto the ground. I pick up both pieces of velvet, holding out one to each of the Warrens. Ronald's eyes dance with delight as he reaches for his.

"Sweet Mother of God," he gushes as he pulls back the velvet material, revealing a pristine gold bar stamped with the Aurora maker's mark. "I always was a sucker for a blonde."

My eyes shift to Hawkman, and he's moving toward the gold bar Reece won't take from me. Reece focuses on me, his hand trembling behind his gun. I look up into his eyes expectantly.

"He's gonna make you do it, isn't he?" I see the conflict chipping away at his stoic face, and I know I'm right.

Reece looks through me, his jaw tight. "Turn around."

My chest feels like lead as Ronald tucks the gold bar into his inside coat pocket. "Hands on the back of your head, please."

I comply, my eyes on Hawkman. This time he's looking right at me, and I see him nod, reaching for his gun.

"Wait." Reece's voice is full of emotion.

"For Christ's sake, Reece. Fine, you don't have to do it, but by God, you will watch. It's time you learn what happens when you neglect your business."

They're bickering again, and Hawk nods once more. Reaching for the tiny gun, I turn and shoot. The blast hits Ronald in the shoulder, and he drops his gun, grabbing at his wound as he falls to the ground.

"Holy—" Reece raises his gun, but another shot rings out in the distance. The planter directly next to my head explodes, sending splinters flying in every direction. The few birds that haven't fled south for the winter bolt skyward, cawing and caterwauling. Hawkman and Reece drop low, guns ready, eyes everywhere. I put my hands in the air and feel Reece wrench the tiny gun from my hand. My mouth drops open as a tall silver fox in an expensive suit walks out of the bush.

It's Senator Franz, and he doesn't look very diplomatic with his rifle aimed directly at Ronald Warren's face.

"Junior—" Ronald's panicked eyes give me a small thrill. Senator Franz backhands him across the face.

"You thought you could double-cross me?" The senator spits at Ronald before turning to Reece.

Reece's jaw is set and his gun is steady as he holds it on the senator. "I wouldn't—"

Junior cracks Reece solidly in the mouth with the butt of his rifle. It's a brutal blow, and I flinch sympathetically. Reece drops his gun and holds his mouth. He keeps his footing, but he spits blood and possibly teeth, though I can't be sure.

Franz hands the rifle to Hawk, then snags Reece's handgun off the ground and points it at me. "Come here, sweetness. I've been waiting a long time to meet you."

Keeping my hands in the air, I inch toward him until he reaches out and grabs me, spinning me until he has me in a headlock. I feel the gun against my temple and his hot breath against my ear.

"You…" He chuckles, trailing the end of his gun along my cheekbone. "You've caused me *all sorts* of aggravation."

"How…how did you find us?" Ronald's pale and clammy, like he's going into shock. I've never been happier to see someone hurt in my life.

"Patrick put a tracking device in your plane," Junior explains. "You've always been a shifty little weasel, Ronald. This time you and your afterbirth here overstepped. You had *years* to fix your screw-up and all you did was track shit everywhere and make a bigger mess."

Senator Franz wipes off his sweaty brow with his sleeve. He turns to Hawk. "Take care of these two, then dig a hole. Gather up the rest of the gold. Delilah and I are going to get to know each other better."

Franz shoves me toward the cabin, and my vivid imagination tells me I'm better off dying right here and now. I turn, and using the force of my momentum, I plant my palm so far up his nose that I'm surprised there's anything left of it. For a little something extra, I knee him hard in the nuts. He drops to the ground in his five-hundred-dollar pants, blood pouring out of his face like a faucet. After that, disarming him is easy. I train the senator's own gun on him, so proud of myself that I fail to notice Hawk until his gun is in between my shoulder blades.

"Drop it." His voice is flat and full of disappointment.

Knowing I'm out of moves, I grudgingly do as I'm told.

"On your knees." Hawk's regretful tone has my heart in my throat. He must have changed his mind once he saw the senator. Out of options, I do as he says.

Franz grabs me by the back of the hair and tugs my head back. He sniffs loudly, his nose still bleeding.

"Beautiful sight, isn't it?" Franz releases my hair and elbows Hawkman chummily. "I got this."

Hawk backs off, and the senator steps in front of me, scooping up the handgun from the grass. He hovers, the zipper of his fly obscenely close to my face. I roll my head back and look up at the expansive blue. Clear skies have always been my comfort zone, and I'd rather they be the last thing I see than him.

"Open your mouth." Franz seems to savor every deplorable syllable.

I refuse to move a millimeter. He slaps my cheek sharply with his handgun. Every nerve ending is on fire.

"You heard me, bitch."

I close my eyes and open my mouth, shooting pain traveling the length of my cheek. When Franz shoves the gun in between my lips, relief settles over me like a warm blanket fresh out of the dryer. Every one of my senses seems heightened, from the taste and texture of the gun to the sound of Reece's frantic breaths.

I open my eyes, but avert them to the incredible green of the trees and the swelling hills beyond them. The vista is as wondrous as always, and I imagine Connor's silhouette emerging from the shadows. I know it's just nostalgia easing me onward, even so, his presence here is strong and comforting.

I think, *I couldn't pick a prettier place to die.* My eyes drop closed, and a hot tear rolls down my throbbing cheek.

I'm coming, Sky. Mommy will be there soon.

The explosive blast that follows is immediate and deafening.

CHAPTER TWENTY-SEVEN

CONNOR

ALL THAT GLITTERS

I'VE BEEN RUNNING at top speed since Ranger Harding landed on the highway at the turnoff to the old homestead cabin. I had to bully him into it. Safety isn't even on my radar. All I care about is getting to Delilah.

I hurdle over fallen trunks and dodge low-lying branches. My knee doesn't hurt at all, and as I push my body to its breaking point, I'm praying for the first time in years.

Please, God. Don't let me be too late.

LuAnn may never forgive me for leaving her behind, but I saw little alternative. Someone needs to survive this...to get the story out. These bastards can't get away with what they've done, and when the authorities hear Lu's version of events, there's no way the Warrens will be able to cover their tracks. Lu was on the phone with Sura spilling her side of things while I was loading the ranger's gun and he was prepping his plane.

I streak through the forest, so focused I see every leaf I brush aside, and feeling the spongy moss on each tree trunk. The access road is now visible through the trees, so I can't be far from the cabin.

I zag so that I can flank the cabin from the right. I finally see part of the "fence" that I now know serves as Aurora 10's final resting place. I'd always thought it odd that Mom built it, but more peculiar that she never completed it, and it only spanned the front of the house. She'd never enclosed the sides or the back. I'd always assumed it was because she got sick before she could finish. Now I know who really built it and the true purpose of its construction.

I slow my approach as I near the clearing, and my mouth hangs open when I see Delilah on her knees in the tall grass beyond. Some flashy-dressed guy has his gun in her mouth.

My brain-scrambling rage is nearly indescribable. Weapon drawn, I charge forward into the open clearing. A shot rings out, and I watch helplessly as Lilah's face is enveloped in an avalanche of sanguineous red.

My heart seizes in my chest, and I stagger. Lilah falls backward, and I hear a bone-chilling sound—half-roar, half-wail. A second later, I realize it's coming from me. Objects in motion tend to stay in motion, and I'm a large, pissed-off object with murder on my mind. Everyone's going to suffer for this, and there'll be no stopping me without a head shot or a Sherman tank. I elbow Reece in the face as I pass him, on my way to Hawkman. I'm able to taste his wide-eyed panic as he fumbles to point his pistol at me. I fire the ranger's weapon first, hitting him twice in the torso before tackling him to the ground.

I realize he's not moving, and snatching his gun from his lifeless hand, I turn both weapons back to my original target. It's only then that I realize the silver-haired man I intend to kill is Senator Franz.

The senator writhes on the ground, howling like a baby. His right hand is shredded, barely connected to his arm by some sadly mangled tendons. Blood spurts from the stump-like remains, and I can't understand what I'm seeing. My eyes swing back to Reece, who's slumped a few feet away against the cabin, glaring at the senator.

Suddenly, gunfire echoes in rapid succession all around us. The wood planters and cinder blocks take a beating as I crawl toward Franz, who's still screaming like a baby. I scan for the gun he shot Lilah with, and spot it a few feet away beside her.

My breath catches when she stirs, her hand lifting to her blood-covered face. She tries to sit up, but struggles. Once again, it appears that she's wearing someone else's blood, this time the senator's. With all the bullets whizzing past me, it's unlikely she'll stay injury-free for long.

I dive for her, shielding her body with my own. Several bullets hit the ground next to us, and I curl around her, covering her to the best of my ability. Lilah's rigid beneath me as gunfire rains down, splintering the ancient cabin beyond. I feel her exhalations against my chest in hot short bursts. Her frantic breath comforts me in the midst of all the chaos. Then, as suddenly as it all began, it stops.

"Put the damn guns on the ground!" The crusty voice of Lieutenant Colonel Floyd emanates from some invisible bullhorn. I'm amazed the aged lieutenant colonel was able to waddle his ass this far out into the woods without a Hover-round. "You too, Garrett!"

Reece cries out for help, and the senator is still keening nearby. The sounds of boots shuffle around us, and I unfurl myself so I can inspect Lilah, brushing aside her untamed hair to get look at her. Even in the midst of this fracas, I revel at touching her. Her frazzled eyes slowly find mine.

"Connor…" She grabs at my beard as if validating my identity.

"It's okay, baby, I'm here."

Her face crumbles. Ever the proud one, she tries to cover it with her hands, but I pull them away.

"Did they hurt you?" I feel my temperature rising at the mere suggestion. Lilah's badass exterior is nowhere to be seen, and when I imagine everything that might have happened since the night before, I'm fit to be tied. "Please say they didn't hurt you, Lie."

"You're…" Her wild eyes probe me, almost as if she's not sure I'm real. "You *came*."

"Of course I did." I wipe at her face with my coat sleeves, and she winces away. I let up immediately, but I've cleared enough of the senator's blood away to see that her cheek is swollen. I want to rage against someone until my knuckles are broken.

"You two all right?" I look up in surprise at Inspector Dixon. Boone is beside him, and they're standing over us, their rifles slung casually over their shoulders, as if they're out duck hunting. I turn back to Lilah with inquisitive eyes and she nods in earnest.

"Look who's still in town," I mutter. Dixon's conveniently well-timed appearance pisses me off for some reason.

"Where the hell have you been?" Lilah demands.

"Protective custody," Dixon replies. "I checked out of my hotel two steps ahead of Warren's thugs and ditched my car at the airport. Lucky for me, the troopers weren't involved."

"E Detachment's here." Lieutenant Colonel Floyd shambles up to join us, huffing and puffing like he's gonna blow the house down. "This is their jurisdiction, thank God. They're gonna take you in for questioning unless you need medical attention like the rest of these yahoos."

"She needs to get checked out." I'm unyielding, but Lilah rolls her watery eyes. "She lost consciousness after a head blow."

"You're the one who got tranqed," she scoffs.

"Fine. We'll both go." I sound grouchy and gravelly, so I smile, even though it hurts like a bitch. "Stubborn little pain in my ass."

She smiles, like she's disinclined but can't help herself. Then she yanks me back down by my hair for a celebratory kiss.

"YOU GONNA EAT your pancakes?" I push my empty plate aside as I notice Lilah ignoring her breakfast. She shakes her head as she settles back onto her pillow.

"It hurts to chew."

I turn on my call light and I switch bedside tables with her, diving fork first into her discarded breakfast.

"I don't know how you do it," Lie says with wonder. "Your face is twice as jacked up as mine."

Our nurse hurries into the room, her concerned expression unwarranted. "What can I do for you, Mr. Garrett?"

"Come on, Diane. Call me Connor."

Her sassy smile may not be professional, but it's appreciated. "What can I do for you, Connor?"

"Lie needs something for pain."

Nurse Diane turns to Delilah. "Are you hurting?"

Lie toys with her blanket, shifty-eyed. I stare her down disapprovingly.

"Pain medicine hurts my stomach," Lilah confesses.

"Maybe some pudding or mashed potatoes might help it go down easier?" I suggest.

Diane seems to approve of my care plan. "I'll see what I can do."

"You're the best." I give her my most charming smile. Considering my face is swollen like the Elephant Man's on one side, I'm sure it's a huge turn-on.

The nurse leaves with an extra swing in her step. Maybe she's into weird-looking dudes.

I turn to Lilah, all smug satisfaction. "That's how you get shit done."

Lilah's amused. "You should run for office. I hear they'll have an opening soon."

I sniff. "Sura would have a field day dragging all the

skeletons out of *my* closet."

Lie frowns at the mention of the *Gazette*'s editor. "She's not coming down here is she?"

"No. She and Dixon scheduled a press conference for next week. She told me to tell you she made sure to invite *People* magazine." I grin, expecting an eye roll or the f-word. Instead, Delilah just nods again, her pensive features making me uneasy. Unplugging my IV pole, I close the short distance and climb onto her hospital bed beside her.

"You're not pissed about the cast, are you?"

Earlier, while she was asleep, I'd drawn "Property of Connor Garrett" in giant red letters on her wrist cast. She shakes her head. She's stuck with the moniker for the next six weeks whether she likes it or not.

"How's Mom?" Lie was off having a head CT when Andi came to check up on us. She's been shuffling between Lu's room and ours, giving updates.

"Bitching and moaning, but otherwise fine," I tell her. "She's pissed about her plane and threatening to file a civil suit against Warren and Franz. She's not too happy about what you did to her ceiling either, but considering you came to her rescue, she's gonna let that slide."

Lilah huffs softly, flashing me a hint of a grin.

"She also told Andi she hid the missing manifest in that frame behind the map. She said we would have found it if we'd looked harder, but we always go off half-cocked."

"Gotta love her," Lilah sighs.

"Your sister demands that you get well soon cause she's about to choke Momma out."

Lilah's glistening eyes and wide smile are telling. Her

family is far from perfect, but she's overjoyed to have them back on a semi even keel. Her rare smile is pure sunshine, and I lean in for a kiss. Lie responds eagerly, brushing my cheek with her fingers. My jaw pulsates and I groan. "Oww."

She cringes. "Sorry. I forgot."

Every nerve in every tooth feels electrified. "It's just...really fucking sore. I can't believe it's not broken."

A playful smile lights up the entirety of her face. "I was looking forward to them wiring that bad boy shut. So much peace and quiet..."

I'm about to kiss her again, jaw or no jaw, when the troopers appear in the doorway. Floyd knocks as an afterthought, and they enter the room wearing matching sober expressions.

"Are you here to arrest me for shooting that man? Because he pointed a gun at me on my property."

Lilah's smile has gone into hiding. "They're probably here to arrest me for hiding the gold."

"No and no." The trooper from Soldotna hooks his fingers through his belt loops, his expression benign. "We're here to get your statements about this mess, since the doctor says you're being discharged soon."

We spend the next hour recapping for the lawmen, and when Lilah gets to the part about Runt, her news hits me below the belt. Luckily, the nurse returns with Lie's pain pills and some mashed potatoes, and I shuffle off to the restroom to pull myself together. When I return, the troopers step out while the nurse checks our vitals, and Lie slips a sympathetic hand in mine. Once the nurse leaves, we finish rehashing our entire experience, censoring out all of our private moments and discussions without even having to exchange a glance.

Floyd turns on Lilah, who's stuffing mashed potatoes into her mouth. "Ronald is singing like a canary, hoping to get a plea deal, I guess. He's telling anyone who'll listen that the senator and his campaign manager orchestrated the hijacking and sabotaged the chutes. The senator lawyered up, so who knows what he'll say, if anything. Oh, and Reece says he shot the senator defending you. Is it true?"

"I don't know. I had my eyes closed." Lilah drops her fork and pushes her table away, resting her head tenderly on my shoulder.

"Pain meds kicking in?" I kiss her forehead. She nods.

"We'll let you rest." The younger trooper says, then turns back, as if with an afterthought. "I understand you refused a rape kit, Ms. Campbell."

Lie doesn't even open her eyes. "If they raped me, you'd have a much bigger body count."

Both men issue forth reluctant grins, and as they leave, I hear Floyd mutter, "She's LuAnn's kid all right."

Delilah doesn't seem to hear him. She relaxes against me once more.

"Are we gonna talk about Dixon?" I ask, and Lie's eyes flutter open. Her complicated expression returns as if I flipped a switch. Boone visited us last night; Dixon rolled LuAnn in moments later.

"I don't suppose you two would mind giving us a moment alone with Delilah." Dixon drawled. Heading out wasn't easy, since I'd vowed not to leave her side again for any reason, but Lilah gave me a nervous grin.

"Bring me back something sugary."

An hour later, when Boone and I got back from the cafeteria, Lilah calmly informed us that Lu had just announced that Dixon was her biological father. I can't say I'm shocked. I've had my suspicions since I watched the two of them argue at the bogus crash site. The similarities of their mannerisms and expressions were uncanny, and later, at the diner, it was like watching two sides of the same coin as the sharp wit flew between them like Chinese throwing stars.

"He says he knew at the crash site. That I have his mother's eyes. He told me that I have a younger brother in New Orleans who just got accepted into law school. He wants me to come to Louisiana to meet them both."

"We should." I lean in and brush my nose against hers. "We can throw beads. Drink some hurricanes…"

Lie peruses my features carefully, reminding me how tenuous our newfound peace is.

"If you like," I add uncertainly, afraid I've spooked her.

"Maybe. I don't know how I feel about *them* yet." She inhales deeply, and gives me another cautious glance. "I have a lot to think about."

She fidgets with her hospital bracelet and I watch the flush spread from her cheeks down her neck to her chest.

She's not just talking about Dixon, and her nervousness is understandable. Thinking about us and all that comes next…it's overwhelming. But I've never been more certain about what I want.

Delilah.

And I'm gonna fight like hell for her this time and keep right on fighting as long as I need to. Hopefully, she'll fight alongside me and not against me.

"Lie?"

"Yeah?"

"Why didn't you turn in the gold? With a reward like that, you would have been set."

She doesn't even open her eyes, she just cuddles up closer to me.

"I was waiting for you, Connor." Her voice takes on that dreamy quality, like sleep's about to claim her. "We're a team, remember?"

"Always." I rest my head on hers and allow her to heal all the parts of me that medication can't touch.

Delilah pulls away, assessing me reluctantly. She must like what she sees, because her eyes sparkle as she uses my beard to pull my lips down onto hers. It hurts like a mother, but I'm riding high on all the love spilling from her into me. She finally releases me, her expression devious. "This beard has *got* to go."

My mouth contorts in a smirk. "You love it."

She snorts and it's obvious that I've missed the mark. "I'm gonna shave you in your sleep."

I feel my wry grin as I pin her golden gaze with mine. "I *dare* you."

The End

If you enjoyed this book, please leave a review at your favorite online retailer! Even if it's just a sentence or two it makes all the difference.

Thanks for reading *True Gold* by Michelle Pace!

Discover your next romance at TulePublishing.com.

TULE
PUBLISHING

If you enjoyed *True Gold*, you'll love Tule's other romantic suspense books!

I Got You, Babe
by Jane Graves

Recipe for Disaster
by Tracy Solheim

No Hero
by Mallory Kane

Available now at your favorite online retailer!

ABOUT THE AUTHOR

Raised in small town Iowa, Michelle Pace is an international best-selling, multi-genre author. After studying theater and vocal music and directing and performing in numerous productions, Michelle went on to earn degrees in both liberal arts and nursing. Determined to avoid shoveling snow, she relocated to the Lone Star State with her husband, author L.G. Pace III.

Michelle is a mother of three, and she enjoys traveling, live music, and is an enthusiastic amateur beer connoisseur. Still most at home while entertaining an audience, her mission is to write gripping fiction, not fairy tales.

Visit her website at MichellePaceAuthor.com

Thank you for reading

TRUE GOLD

If you enjoyed this book, you can find more from all our great authors at TulePublishing.com, or from your favorite online retailer.

TULE
PUBLISHING